All Timelines Lead to Rome

Dale R. Cozort

Other books by Dale R. Cozort

Exchange
American Indian Victories

Stairway Press
www.stairwaypress.com
1500A East College Way #554
Mount Vernon, WA 98273

www.DaleCozort.com

To: My Family and My Online and Real-World Writing Groups.

ISBN 978-0-9849070-9-0

Published by:
Stairway Press
1500A East College Way #554
Mount Vernon, WA 98273

Author's Notes

If you enjoy the novel, feel free to drop by my website at www.DaleCozort.com or my blog at http://dalecoz.livejournal.com.

I would like to thank David Johnson for his work on the cover art.

Front cover photography courtesy of C. C. Ward
www.ccwardphotography.com

Chapter One

SCOTT WHITE RAN into a wall of Metallica blasting from a jukebox when he entered Dickey's Bar and Grill. The guy behind the bar loomed like a wall too, at least five inches taller than Scott's six feet and bulky in a Harley T-shirt with the sleeves ripped off to reveal bulging biceps. A scar ran from his eyebrow to his chin. Harley Guy rubbed his shaved head and gave Scott a friendly smile.

"Bill Dickey, owner of this fine establishment. You here to pick up the lady?"

Scott nodded. "Yeah, the detective."

"You a boyfriend? Husband?"

"Nope. I'm from the BTI. Just picking her up. She busted an axle on her rental car."

"She checked you out big-time when you walked in," Bill said. "That's a lot of trouble sitting over there. I'll have a go at her if you don't mind."

Scott shrugged and turned away, but Bill said, "Tell the Bureau your public relations suck. You make portals to another dimension boring."

"Not my department," Scott said. "I'm an analyst." He strode over to the twenty-something woman with dark purple hair and East Asian features Bill had pointed out. She snapped a lighter open and shut as Scott held out his hand. "Scott White, Bureau of Timeline Integrity."

Darla Smith looked businesslike in spite of her dark purple hair; tall and slender in blue dress pants and blue and white shirt.

She didn't take his hand, but patted the chair beside her.

"Have a drink."

Bill Dickey joined them uninvited. "I heard you say Boston earlier. What's a Boston detective doing in Illinois?"

Darla flicked her lighter again. "Investigating a murder."

"No smoking here," Bill said. "I'm a law-abiding type."

Darla stared at the flame. "I don't smoke."

"You're hot enough to."

Darla grinned. "Don't you have a bar to run? Better pickup lines?"

He winked and strolled away.

Scott said, "A murder?"

"Yep. And a Roman scroll." Darla pulled up a picture on her cellphone as the jukebox went temporarily silent. "It's a volume in Livy's *A History of Rome*, probably from Timeline X. They tell me this volume didn't survive in our reality. Chad Summers said you're assigned to the case."

"That's the first I've heard of it. Tomorrow I go into quarantine for Timeline X Indian country. Where did you get the picture?"

"From a body. A Jane Doe."

They finished their drinks when the jukebox started again, making further conversation impossible. As they left, Scott spotted a young East Asian woman in dark sunglasses wafting cigarette smoke out the driver's side window of a late model black Mercedes. Her car sat at the fringe of the parking lot, rigidly segregated from the pickup trucks under a faded sign on the side of the bar: "UDE GIRLS EVERY NIGHT."

Darla glared at the Mercedes and her lips tightened. "My personal cloud."

Scott glanced at her, but she didn't say anything else.

The Bureau of Timeline Integrity's Midwest office stood six stories, a pygmy among the office buildings surrounding

Oakbrook Mall in the middle ring of Chicago suburbs. It discreetly bore the bureau's logo.

Scott barely noticed the handful of demonstrators near BTI's underground garage, a tiny remnant of the thousands that gathered there when the portals opened seven years ago. As he drove his four-year-old green Chevy past them, they chanted, "Close the Portals. Timeline X for the Indians." A tall bearded guy brandished a sign that read, "Jesus Died For TimeLine X Too."

They met Chad Summers in a conference room on the sixth floor. Chad pulled Scott from his Timeline-X gig and assigned him as Darla's liaison. Scott felt a mixture of irritation and relief. Three week quarantine, boring. Working in Timeline X, great. He asked, "Why did BTI route this here instead of New York? And why are you sending it to me instead of having the powers-that-be declare martial law?"

"They want it low-key until we know it's not a scam, but they also want something to happen," Chad said. "New York would slop coffee on the file and toss it in a drawer." He projected the scroll picture onto the conference room wall. "If this was Aztec or Inca, I'd say it was genuine. With Roman stuff, the burden of proof gets higher. Being Roman makes it a scam or a national emergency."

"Why?" Darla asked.

"Disease. Scott can talk details with you."

Darla pulled a package from her briefcase. "So...BTI. Bureau of Timeline Integrity. I hear you hire the best people the FBI doesn't want."

Chad's face went expressionless. "We own turf the FBI wishes they had. If it involves TLX, it's ours. I'll touch base later."

After he left, Darla grinned. "Methinks I hit a nerve. TLX?"

"Timeline X," Scott said. "How much do you know about it?"

"Alternate reality. Roman Empire stuck around, never got to the New World. No Columbus. Lots more Indians."

"Yep. TLX is *the* alternate reality—the only one we know of. And TLX Rome is a lot like Rome in the first century AD, which is one of the mysteries of TLX."

"Why is a book from Rome less likely than an Aztec one?"

Scott went over the basics: portals located at weak spots in the wall between the realities, with seven in the Western U.S., twelve in Australia, and one each in Siberia and Iceland, but none in mainland Europe because of the huge power requirements—it would take all the power from two nuclear power plants to make a dime-sized hole anywhere in Europe and most places in Asia.

"Too expensive. Portals are only at the weak spots and without portals, you can't have artifacts."

"So why would something from Rome be a national emergency?"

"Smallpox. It would kill millions if it got loose here. And who knows what other diseases they have." Scott turned to the picture on the screen. "Your turn. Where is this from?"

"A removable cellphone camera chip hidden on a headless, handless, naked Jane Doe, murdered and mutilated to prevent identification. Never found the cellphone, just the chip. Chip also contains a thousand-plus pictures of twenty-year-olds having fun. Nothing that identifies her so far."

"What killed her?"

"Other than having her head cut off?"

"Didn't that happen after she died?"

"Yeah. Just being a smart-ass. It'll be a while until I have the autopsy report."

"On a murder case?"

Darla pulled the chip out of her briefcase. "You obviously haven't worked with big-city law enforcement."

Jeni Burgen drove the hundred miles to her portal in eastern Ohio alone. The portal was hidden in a small, windowless building in a forty-acre warehouse and data center complex. A seven-foot fence surrounded the complex to keep out casual trespassers. Cameras and motion sensors discreetly backed up the fence, adding unobtrusive but potent layers of security. A long, straight access road led from the nearest county road into the complex, adding a mile-wide flat and treeless buffer zone from that side. From a security standpoint, the back of the complex worried Jeni. One of the landowners there had promised to sell, but got bogged down in a lawsuit, legally encumbering the property. Scrub trees grew in the fields, and security often scrambled when hunters approached the fence.

Jeni presented her badge at the gate. The security guard glanced at it and waved her in with no sign of recognizing her as anyone special. Bernhardt Sloan met her at the front door. He studied her unsmilingly.

"An unexpected pleasure. You should let me know about these trips so I could give you a proper escort."

"Don't be so modest. I'm sure the guards at my house phoned you when I left and somebody discreetly followed me with enough firepower to ward off kidnappers or assassins."

Bernhardt smiled. The expression looked like it made his face hurt. "Perhaps. The constant security undoubtedly gets on your nerves, so I try to maintain the illusion it doesn't exist."

"Thank you. I don't think there's been a minute in the last three years when you didn't know where I was."

"Actually, I lost track of you for three months. I hope we don't repeat that experience."

Jeni smiled. "You really didn't know where I was that summer? Good. As to repeating the experience, I so wish I could. Now, if you'll excuse me, I'm going across."

Bernhardt nodded. Before she could walk away, he said, "About the young woman who snuck into your compound..." He hesitated. "Be careful."

"I will. Something you want to tell me?"

Bernhardt's face went back to its usual inexpressive mask. "Just to be careful."

"Yeah. I need time away from everything."

Bernhardt nodded. "I'm going over this afternoon."

Jeni went into the portal building. It looked like a power substation, which, along with its covert function, was exactly what it was. Dual overhead doors allowed trucks to enter, though the actual portal was one-way only for truck traffic, to reduce the power needed to keep it open. Jeni watched the doors to the portal tunnel slide up. They were heavy, over a foot thick and made of a shell of high-quality steel around a mix of ceramic materials sandwiched inside. A similar door slid open at the other end. A second pair of identical doors was set on each side of the portal itself, poised to swing shut in an emergency.

Jeni walked along the pedestrian walkway that led to Timeline X. There was no sign marking the transition from one timeline to the other. Some people claimed to feel disoriented when they went across, but Jeni never felt anything unusual.

On the other side, she found herself in a thunderstorm. She dashed from the portal door to the door of her house. Or more properly, her mansion.

Power was out in the house, but backup lights were on. Her housekeeper looked up casually from some kitchen task and then doubled her efforts when she recognized Jeni. Jeni went upstairs to her bedroom and changed out of her wet clothes. The thunderstorm ended a few minutes later. She strolled outside and glared back at the main house, built into the side of a hill, with retractable shutters to camouflage the windows, doors, and solar panels. Yeah. That monstrosity was really going to be invisible from the air. If the pilot was blind. Even with the shutters down, thermal imaging would find it.

She could only spot one other building from the low hill

where she stood. The top of a white frame house—temporary housing—peeked out of the woods. Her stomach churned at the sight, and not just because it was clearly visible.

I don't want them here.

The rest of the buildings sat invisibly underground, including Jeni's "Indian College" half a mile away. No roads connected the buildings, just camouflaged paths for electric carts.

Jeni chased down a plastic grocery bag blowing across the path in front of her. "Great. We're already trashing the timeline."

She marched to the white frame house. A guard sat at the gate of a nine-foot-high chain-link fence topped by barbed wire that surrounded it. He glanced up from his portable videogame, did a double take and hid the game beneath his logbook.

Jeni smiled. "It's a boring job; I get that. All jobs are boring eventually."

"Most of them are grounds-keeping, but there is one here."

"Who authorized the grounds-keeping?"

"Mr. Hollsworth."

"I'll need to chat with him. I don't do slaves."

"He said they're getting paid. I don't know what they would do with money, though."

The guard walked her in. A young female about three feet tall stood up when the door opened, got an eager expression on her face and picked up a notepad. "Draw?"

"They call this kind *Eyes*."

Jeni stood by the door until the "Eye" toddled over with her picture. If the female had a tail, she'd be wagging it. Jeni stared at the picture and didn't have to feign amazement. "Impressive."

The Eye grinned from ear to oversized ear. Jeni impulsively reached down and almost patted her on the head. She stopped herself. "I've got to get out of here."

She rushed out of the house.

Chapter Two

SCOTT CRINGED WHEN he noticed Darla eying the chipped conference table and elderly laptop computers.

Probably thinks we got them at a garage sale.

He flipped off the lights so he could examine the pictures from the cellphone chip that Darla projected onto the wall.

"You saw the last picture she took," Darla said. "She shot a video of the same scene."

Scott studied the picture. Other than the scroll, nothing. The table was oak and new. That meant expensive. "Wait. There's a mirror. Is there anything in it?"

Darla zoomed in on the mirror. "Nothing." She ran through the video, checking out the mirror there too. "And nothing."

"Wait. Go back." Scott thought he saw a flicker of motion in the mirror. "Slow it down."

A distorted face appeared in the mirror for a dozen frames, less than half a second in real time. Darla brought up the frame where it showed the clearest. Scott studied the image. Not a mask; the expression changed. And not a gorilla. "I think it's a man." But the forehead was wrong. The ears were wrong. "What is four feet tall with a face like a gorilla and hangs around rich people's houses?"

"I don't know."

Scott ran the twelve frames in a loop and studied the slight motions, fascinated. Not much room for a brain in that forehead.

Finally Darla said, "I'm ravenous. I skipped breakfast to catch the plane and didn't trust the food at Dickey's."

Scott glanced at his watch. "It's early for lunch, but I'll make hard copies of the twelve frames, then treat you to BTI cafeteria food. It's fast and not completely awful. Greasy burgers. Skimpy salad bar."

As they ate, Darla asked, "What does a BTI agent do when he isn't looking at mirrors?"

"I'm an analyst, not an agent. There's a huge difference. Bigger than detective versus beat cop." Scott glanced around the nearly empty cafeteria. "Agents are too good to eat here. They have big egos, guns and police powers, God help us all. And small manhoods—so I hear."

Darla grinned. "And let me guess; analysts play with computers. That explains the geeky look."

"I run marathons. I'm working up to Ironman competitions. And I've been to Timeline X a dozen times."

"Wait, didn't you just say we couldn't go there because of the diseases?"

"The diseases are in Europe. Indians don't have the nasty ones. That's why Indians died in heaps from European diseases when the Europeans came over but Europeans didn't die from Indian diseases."

"Definitely a geek answer. No offense. I poke at people. You'll get used to it." Her grin widened. "Besides, I like geeks." She pulled out her lighter and flicked it. "So the Indians are changing, doing what they would have done if your ancestors hadn't taken over. The Romans aren't. And that's a mystery."

"My ancestors?" Scott laughed. "I'm a quarter Indian. And you're part Anglo."

"Vietnamese-Irish."

"Yeah." Scott glanced up at the sprinklers, half expecting them to go off as Darla stared at the flame from her lighter.

"Could you put that away?" He pointed at the sprinkler head above them.

"Sorry. Nervous habit." Darla flipped the lighter shut, but held it poised in her hand. "Romans. No change. Tell me more."

"Not much to tell. The Romans stopped changing. A couple of hundred years later so did China and Japan. Looks like something spread from Rome. If anyone knows what spread, they haven't told me."

"Indians. Change. Tell me more."

Scott tried to sum up the five hundred years worth of changes as succinctly as possible: bigger towns, use of bronze, the spread of pigs and chickens from Polynesia. He started to mention butterfly effects before 1492, but caught the glazed look in Darla's eyes.

All she's hearing is "Yada yada, blah blah."

He finished with, "And that's the most intense sexual experience I've ever had."

"Huh? Okay, you got me. I zoned out."

"I'm used to it. Recovering Anthropology professor."

They finished eating and headed back to the conference room.

"The walls are thick in Europe and Asia, thin in the western part of North America and Australia. Does very different history in an area make the wall between the universes thicker?"

"That's a geek question, and a good one." Scott shot her a searching look. "The data says yes, but theory says it's a coincidence."

Darla smiled when they walked into the conference room, a smile with a mix of humor and malice.

"How is Dr. Scott White, history geek, going to help me solve a murder?"

"Scott White, marathoner, may have already spotted your murderer."

"Running is a geek hobby. And I would have spotted him."

"Maybe. What do you know about Jane Doe?"

Darla pulled a set of photos out of her briefcase. "Caucasian, in her twenties, in good shape, natural blond, light skin, wore high heels a lot. We found the body based on an anonymous tip from a disposable cellphone. The guy gave a location and hung up. No other calls from that phone. She was in the water two days before he called, so he didn't just see the body dumped and call it in. Body was weighted, so he couldn't have seen it floating. I'll figure it out. Nobody gets away with murder with me on the case."

"Ah, a master detective. How many murders have you solved?"

"Technically, none. But hey, perfect track record so far."

"Or no record at all."

They spent the next four hours scanning candid shots of what Scott mentally labeled "Ken and Barbie people," young adults spending mommy and daddy's money. Not a pimple or inch of cellulite in the bunch.

He did spot two first names on birthday cakes.

But I'm missing something else.

Scott closed his eyes. Nothing. They were evidently allergic to taking pictures by landmarks, road signs or the license plates of their Porsches.

Darla leaned back and stretched her legs. "No landmarks until she moved to Boston three months ago. But where did she move from? And where *to* in Boston?"

Chad peeked in. "Anything?"

"Not much," Darla said. "No labels. She probably downloaded the best pictures to her computer."

And deleted the blurry ones. Scott blinked. Then he sat up. "No blurry pictures because she deleted them."

"So?"

"So that's why you need a geek, not that I am one. If you delete a picture, the camera's file system makes the space available, but the picture stays until the space is reused."

"And you have software to get at those pictures?"

"Are bears Catholic? Does the pope sh—um—take walks in the woods? In other words, yeah." Scott plugged the chip into his computer. After a couple of minutes, he grinned. One hundred deleted files.

He showed the expanded directory to Darla. She groaned. "Four o'clock now. Figure another two hours to get through them."

Chad waved. "Have fun. I have to pick up the kids."

Most of the deleted pictures were blurry or partly written over. Finally Scott hit possible pay dirt: a TV van with the call letters visible. He found the call letters on the Internet. New Bristol, forty miles west of Boston. "Okay. Progress."

As he walked Darla through his discovery, Scott's feeling of triumph faded. Jane Doe could have been visiting New Bristol. The TV people could have been covering a story out of town. "If we find New Bristol landmarks in the pictures, we have to find Jane Doe in a population of a hundred thousand instead of millions." Scott sighed. "Maybe a little progress."

"We'll find out tomorrow." Darla brushed Scott's arm as she retrieved her briefcase. "Want to be my native guide for supper? I don't have another rental car yet."

"Sure. And I'll even drive you to the hotel."

"Okay, but the evening ends at the door. You're cute but not that cute. Let's try Dickey's."

"You said you didn't trust their menu. Lots of good restaurants near here."

"Yeah, but I want to keep my illusion of superiority. I'm in flyover country, so we eat in a redneck bar."

"Chicago isn't flyover country."

"Not to you, I'm sure."

Dickey's wasn't much more crowded than it had been in the morning. Bill Dickey waved to them from the bar, then rejoined a cluster of guys around a chubby blonde in a black miniskirt and red stiletto heels.

At the table, Darla smiled. "Tell me everything about yourself."

"You first."

"I don't pour out my life story to strangers."

"You just asked me to."

Darla grinned. "Fair enough. Let's start small. You're part Native American, right? How much and what tribe?"

"One fourth and I wish I knew. My grandmother claims she's pure-blood Natchez."

"And that's a problem because…"

"No records of Natchez ever living in northern Ohio. And she claims we're direct descendents of the Great Sun, which means that she's full of—let's call it *misinformation*. But I grew up thinking I was a Native American prince, which is why I'm an anthropologist instead of a factory worker like my dad."

"I have no idea what a Great Sun is, but it sounds cool."

"It would be if it was true." Scott glanced up and gave the waiter his drink order. "Your turn."

"Not much to say. I'm plain Darla Smith. My ancestors came over on the Mayflower—both sides. I went to Harvard, then gravitated to police work."

"Somehow I doubt that."

"What part of it?"

Scott laughed. "All of it."

"Little known fact: there was a Vietnamese woman on the Mayflower."

"No there wasn't."

"My birth mother was Vietnamese-American. My adoptive parents actually were ancestors-on-the-Mayflower types. I did community college, Marines, then an oops or two before I got my degree."

"No Harvard? Were your adoptive parents scandalized?"

Darla laughed. "They've been continuously scandalized from the time I was twelve until—well, until now, I imagine. I haven't talked to them in years."

Bill Dickey brought their drinks. "Did I hear the word scandal?"

"Probably," Scott said.

"I told you she was trouble. You've been here twice, so you're regulars. Any time you want to get drunk and tell me your darkest secrets, I'm here for you."

"We'll keep that in mind," Scott said. He gestured to the stage. "No 'UDE' girls."

"You're not drunk enough to appreciate the girls I get here," Bill said. "Speaking of deep, dark secrets, when are they going to bring oil through the Portals?"

"Hopefully never."

Bill grinned. "Ah, tree hugger. Leave the Indians alone? Well your money spends as well as anyone's, but remember, screwing over Indians made this country great."

"That's one way of looking at it."

Bill stretched his long arms. His shirt rode up, revealing a pot belly. "We're a plague of locusts, all of us, Americans and Europeans, Asians. We eat the land bare. Stop moving and we starve to death. Now we have the portals—a whole new world to ravage. We're a Biblical plague. No use pretending we aren't." He strolled away, grinning.

"Cheery thought." Darla turned to Scott. "Where were we?" She cautiously sipped her drink. "How have you scandalized your parents? Scratch that. What's the most Native American thing you've done?"

"I made an authentic Native American bow."

"A Natchez bow?"

"No. Plains Indians made better bows. They were sinew-backed and—you don't care about that, do you?" Scott scanned the menu. "Your turn. What's the most Vietnamese thing you've done?"

"I ate Vietnamese egg rolls."

"That's the best you can do?"

"It's the best I want to do until I know you better."

"You're such a cheat."

"You never told me what you've done to scandalize your parents."

"You said scratch that."

Darla laughed. "Yeah, but I think you have a good scandalizing or two up your sleeve."

"Not really. Dad wanted me to work in the factory like he did. He still does, even after the factory jobs got outsourced."

"Is that the best you can do?"

"It's better than you did. All I know is your parents were scandalized." Scott grinned. "I may tell you more once I get to know you."

"Touché. So there is more."

They finished eating and drove toward the hotel. Scott glanced in the mirror. "Is someone following us?"

"Wouldn't surprise me."

"Your personal cloud again?"

"Probably."

A fire truck roared down the street behind them, siren blaring. Darla grabbed Scott's arm. "Let's follow it."

"Why?"

"Why not? I'm wired."

Scott followed the truck. Flames rose from a church steeple

blocks away. "Looks like a big one."

"Park and get closer."

"Aren't you exhausted?"

"Not anymore." Darla grabbed his arm. "Come on."

The fire burned out of control as they hurried toward it. Half the roof collapsed and the firefighters pulled back. Darla wrapped her arm around Scott's waist. He glanced at her. "What—"

She kissed him, pressing her body against his. Scott returned the kiss, but she suddenly pulled away and ran to the car. Scott ran after her. "What was that about?"

Darla snapped, "Get me to the hotel parking lot. And don't walk me in."

Chapter Three

JENI BURGEN LEANED back in a soft chair in her virtual-presence room.

"So the Boston Police found a body," she said. "Why do I care?"

Andy Hollsworth was in Boston, but the wall-sized video panel gave the illusion that the round-faced, balding company lawyer was sitting in front of her. "Not sure. What did Bernie Sloan do to our visitor?"

"I told him to get her out of there and destroy any pictures. Why do you think this body has anything to do with her?"

"Samantha Murphy never showed up at her apartment. The police figure Jane Doe died the night Murphy snuck into the Ohio complex. And her boyfriend died two days ago."

"The security guy we fired for letting her in?"

Andy nodded. "Apparent heart attack at only forty-six years old—didn't smoke, wasn't overweight."

Jeni sighed. "You aren't a big fan of Bernie Sloan. Are you saying he killed them?"

"Why not? The guy's a thug. Keep an eye on this, Jeni. Don't get blindsided."

"I'll look into it. Don't attract attention. And remember, coincidences happen."

Andy laughed. "I'm the lawyer. I'll be discreet."

"Do that." Jeni blanked the screen and strolled to the pool.

She turned on the security monitor. “Morning swim. Monitor me.” In the locker room, she studied herself critically in the mirror. One advantage of being among the fifty richest people in the world: appearing over a decade younger than her forty-one years. She swam a quick mile, thinking about the conversation with Andy.

I'll have Adam look into it.

She paused. “But he's in Rome.”

A voice came over the monitor. “Did you say something?”

“Talking to myself.”

And getting depressed.

Bernhardt Sloan looked the part of a security chief. It wasn't just his height and weightlifter build. It was also his perpetual scowl and the dark expressionless eyes. Those eyes gave away nothing as he stared at Jeni Burgen through the virtual-presence screen.

“From a legal standpoint, you don't want to know what happened to the young lady.”

“What did you do to her?”

“I took care of it. And I take full responsibility for the problem.”

Jeni matched Bernhardt's scowl. “You aren't going to tell me?”

“No.”

“Not even if your job is on the line?”

“If I no longer have your confidence as head of security, I'll submit my resignation.”

Jeni sighed. “I figured that. I'll let you know.”

A half-smile crept over Bernhardt's cold face. “Please do.”

Jeni fought back a surge of anger and smiled back coldly. “Ever wonder how I got to the top and stayed here?”

Bernhardt's smile faded only slightly. “I know how you did it.”

"I wonder if you do, really."

Jeni turned off the screen and avoided the issue the rest of the morning—not procrastinating, she told herself, but working on more important issues.

I need to know what happened that night, but part of me doesn't want to know.

After lunch, she linked to Andy's office. "Any developments on Jane Doe?"

"My contacts say the detective assigned to the case is now working with the Bureau of Timeline Integrity. Jane Doe is probably Samantha Murphy."

Jeni swore. "Even if the body is hers, how did they connect her to Timeline X?"

"She saw a scroll."

"She saw a pixie too. Why did you bring those creepy things back?"

"Not my call. I said you might be interested and boom, half the yacht was filled with them."

"I don't do slaves," Jeni said. "Not in any form. We need to get rid of them."

"They're totally loyal to you and they work hard."

"But they're slaves."

"Or pets. I know you don't want them, but what can we do? Kill them? They're human enough a court might call that murder." Andy grinned. "Talk about a media circus."

"Don't kill them. Put them on the next ship to Rome."

"Will do. I don't think BTI even knows about pixies. They should, but if they do, they're keeping it close to the vest. I'm not sure why."

"Because quasi-human slaves screw up everything—law, religion, economics. Any self-respecting bureaucrat would want them to go away. I want them to go away and I'm the antithesis of a bureaucrat."

"Did you talk to Sloan?"

Jeni nodded. "He claimed I'd be better off not knowing what he did with Murphy."

"If he cut her head off, he's right."

"He does a good job." Jeni leaned back in her chair. *But I'm not entirely sure he wouldn't kill someone or cut off her head.* "Keep an eye on this, but cautiously."

They chatted briefly about how Andy's cabin on the other side was progressing. Andy assured her that the workers were legal, in from Guatemala on work visas and slated to return to Central America when they finished.

Jeni grinned. "And all of this is so you can go bird-watching, huh?"

"It's a hobby." Andy looked embarrassed. "The workers' arrangement: Good. Not foolproof."

"Just another risk of doing business," Jeni said. "What's the point of having money if it can't buy you things nobody else has?"

"Well, you've certainly done that. You realize how big a risk this portal is?"

"You don't get where I am without putting yourself on the line," Jeni said.

"This does put you on the line. Your money, your freedom. Everything."

Chapter Four

TWO EAGLE TRACKED the strange footprints from the bank of the Ohio River inland to a thicket where an undetected spy could have, and apparently had, watched the Wenroh people. The footprints puzzled Two Eagle. They were pressed into the mud near the river leaving an intricate pattern of ridges, with each foot shaped differently.

He followed the return trail to the river. On the bank, he spotted marks where a canoe had been beached and then launched. There was no sign of the odd-footed watcher or his canoe on the river, but he found a round, flat, shiny object about the size of his thumb, glinting at the edge of the water. He picked up the disc and examined it. A sculpture of a man's face stared back at him, protruding slightly from the disc's surface.

Two Eagle trotted back to town, carrying his find. He carefully avoided the ankle-high corn in the huge fields that surrounded the palisaded town. The guards on the nearest watchtower looked him over as he approached, then relaxed. He told the guards about the footprints. A group of warriors went to check them out, but found nothing more. The council doubled the night guards, but nobody could think of anything else to do, so life went on, with a hint of uneasiness.

Scott did his usual six-mile morning run along the Prairie Path nature trail from his apartment in the Chicago suburb of

Wheaton. Darla called while he was dressing and asked him to give her a ride. She didn't apologize for her outburst the night before. *Find your own ride*, he wanted to say. But he settled for saying, "Yeah, sure."

Darla glared at him when he drove her to the office. "You're wide awake. I hate you."

"I run in the morning. It wakes me up."

"I really hate you. How far?"

"Six miles."

"I did tell you I hate you, right?"

"Yeah."

"Just wanted to make sure." She stared out the window, arms crossed.

When they got to the conference room, Scott searched for landmarks from New Bristol on the Internet. Finally he sat back and studied the printouts of the twelve video frames showing the *gargoyle*. "It's not an ape, but that brain isn't going to have a lot of light-bulb moments."

"Hobbits? They were in headlines a few years ago. Someone found bones of little people in Indonesia. Three feet tall. Tiny brains. They called them Hobbits."

"Yeah, I know. They lived on our version of Flores. I have a doctorate in Anthropology, remember."

"Well, aren't you the educated one? Should I call you Doctor White?"

"Scott works. Hobbits, huh?" They could have survived over there. That was a lot of speculation to hang on blurry pictures though. Scott turned back to his computer. "Was the kiss that bad?"

"The kiss was fine."

Peter Kindahl stuck his square-jawed, well-groomed face into the room. "I hear you have a spot of a mystery."

Scott glared at him. "That's more than you need to know, *old boy*."

"Hmmm. Mr. Summers thinks Ms. Smith needs an actual agent on the team. Sounds like a capital idea to me. Aren't you going to introduce me?"

"Peter Kindahl, meet Darla Smith. Darla, Peter is an agent, as I'm sure he'll tell you. He'll tell you a lot about himself."

Darla grinned. "And you two are great buddies, I see."

"Yeah. I'm so looking forward to having Petey on the team."

Peter sat on the table next to Darla. "So you're the Boston detective."

"And you're in my space. Shoo."

Peter shrugged. "I'm getting coffee. I'll be back for a briefing in ten minutes."

As the door closed, Scott laughed. "Wow. I haven't seen him get shot down like that in, well, ever. Women fall for the pseudo-British thing, at least for a night—two at the most."

"Maybe I will later. Now shut up before I tell you to shoo too."

Hobbits. Scott decided to take another look at how the mystery creature moved. He went through the clip frame by frame. "I don't see the beastie in the mirror."

Darla looked over his shoulder. "Huh. That's the right spot."

"But no beastie."

Darla searched her briefcase but couldn't find the camera chip there or in the computer.

Scott checked the computer. "Not there. Great. You realize the original chip will be vital if this ever goes to trial."

"Yeah. Me police officer, remember. Took classes. Got a badge. I didn't lose the chip. If it's gone, it's because your security sucks."

"Well until you find it, I'll use the copy on my computer." A couple of seconds later he said, "The beastie isn't there either."

Chapter Five

SCOTT LET THE soothing endorphins from his run wash through him as Darla briefed Peter Kindahl. Peter tossed a quick "I'll see what I can do" over his shoulder as he left. Scott and Darla spent the rest of the morning silently working at their computers.

Darla found the missing chip on the floor beneath the table when they got back from lunch. "So I'm not a total screw-up."

She loaded the video from the chip. The same frames were there, but there was nothing in the mirror. "Not there either."

Scott checked the file's change date. "No changes. Did we imagine it last night?"

"You might have. I didn't." Darla put the chip back in her briefcase. "Someone in your agency doesn't want my investigation going down that road. You have people who could edit a video and spoof a file date." Darla zoomed in on the mirror and circled an area near the top. "They were in a hurry—used this to paint over our beastie. It's good enough to fool someone who isn't looking for it."

Scott examined the frames again. She was right. "I'll ask Chad who had access to the room."

"I wouldn't. Keep it between us until we know who's doing what and why."

"Fine. I don't know what I'd say to him anyway."

Scott tried to set the issue of the mirror aside and work on identifying Jane Doe's friends, but the possible security breech worried him. He mechanically copied the faces of Jane Doe's friends onto a single screen, then searched social networking sites and blogs for New Bristol. No luck. He expanded the search to surrounding towns. After a while he found a match, "Got one," he said.

He compared a cellphone picture to one on a social network. "What do you think?"

Darla leaned over his shoulder. "He's older and has longer hair, but maybe. What's his name?"

"His screen name's Bowwow17."

"Any way we can use that to find his real name?"

"We could subpoena the email address he used to open the social networking account." Scott grinned. "Or we could email him through the social network and ask for his name."

"Why would he tell us?"

"Because I went to school with him and stumbled across his picture, as far as he knows." Scott typed a quick email. "I'll see if Jane Doe's other friends are in his pictures. You check his friend list for matches." He glanced at Darla and added hastily, "If you want to."

Peter Kindahl came in. "Any progress?"

Scott and Darla spoke at the same time. Scott said, "A little." Darla said, "Nothing important."

Darla added, "A long shot. Not something we'd look at if we had anything real."

"You can tell me about it over dinner."

"I could, but I'm not that bored." Darla smiled. "Besides, I'll be busy counting ceiling tiles in my hotel."

"Ouch. Again, your loss." Peter strolled out.

Scott stared at Darla. "Ouch indeed. A hard left jab to the ego. Maybe I shouldn't take the stuff you say personally."

"It's more fun if you do, but good job on finding Bowwow17."

"Why didn't you tell him about that?"

"Mr. Shaken-Not-Stirred wannabe? Because I don't know who screwed with my evidence. I wouldn't have told you except you already know. This isn't some misdemeanor case. If that scroll is genuine, it's priceless. Getting it took resources only governments usually have. Someone with that much power committed murder. And now we have evidence tampering. When the stakes are that high, and we don't know who the enemy is, paranoia is common sense. Someone with those resources could effectively be above the law."

"I don't believe that."

Darla shook her head. "So naïve. A district attorney only has so much money. Who is he going to prosecute? Two dozen poor but vicious slubs with public defenders or one rich guy with the best lawyers money can buy and enough tricks up their sleeves to keep the case in court for years?"

"Rich people still go to jail in this country."

"Yeah, if the case is strong enough and the people they hurt matter enough."

"So cynical."

"That isn't all. Prosecutors know their opponent will have lots of money in the next election if they go after the wrong people."

"Okay. This isn't a perfect world. Why don't we give up and go home?"

"I'm not giving up. I want whoever did this to rot in jail. But we need to dot every 'i'—prove the case so even the sneakiest defense attorney can't get the murderer out of it."

Chapter Six

THE HOUSE ON the Timeline X side of the portal had a virtual presence room identical to the one in Jeni's house on the other side, with a video cable running through the portal. Jeni used it to buzz Andy Hollsworth in the Boston Office.

"Back from your bird watching?" she said.

Andy grinned. "I don't care how much the portal costs, it's worth it. An unspoiled world. When I go there, I don't want to come back."

"That's easy for you to say. It's my money."

"Mostly. And it's your butt on the line if this Samantha Murphy investigation leads BTI to your portal."

Jeni felt something crinkle in her pocket. She pulled out the drawing from the Eye. "Any word on the investigation?"

"We can't get inside it, but we know who's involved. Boston PD sent a detective named Darla Smith to the BTI office in Chicago. She ate dinner with BTI analyst Scott White. We think he's involved from the BTI side."

"Scott White? Doctor Scott White? I know him. And no, you don't need to know how." She smoothed the creases out of the picture and thought about confronting Andy about using the pixies as groundskeepers, but decided to avoid that confrontation for now.

Andy said, "Ah. You probably met him during one of your 'I want to live like normal people' phases."

Jeni sighed. "There's nothing wrong with that."

"I don't see the appeal. You're one of the wealthiest people in the world. You worked your butt off to get there. Why look back? Why try to be anyone else?"

"It's necessary. Sometimes I have to take a break. Actually, this was work."

Andy gave her what he knew about Darla Smith, then added, "There's something weird about her background. I haven't been able to trace her before the Marines yet, but I will. Smith moves fast. She was all over Scott White in a parking lot. Didn't go home with him though."

"You had them followed?"

"Nothing anyone can tie back to us. Somebody else is keeping an eye on them too."

"Who?"

"The obvious guess would be Bernie Sloan. You might want to check out his budget."

"I did. Unless he hired somebody out of his own pocket, it isn't him."

"Then I have no idea. That's not a comforting thought. I hate to bring this up, but you might want to hide some assets."

"You think it's that serious?"

"Probably not. A wrongful death lawsuit is the biggest threat. If Samantha Murphy's family hits you with a civil suit, they don't have to prove their case beyond a reasonable doubt. They just have to prove a preponderance of evidence. Put it in front of a jury and who knows what will happen."

"Look into it and make a contingency plan." Jeni leaned back and rubbed her neck, which had tightened as the conversation went on. *I so want this to go away*. "I'm not pushing Sloan too hard. I don't want him on the outside with nothing to lose."

"That's the nightmare scenario. You'll want to vet anything you say to him with an eye to how it might get twisted in front of a jury."

"Right. I have a bunch of companies to run. Remember to keep me posted."

Jeni closed the link and turned to an email her computer just finished decrypting.

Hi, Jeni.
We made port in the Timeline X version of Lisbon this morning. Your yacht's a bit the worse for wear, but nothing that'll keep us from making it back. Sailing's a challenge without GPS or weather satellites. The link to our timeline's weather satellites was useless—the weather here is totally different.

The fuel tanks in the Azores are ready, and we have a bare-bones shelter there. A rustic cabin. That means limited electricity, Porta-potties and bottled water, which we left quite a bit of. We also set up a navigation beacon. So, our end of the air route is available when you're ready at your end.

Miss you.
Adam

Jeni flushed all traces of the message from her computer. She stared hungrily at the twelve digital pictures that accompanied the email. Finally, she deleted the pictures too.

She shut down the computer and let the silence wash over her. It wasn't complete. The guards and groundskeepers went about their tasks, though more quietly than they would have on the other side of her rogue portal. Even the reduced noise grated on her nerves.

She strolled outside and stood in the sunshine. Her compound on the Timeline-X side of the portal was almost identical to her home compound a half hour away from the data center in Ohio—so close a casual visitor wouldn't notice the difference. The defenses were stronger here, but that wasn't obvious unless you knew where to look. The oak trees on this side were taller. She insisted that the workmen leave as many as possible in place as they built the compound, though the trees made placing solar panels difficult. The equipment for the high-altitude tethered balloon that gave her intermittent communications with her yacht was hidden from casual observers.

Jeni wandered through the trees to a canopied swing by a fish pond. She sat and gently swayed in the breeze. The silence soothed her, giving her a break from the pressures of being Jeni Burgen. It wasn't a complete break; she still felt the ever-present security, though she saw no sign of it.

The first of two flying boats was assembled and tied up along the Ohio River on this side. The second of the two boats was also assembled, but in need of a couple of shakeout flights before it was ready to go, no more than a day according to her mechanics. She pushed aside a wild impulse to order that the first boat fly this afternoon. Too risky. Not until the second flying boat was ready. Tomorrow would be soon enough. And Bernhardt would have his people on board anyway. She sighed. "Even there I can't really get away," she whispered to herself.

Chapter Seven

SCOTT GOT A response to his email at five o'clock. That gave him a name: Ralph Worster. He searched for Ralph on the Internet. Ralph Worster had been a high school football star in New Bristol. The cellphone pictures appeared to be a bunch of twenty-something ex-football players and their groupies. Scott spotted at least four of the faces from the cellphone on Ralph's friend list. All they needed was a yearbook to map out the football players, figure out who hung around them, put names to people in the pictures and ask who had been behind the phone camera.

He showed Darla the pictures.

"Okay, *now* I'll admit you've got something. We need a yearbook. And that should get us to square one, putting a name to Jane Doe."

"Yearbooks are dead tree stuff. The school may have an online yearbook. Or I could send young Mr. Worster the picture with him on it and ask him who was behind the camera." Scott grinned and typed "Hey, Ralph, somebody forwarded me this picture a couple of months ago. I want to put it on my front page but I can't figure out who took it and I want to make sure it's okay." He sent the message. "Isn't social networking wonderful?"

"Who does he think you are?"

"He has no idea, but he thinks he should know me so he won't admit that he doesn't." Scott stood up and stretched. "Now I have to catch my boss before he leaves so we can figure out what's going on with the disappearing mystery beastie and why he stuck me with Peter Kindahl."

Darla shook her head. "I told you, don't do that."

"I remember the conversation, but you don't sign my paychecks. Chad Summers does. You're being paranoid again."

"You really think so? You do realize someone in the BTI altered those pictures, right? If it was somebody inside the bureau, how do you know it wasn't Chad Summers? I know you would dearly love for it to be Peter Kindahl, but it may not be."

"If whoever killed Jane Doe has a way into the investigation, why would they erase just the beastie? Why not erase the chip or steal it and erase our backups?"

"That, my friend, is a good question. Maybe I'll find a use for you after all, like letting you take me to supper."

"I thought you needed to count ceiling tiles."

"Maybe later."

Scott nodded. "Okay. Supper. As soon as I talk to Mr. Summers about Peter Kindahl."

"And the missing thing in the mirror?"

"I'll hold off on that until tomorrow and sleep on it."

Scott strolled to Chad's office. "I hear I'm working with Peter."

Chad grinned. "He gets things done."

"I get things done too."

"That you do. He gets a different class of things done."

"He's a pompous ass."

Chad stood and closed his briefcase. "Okay, he's a pompous ass who gets a certain class of things done. Work with him. How is the investigation going?"

"We may be closing in on a name for Jane Doe."

"Great. Any sign of anything else from TLX in the pictures?"

Scott hesitated for a fraction of a second. *I should tell him. Trail is going cold.* "No other artifacts. We're dealing with wealth.

Nobody without a lot of money would have the scroll long. Who has that kind of money around Boston?"

"That's a long list and no easy way to narrow it." Chad glanced at his watch. "Got to go. What do you think of Detective Smith?"

"She says what she thinks without much filtering, but she's not stupid."

"Boston PD seemed to like the idea of her being gone. They suggested we assign her to a task force. There may be things in her background she isn't telling us."

Scott nodded. "I've seen signs of that."

When Scott got back to the conference room, Darla was gone. A note on his computer read, "Decided to fly to New Bristol. Had to run to catch the flight. I'll take a rain check on supper."

Chapter Eight

JENI'S KNUCKLES TIGHTENED on the seat in front of her as the flying boat circled while the pilot studied the area and then made his landing approach in a small natural harbor in the Azores.

The approach gave Jeni glimpses of forest stretching almost unbroken across the island. Ordinarily she would have been fascinated by her first glimpse of a fragment of the world still mostly untouched by humans except for a minimal, hopefully benign, presence around the harbor. That fascination was more than counterbalanced by fear. She tried to push that fear to the back of her mind. *Adam is careful. No coral reefs where we'll run into them. No rocks.* Her mind believed that. Her body didn't, not until the plane came to rest, swaying faintly in the waves.

Bernhardt leaned back in the seat in front of her. "Going to be able to pry those hands loose from the chair back?"

"Eventually." Jeni glanced around the plane. The half dozen security team members all seemed relaxed and casual about the landing. They seemed more impressed by the forest that reached almost to the beach, with little transition, and the throng of birds that sat thickly on the beach eyeing the plane with apparent curiosity but no sign of fear.

Jeni glanced back at Andy, expecting the lawyer to be staring avidly out the window. He was skimming notes on a legal pad.

"I figured you would be leaning out the window. That's bird-watcher paradise out there."

"No challenge. And I'm a tad busy keeping the human vultures at bay."

"They've never seen a human," Jeni said. "Except for Adam and his team, I guess, which is appropriate in a weird sort of way."

Jeni and four of the security detail rowed ashore. The birds in their path still showed no sign of fear. They didn't even hop out of the way when the humans reached them, and Jeni had to circle around them. Other than the birds, there was little in the way of wildlife to see on the island—no mammals other than bats and only a few lizards. Insects there were in large numbers, but they were more annoying for their presence than for any harm they inflicted. The island seemed devoid of biting or stinging insects.

"Almost a paradise," Jeni said. None of the security people said anything. They kept their eyes turned to the sky, watching for large hawks or buzzards, which according to Adam had persistently attacked one of the men from his party. Jeni added, "I know Adam claimed there was a hawk, and some of the Portuguese settlers from our timeline talked about them, but there is no solid evidence there were ever hawks here."

The security guys didn't respond and kept searching the skies.

I guess it gives them a hobby.

The cabin was certainly rustic, an actual log cabin in a clearing made by cutting the trees used to build it, with shingles cut from those same trees. A little garden of corn and beans had not sprouted yet. A rubber "Big John" outhouse struck a dissonant note in the otherwise pioneer-like scene.

They left a skeleton crew on the flying boat and bedded down in the log cabin, in sleeping bags. Jeni stared at the ceiling dimly lit by a rechargeable lantern.

I'm going to turn this into a home, but one that blends in, that lets me live light on the land.

One of the security guys spoke. "This place needs animals.

It's way too empty."

"It's not empty," Jeni said. "It's a miniature laboratory. Put a few of these and a few of those on an island and give them a few million years to see what happens. Just like the Indians are a natural laboratory. How many ways can humans put a culture together? What things does one culture invent that no other culture could figure out because of the blinders of their own cultures? That's what I love about being here." She sat up and turned to Andy. "That's why I'm here."

"So, what is your business plan?" Andy asked.

"Does everything have to have a business plan?"

"If it costs multiple millions of dollars, yeah. At least that's the way I've always heard it."

"Sometimes you do things because you want to do them," Jeni said. "When it's stockholder money, there's a business plan. When it's my money, I buy things that bring me pleasure. Seeing something like this—an island that has never been touched by humans, that's still the kind of laboratory most of the big islands were before our ancestors came along—that brings me pleasure. Going to Rome, that brings me pleasure." She snuggled into the bag and went to sleep.

The next morning they refueled the flying boat and flew on to the Roman port of Olissipo, on the site of home dimension Lisbon. They landed outside the view of the Romans and came in the last couple of miles as a boat.

Jeni stared out the window at the late afternoon sun glinting off long, slow waves pushing the flying boat toward land. She could see parts of a Roman harbor from the window. Her yacht was at a berth deep within the harbor, dwarfed by half a dozen trireme warships. Two of the triremes cast off in the harbor but hung back as a ship half the size of the yacht glided toward them. The part of the sky she could see was cloud free.

The rain in Spain falls mainly in the plain.

She grinned, partly out of relief that the plane trip was over.

Jeni caught a glimpse of the oarsmen in the ship headed toward them, massively muscled near-humans. Based on their upper bodies, they were probably a little under five feet tall and nearly as wide. The oarsmen's burly muscles propelled their ship almost as quickly as an engine. They looked like orcs.

Jeni walked up to the flying boat's pilot, Ben Dunham, who grinned at her. "I got us here. Flying's a challenge when you don't have GPS or weather satellites."

"Couldn't you link back to our timeline's weather satellites?"

Ben shook his head. "We did until the link went down, but it was useless. The weather over here is totally different."

A fat, dark-haired man in a toga and a cheap pink digital watch hailed them from the ship. Jeni spotted Adam Stine standing beside him. Adam smiled at her and then translated the other man's oddly accented Latin.

"Welcome, friends of our old friends and partners."

Andy laughed. "We've been here once before. I wonder what he would consider casual acquaintances."

"Someone he doesn't want to trade with." Jeni studied the guy in the toga. "That watch is quite a fashion statement."

"Over here it is." Andy nodded to the man in the toga. "That's our host. Severus something-or-other. He's head of a politically connected merchant family. The Emperor gave him a trade monopoly."

Jeni mentally nicknamed the merchant Severallus Doublechinus and fought to keep a grin off her face. Being this close to land and in view of a Roman harbor raised her spirits.

I made this possible. I did it.

The amateur archaeologist in her ached to be in the city. She didn't, however, care for the smell. Based on the odor, the Roman sewer lines must terminate in or near the harbor.

But the stench only reminded her of where she was. The grin

broke through.

Andy stared at her. “I’ve never seen you this happy.”

“Yeah. Weird, huh?” Jeni spotted a Roman merchant holding an old off-brand CD player. “Isn’t it a bad idea to sell them things that require batteries?”

“Keeps them coming back for more.”

“If they’re anything like our Romans, these are proud people. If you make them look stupid, you may lose body parts. And believe me, Romans are good at cutting stuff off.”

Severus shouted instructions for the flying boat to follow his ship and assigned it a berth. Bernhardt glared at the bulks of the triremes looming uncomfortably close. “I doubt if we could get out of the harbor if those things came after us. It would be nice to have a cannon or two or even a machine gun.”

“That would raise eyebrows back home if anyone traced them back to us,” Jeni said. “We’re already taking enough risks.”

“Enough money can buy anything, including discretion on who the buyer is.”

“It can, but that kind of firepower could get you attention you don’t want,” Jeni said. She turned toward the dock where Severus shuffled up to greet them, Adam by his side.

Andy said, “Time for a round of feasting, drinking and pixie prostitutes.”

Adam came up behind them as Andy said that. He shuddered. “I’ve been at sea a long time, but I won’t have any problem saying no to that. It’s like sleeping with a monkey.”

“You’d be surprised,” Andy said. “The Romans had over two thousand years to breed them to look good, smell good and make a man feel good. Most of the crew indulged last time.”

“Not all of it,” Adam said. He turned to Jeni. “And you made this all possible, including the indulging.”

Scott ate a microwave dinner in front of the TV in his apartment.

He read Darla's note again and said to his empty apartment, "The woman's a bitch. She could have at least left her number. 'Get to know you better' my butt." He flipped through channels for a while, then checked his email. *Yes. Ralph the ex-football star. What do you have to tell me Ralph?*

The email said, "I think it was Samantha. Do you have her email? It's SMurphy. I think she's on jmail. Have you heard from her in the last two weeks? I haven't, and we're getting worried. By the way, I've been trying to figure out who you are. Sorry dude, but I can't place you."

Scott laughed. "And you never will, my overly trusting friend. But thanks. You gave Jane Doe back her name. And what do we know about Samantha, last name probably Murphy?" He searched for the name on the Internet and social networking sites. He found a picture of a Samantha Murphy in a cheerleading outfit and stared at the blond-haired, blue-eyed missing face of Jane Doe.

That's eerie.

He pieced together parts of her life. A blog chronicled Samantha Murphy's friendships, her travels, her boyfriends and her troubled relationship with her parents in excessively intimate detail. The blog also talked about her new life in Boston and her latest triumph: a story published in *Celebrity WebBeat*, an online magazine. Scott followed her link to the article. It was a puff piece about John Peltz, a software multi-millionaire, published two months ago.

Scott combed the article for signs John Peltz might be interested in collecting Timeline X objects. At the end, he shook his head. Probably not the type. Scot matched a couple of pictures on the chip to some in the article, then looked for pictures of the Peltz residence dated after the article. He sighed. Nothing in the article anyone could object to and no sign she went back later.

The blog entries ended ten days ago. Scott reread them. He

found the name of Samantha's most recent male friend, Irwin Boyer. Reading between the gushing lines, Scott figured out that Irwin was almost twenty years older than Samantha and that her family and friends disapproved. Scott downloaded the blog entries, then went to bed.

Jeni stayed on the flying boat while most of the crew went into Olissipo that evening. Adam stayed with her, catching her up on the details of the trading. Bernhardt and his security people moved to the front of the boat or deployed nearby.

Jeni and Adam sat next to each other on the seat, their knees touching, but with no hint of the attraction they once felt. From husband and lover to friend. How often did that happen? Jeni smiled at him. "Happy?"

"I'm in my element here," Adam said. "Archeology all around me, plus a manageable little business. A few million worth. Why would anyone want more?"

She did. And that was one of the many reasons he was here and she usually wasn't. They caught up on business, and Adam left for the yacht.

Andy climbed back aboard the flying boat a little before midnight local time. He sat across from Jeni. "Yacht got in touch with home."

Her neck stiffened. "It better have been good news."

Andy took a deep breath. He glanced at Bernhardt and lowered his voice. "I think they've identified the corpse as Samantha Murphy. If they haven't already, they will soon. Darla Smith flew to New Bristol this evening. That's Samantha Murphy's home town."

Jeni felt her muscles tighten. Black spots wavered in front of her eyes. She took a deep breath and they faded. She heard Andy's voice "Are you okay?"

She nodded. "Yeah. Stiff neck. So it was her?"

"Sure. I've been operating on the assumption it was from early on."

"And *I* kept hoping it wasn't. You wouldn't believe how much I hoped it wasn't. Where does this leave us?"

"Once they know who she is, they'll talk to her friends. That could lead them to Irwin Boyer, and if they know Timeline X artifacts are involved, which they apparently do, we'll be on the suspect list."

"How can they know she was connected to Timeline X?"

"I still have no idea. I can't even figure out how they put a name to the corpse."

"We need to get inside the investigation."

"How? Pay somebody off?"

Jeni shook her head. "Too risky, and illegal in its own right."

"Then there's not much I can do. Someone else *is* tracking Darla Smith. That went from a probable to a one hundred percent." He stared out the window into the dark harbor. "How good is your cover story for the portal?"

"As good as we can make it," Jeni said. She went over her precautions. The data center ran on much more efficient processors than the books said it did, letting them hide the portal's power draw. "It would take a hardware guru to figure out the swap."

"Will the new processor boards show up on the paperwork?"

Jeni nodded. "But they're officially at another data center, which is officially experiencing technical difficulties."

"I understood less than half of that, but the bottom line is we're covered, right?"

"As well as we can be. The equipment for the portal could be traced to us if somebody with enough resources kept digging." Jeni shrugged. "You can't do something on this scale without leaving some trail."

"You may want to scale up construction in Timeline X and

move up your timetable."

"That would increase the risk."

Andy nodded. "I know. Here's a worst case scenario though." He glanced to the front of the flying boat, where Bernhardt Sloan sat, his eyes closed. "What if Bernie up there knows how Samantha Murphy ended up dead. Boston PD and the BTI lean on him. He says, 'Gee I'm just a little fish following orders. What you really want is the big fish.' And you know who the big fish is."

"I get the picture. So what does that have to do with building faster over here?"

"If the worst case scenario played out, you might want a hidey hole here. And if you need it, you'd probably prefer a mansion, not a mud hut."

"I've got a state-of-the-art, super-efficient partly in-ground house over here already."

"Right, but it isn't self-sufficient. You're bringing in food, electricity, gas, just to mention a few necessities. For Timeline X to work as a bolt hole, we need to make your compound here self-sufficient or stock up on what we need to keep a reasonable lifestyle going."

Jeni leaned back and closed her eyes, feeling the flying boat sway gently in the waves. "Okay. Have a contingency plan. Don't move on it unless I say so. Do you have a plan together for hiding assets?"

"On your desk when we get back."

"Good. Could this actually get that serious?"

"Probably not, but making the compound on this side self-sufficient would cut portal traffic anyway, and make it harder to detect. If we could shut down the portal for a year or two, or even five years, that could help in a lot of contingencies."

"True. More chance of detection up front though. Speaking of detection, review our email and erase anything we don't have to keep before any subpoenas hit us."

"Spoken like a lawyer," Andy said. "I have it under control, but I'll look at the procedures again."

"Actually, spoken like a law-abiding woman who doesn't want jail time for something she didn't do."

"Mostly law-abiding. Building a private portal was illegal last time I checked."

"For the time being. By the way, I hear you're using pixies as groundskeepers. What part of no slaves didn't you pick up on?"

"Sorry. We're scrambling for labor and the pixies were sitting around getting bored and fat. They're bred to work and don't do well just sitting."

"Go back two hundred years and I bet a lot of plantation owners were spouting the same nonsense."

"Except this time it isn't nonsense. Pixies aren't human. They really have been bred to work hard. I have problems with doing that to arguably human creatures, but what's done is done. I set up accounts for them and we're paying minimum wage. I don't know what they could buy, or if we could even get them to understand money, but it's there."

"I don't like it, and I especially don't like finding out about it after the fact."

"You're the boss. I can put them back in a cage if you think that's better."

"No. Keep them doing what they're doing, but send video of everything they do to my computer on the Timeline X side. If I see the slightest evidence of mistreatment or neglect, they stop working and you're no longer working for me. Are we clear?"

"Completely. One other thing. Do you keep records of our video conferences?"

"I edit them myself at the end of the day and destroy the originals."

Andy nodded. "Be ruthless on the editing. This is serious

stuff."

"I know. Keep me posted." Jeni sat back in her chair and tried to rub the stiffness out of her muscles. The slow movement of the flying boat on the waves gradually lulled her to sleep.

The next morning Jeni went into the city with Adam, Bernhardt and three of his men. Their host, Severus, insisted that they ride in elaborate gold-encrusted chairs carried by pixies. Two short burly pixies almost as wide in the shoulders as they were tall hoisted each end of the two poles, moving so smoothly that the chairs almost floated. Physically comfortable. Morally? Not so much. At least the chair gave her a good view of the city.

The raw sewage odor of the harbor faded as they rode inland. The houses became larger and more ornate as the sewer odor faded, replaced by that of unwashed bodies with a distinctive but not unpleasant odor. The pixies smelled different, with a vague hint of spices to them. Throngs of pixies packed the streets, making up more than half of the crowd. The streets grew cleaner but more jammed and noisier as the harbor odor faded.

"They breed pixies for different hair and skin colors," Adam said. "Though I haven't seen anything darker than light brown in the skin color department. About as dark as you."

Jeni noticed quite a few pixies with red hair and green eyes along with a high percentage of albinos. The breeding seemed to be for varying amounts of hair too, from entirely hairless to thick hair of various colors all over the visible part of their bodies.

Pixie prostitutes, both male and female, lounged in front of a temple Jeni recognized.

Still worshipping the old Roman Gods.

Another breed of pixies, almost five feet tall and muscular, bustled along effortlessly carrying seemingly impossible loads on their backs. Others carried chairs like the ones Jeni and the men rode, bearing men and women wearing elaborate togas. Troops of taller, slightly less robust but even tougher-looking security pixies surrounded the chairs, accompanied by stern-faced middle-aged men in togas, men who reminded Jeni of Bernhardt.

The number of security pixies in a retinue seemed to be a sign of status. By that measure, Severus was high in the local hierarchy. His security detail forced pedestrians to the brick sidewalks and made other big retinues move aside to let him pass. Not exactly winning him friends, judging from the glares they got.

One of Bernhardt's men gestured at the security detail. "Man, I'd hate to have to fight those suckers. You can almost smell the testosterone from here. I'd so like to see a couple of them in the NFL. Just for the Eagles though."

Jeni said, "They're not that big. Maybe five feet tall."

"A pit bull isn't that big either. Any one of those guys, or whatever you call them, could probably make your average NFL linebacker cry like a baby."

Jeni scanned the street in front of them. No chariots. No horses. Actually no animals except birds and pixies. And she wasn't sure if she should call *them* animals. She spotted pitted scars on the face of one of the human security minders.

Smallpox scars.

Severus gestured and his retinue turned down a side street that led to a compound surrounded by an ornate but strong-looking ten-foot-high iron fence. Security pixies jumped, bristling at the approaching group, then relaxed and sat as they apparently recognized the party. Severus gestured again and the pixies carried his chair over to Jeni and Adam. Adam translated as Severus said in his oddly accented Latin, "Eat, drink, satisfy the urges of man or woman tonight, old friends. Tomorrow we'll indulge in the banalities of trade." He glanced at the pink digital watch on his wrist and added, "At nine in the morning."

Chapter Nine

SCOTT DID A long run the next morning—twelve miles—then drove to work and tried to find out more about Samantha Murphy and Irwin Boyer. He came to a point of diminishing return on that and decided to follow up on the mystery beastie in the mirror. He did a series of searches on hobbits, looking for reconstructions of what they looked like. None of the reconstructions looked like the creature in the mirror.

Darla called shortly before noon. "You should get out of your office more. Do a little fieldwork. I know Jane Doe's real name. She's—"

"Samantha Murphy."

"How did you know?"

"The Internet's a wonderful thing."

"Okay. Well I bet you didn't know that she was writing for—"

"Celebrity Webbeat. It's on the Internet."

"You sure know how to let a girl bask in her triumph."

"And you sure know how to make an exit."

"I had a plane to catch. I guess you already know she did an article on John Peltz."

"Yeah. He's probably not our guy though. I figured that was the last I'd see of you."

"I don't think he's our guy either. The timing doesn't fit and she didn't say anything that would hack him off. I don't see how you could possibly know that she was dating—"

"Irwin Boyer. Internet again."

"You're downright scary. And you ought to know I'll be back. I still don't know your scandalous secret."

"It'll be a while on that."

"I can be persuasive. How did you know about Irwin Boyer?"

"Like I said, Internet. Wonderful place. People tell the world all sorts of things about themselves."

"I suppose you know he's dead too."

"Just a second." Scott brought up an online version of a Boston paper and searched for the name. "Irwin Boyer? Yep. Apparent heart attack, right?"

"You just looked that up, didn't you?"

"Maybe." Scott laughed. "And you just flew to the coast when you could have let your mouse do the flying."

"He was older than she was but he was only—"

"Forty-six. Were there any risk factors?"

"I don't know yet. I suppose you already know he worked security for Jeni Burgen."

"I didn't know that." Scott jotted the name down and turned to his computer. "I also have no idea who Jeni Burgen is."

"She's number forty-something among the fifty wealthiest people in the U.S."

Scott grinned. "I think we have ourselves a bingo. Does she seem like the type who would collect Roman books or random heads and hands?"

"Not really, but when you get that wealthy, you can manufacture your own image."

"Who is she? What does she do? How did she get that rich?"

"She's a computer type," Darla said. "No degree. Dropped out of college to work for a software startup, cashed in when the company went public, and was wildly successful with her investments—rode the booms, got out before the busts. She's as reclusive as they come. No recent pictures. No interviews. Keeps her private life very private. Apparently doesn't fly much—ecological reasons. Runs everything by videoconference."

"That fits." Scott did an Internet search for Jeni Burgen pictures. "I'm finding out how good she is at avoiding paparazzi."

"Very good. You won't find anything less than twenty years old."

Scott pulled up a picture of a twenty-something Jeni Burgen. "Yeah. Found something from twenty years ago. Looks like a nice wholesome type. She also looks vaguely familiar. Are you coming back?"

"Yeah. I'll be flying in this evening. Pick me up at the airport?"

"I guess. You owe me supper and a scandal though."

"I'll let you buy me supper when I get in."

"Yeah, I've heard that before. Is this Jeni Burgen above the law?"

"If she had Samantha Murphy killed, she'd better not think so."

Chapter Ten

JENI WATCHED IMPATIENTLY as the work of filling the yacht with trade goods slowly proceeded. The Romans feasted and otherwise celebrated on a bewildering array of occasions. The crew rotated between standing guard on ship to prevent casual pilfering and enjoying life in port.

For a port city, Ollisipo was clean. Elaborate systems brought in fresh water from the countryside and carried sewage away to the ocean. The relative cleanliness didn't mean that the food and water were safe. Jeni ate only well-cooked meat and fresh vegetables at the feasts. Some sailors were less careful and Jeni hoped that they wouldn't die of their long, painful bouts with dysentery. They all stayed on the yacht or the flying boat at night to minimize their vulnerability to microbes and human predators. They did have a doctor on board, and a supply of broad-spectrum antibiotics, but Jeni worried about the effectiveness of the smallpox vaccinations she had scrounged up.

There were signs of diseases in the city, including mumps and measles. Jeni spotted more deeply scarred faces that showed that smallpox had visited the city. Through Adam, she talked to the local equivalent of a doctor and discovered they used a form of inoculation with weakened smallpox virus to ward off the disease. Beyond that, their only treatment involved putting smallpox victims in rooms furnished entirely in red.

Jeni and Adam surreptitiously took pictures of as much of the city as they could as they went back and forth between the harbor and Severus's compound. Adam was still trying to sort out the local political situation, but passed what he knew to Jeni. Severus informally controlled or strongly influenced the local government, though he held no formal position. The city government had a great deal of autonomy, but provincial or imperial authority could override that if either wanted to. On the second day, they saw a body of several hundred guard pixies in black uniforms riding toward them on horseback as they rode through the streets on Severus's golden chairs. Severus's normally arrogant retinue quickly made way for the imperial troops. It wasn't just a token gesture of submission; the guard pixies and their commanders looked genuinely relieved when the imperial troops passed without incident.

Jeni wondered how much the higher levels of the imperial administration knew about the strangers from across the sea. Severus complained loudly and often about taxes, but never criticized or even mentioned the provincial or imperial administrations.

The only sign of imperial or provincial interest that Jeni saw was the quiet presence in Severus's compound of a thin man accompanied by a frail old pixie in a plain black tunic with an eagle standard prominent on back and front. The man occasionally pointed at some part of the compound and the pixie immediately drew a sketch of the scene the man had pointed to. Jeni caught a glimpse of one of the drawings and was stunned at the detail the pixie was able to achieve in a few minutes. She had Adam ask Severus about the sketches and was rewarded with a startled look and a comment about not looking into the eyes of the emperor.

Adam was able to buy a few sketches of a somewhat lesser but still stunning quality from his host. The Eyes appeared to be a separate breed of pixie, available to anyone with enough money, but with the most capable reserved for the emperor and his court.

Eyes were one of many breeds they saw around the city. Some of the breeds were utilitarian—guards, beasts of burden, prostitutes, scribes, messengers, or more rarely, helpers for blind or lame Romans. Others seemed to be purely status symbols—the Roman equivalent of lapdogs. Jeni also heard whispers of illegal breeds used by the Roman underworld as stealthy thieves and assassins, but saw no evidence of their existence.

In the evenings, Severus brought in singers and other musicians, all pixies. Female pixies hit inhumanly high notes while male pixies hit high pure notes with a power that no human male could have matched. One evening one of the sailors leaned over to Jeni and said, "I can't imagine any guy hitting notes that high."

Adam grinned. "I'm guessing that they aren't quite male. Not anymore anyway."

"Oh, that's not good. At least they're not human."

"They used to do it to human boys back in the Middle Ages," Adam said. "Catch them before they hit puberty and *snip*. The voices got stronger but they never got deep like normal guy voices. That supposedly made for voices like nothing you've ever heard—like nothing we would have ever heard if we hadn't come here." Adam unobtrusively made video and audio recordings of the performances.

The pictures and audio recordings were more valuable to Jeni than any of the physical goods they traded for. As to what objects and products they were going to take back, that was proving to be a problem. Books were a top priority, but without printing presses and mass production of paper, they were scarce and expensive. Pixie scribes were available to copy select books, but prices were high enough that the copper/gold eagle coins that the Romans paid for the trade goods didn't go anywhere near as far as Jeni would have liked. Adam also had trouble getting access to some of the books to have them copied. Adam admitted to covertly taking pictures of books in the city's library, though it didn't have a lot of the books Jeni wanted the most. "I feel like a cheat for taking pictures, but the Latin scholar in me can't stand leaving all of that knowledge on the table."

Severus had a good handle on what trade goods would sell on the local market. Digital watches went well, especially gaudy ones, just as they had on the first trip. Cheap digital audio recorders sold even better than the watches. T-shirts had been in high demand on their first trip, but didn't sell as well this time, although for some reason shirts with a couple of band logos on them were worth several times more than their weight in the heavily debased Roman currency. Sunglasses were in high demand, the darker, and to some extent the cheaper, the better. Reading glasses and hearing aids sold moderately well, but not as well as the sunglasses. Costume jewelry also went well. Tennis shoes, nylon stockings and cigarettes were quickly and avidly snapped up, but Jeni suspected none of those items left Severus's compound. Oddly, the Romans showed no curiosity about their visitors' weapons other than the short swords they had armed themselves with before the trip. Severus had one of his retainers examine Adam's sword. The retainer dismissed it with a look of contempt, and Severus offered Adam a genuine Roman sword in exchange for another cheap pink digital watch.

The two days Jeni had allotted went too quickly. She forced herself to say goodbye to Adam and watch as the flying boat took off and Olissipo first dwindled to a dot behind them and then disappeared.

Jeni slept through most of the trip back. She dreaded what she would find in her email box, but went straight to her Timeline X office when she got back. As she expected, she'd been deluged with messages, in spite of several layers of filtering. She worked at the most urgent ones for several hours, her neck gradually stiffening. When she got up to stretch, she noticed an odd bulge in the long drapes in front of a balcony window. She stepped over to straighten the drape. When she moved it, she came face to bare chest with a tall Indian. He grabbed her hand with one of his, reaching for a bronze knife with the other.

Jeni jerked her arm back, pulling the Indian into her knee, which was already rising toward his groin. The man's bronze face went purple as the knee connected. He lost interest in his knife, which was mostly out of its scabbard. Jeni grabbed it as it fell and stepped back. At that point she yelled for help. Her voice came out cracked and weak. She reached to her waist and pressed her panic button.

The Indian lay writhing on the floor, but silently. Jeni drew back her foot to kick him in the head, hesitated, then put the desk between her and the injured man. A security team arrived while the Indian was still on the floor, Bernhardt in the lead. He stared at the Indian.

"What happened?"

"That's what I want to know. I thought we had security around here."

Chad stopped by shortly after Scott got off the phone with Darla. "Any progress?"

"Lots of it. We think we know who the Jane Doe is and we have a potential ID on the collector."

"Who and who?"

"Jane Doe is probably Samantha Murphy. Our scroll collector may be Jeni Burgen."

Chad whistled. "She fits. Reclusive. Computer and technology geek. How sure are you?"

"Not very. Murphy was dating a Burgen security guard. The security guard is dead. Apparent heart attack at age forty-six."

Chad nodded. "Yeah, that's tentative all right."

"So if it is her, do you have a problem going after her?

There's a lot of money there, maybe political clout."

"If she's bringing Timeline X stuff here, yeah we take her down," Chad said. "Get the evidence on her and I'll deal with the politics. You keeping Peter in the loop?"

"I'm not going out of my way to do it. If he stops by and asks, I'll tell him."

"You two need to work together. Where's Darla?"

"Flew east for some hands-on. She stood me up for supper last night." Scott turned back to his paperwork.

Chad sat down across the table from him. "We need to chat, seriously and off the record."

"That can't be good."

"I get Internet usage reports twice a day. It seems you were looking up Flores hobbits this morning."

"It's for the case. I—" Scott had an instant premonition of where Chad was going. "Just a wild theory."

Chad nodded. "That's what I was afraid of. I think you saw something you shouldn't have. We tried to clean up the situation, but if you're looking up hobbits, you got to it before we did."

"I saw something. I'm not sure what it was."

"If you knew what it was, I'd have to shoot you." Chad grinned. "I'm kidding. Well, exaggerating. I've always wanted to say that. You should have seen your face." The grin went away. "You saw nothing. Got it? Matter of national security. Talk about it and you don't work here anymore. You don't work anywhere that requires security clearance anymore. Maybe you even disappear to some village like that spy in the old TV show."

"You're kidding about that last part, aren't you?"

Chad shrugged. "I don't know. I hope so. But I can't help thinking that Timeline X would make a nice place to dump anyone with inconvenient knowledge."

"Why are the portals public knowledge when whatever this is, is a national secret? And why does everyone always change the subject when I ask why Timeline X's Europe never found the New World?"

"I didn't ask," Chad said. "Look, I'm taking a chance, but you're a good analyst and I'm going to trust you. This conversation never happened. You didn't do a search on hobbits. You never saw anything that would cause you to do a search on hobbits. And you never mention this to anyone. Got it?"

"Got it. Six isn't my lucky number anyway." Scott grinned. "I can do really obscure pop culture references too. So Peter Kindahl doesn't get in on this part of the investigation?"

"No."

"Too bad. He would make a good number six."

Chapter Eleven

JENI WENT BACK through the portal and drove to her compound. She watched for the normal discreet security detail. As usual, she didn't see any sign of it. When she got back, she went to the pool and swam a fast mile. That didn't provide the usual level of comfort, and she started at every noise as she showered afterwards.

She dressed and went up to her virtual-presence room. She stared at the panel and said out loud, "Adam, get back soon." The lack of radio contact from the yacht worried her, though she knew that without satellites, radio transmissions to and from Europe were iffy. She also knew it would be weeks at best before Adam and the yacht returned.

She hesitated, then pressed the button for Andy Hollsworth. After a couple of seconds, he came on screen. He stared at her. "You look—I don't know—shaken up, I guess. Are you okay?"

"No." The story of the Indian in her room came pouring out. When she finished she said, "Bernhardt offered his resignation. I'm thinking about accepting it."

"Understandable. How did the Indian get in your room?"

"Supposedly Indians have taken to sneaking in and stealing stuff, mostly metal and clothes. Security usually stops them just inside the fence, but the outermost camera malfunctioned and the guard at the next station missed him."

"How did he get into the house? How did he get into your

room?"

"A series of malfunctions and screw-ups. Each one of them is possible. All of them together—well I guess they're still possible but—"

"You don't believe it. Do you think Bernie set you up so he could be the hero?"

"I don't know. If he did, it backfired. I don't see how he could have thought it would do anything else. He's not dumb. If he let this happen, he must have had something else in mind."

"The Indians actually have been sneaking in. I've had trouble with that at my cabin."

"I thought we took care of that by leasing land the locals didn't use much and paying them well—at least in their terms. I feel guilty about how little we're paying them."

"In their terms we're paying them way too much," Andy said. "Which is part of the problem. Old clothes or a handful of nails are enough wealth to them that the neighbors try to figure out how to get in on the action. A young warrior wants to make a name for himself. He can raid enemy tribes, or he can sneak in and filch our garbage. Since we don't kill people we catch trying to filch our garbage—"

"It's their land. There are non-lethal ways of dealing with them."

"We've agreed to disagree on that," Andy said. "What happened to the Indian you took out of the gene pool?"

"I didn't—well, I probably didn't take him out of the gene pool. Bernhardt has him locked in a storage room. He wants to question him about how he got through security."

"And you're over here, not over there?"

"I know I should have stayed, made sure he asked the right questions, but I didn't feel safe there. You could go, except you don't know any of the languages over there."

"I just know one language, but I'm really good at using it.

Being scared is understandable, but killing you or letting you get killed makes no sense for him. You're his meal ticket and reference for the next job."

"Unless he thinks I'll find out he murdered that poor girl and wants to get me first."

"Have you given him any reason to think that?"

"I did ask him what happened to her. I haven't pressed it."

"You've got to be paranoid to be a good security person. You're one of a handful of people who knows a piece of what happened that night. The fact that you haven't pressed it may be sounding alarm bells in that messed-up head of his."

Jeni shook her head. "What am I supposed to do? If I press it, I make him paranoid. If I don't press, he wonders why. You know I don't fire people lightly, but I feel less secure with him around than I would with no security at all."

"Rightly so. As to firing him, that's your call of course," Andy said. "As your lawyer I advise you to hold off on that. He's a problem on the inside, but he's even more of a problem on the outside. Firing him would draw the BTI to him."

Jeni brought up her email and sorted it as she talked. "Do you think he would tell them anything?"

"If he thought he was going down for murder and you weren't backing him, yeah, I think he would."

"Is he less likely to talk if he's on the inside?"

"I don't know."

"Keeping him on means I'm dependent on him for security. What if he wanted the Indian to kill me? I don't know what his motives were today if he did let the Indian in, so how can I leave myself at his mercy?"

"Maybe you don't have to. Maybe you can bring someone in to 'review' your security procedures and in the process give yourself security tricks Bernie doesn't know about."

"Isn't that going to make him more paranoid?"

"Probably, but I can't think of anything that won't."

Jeni thought about that. "I don't know. We have a big secret. We don't need more people knowing about it."

"True, but if you fire him you'll either have to promote someone who worked under him or bring someone in from outside anyway. What if I find someone discreet and work out a way for him to beef up your security without knowing about your secret?"

"Put together a plan and I'll look at it." She sighed. "Anything I should know about the investigation?"

"Nothing new. I don't know if they've linked Samantha Murphy to her boyfriend or not."

"Okay. I may have to do get inside the investigation myself."

"How could you do that?"

"I'm not without resources." Jeni started to cut off the virtual presence. "Thanks, by the way."

Scott got a call from Darla just before he left work. "Don't bother picking me up. I got a ride."

Scott sighed. "What about supper?"

"I'll take a rain check on that too."

"Any reason?"

"Do I need a reason?"

"I guess not. Anything work-related you need to tell me?"

"Nothing new." She paused for a second and then said, "Look, you're cute and all, but Shaken-Not-Stirred gets the girl. Works out better for everybody that way."

"Petey? Good luck with that. Good luck with him calling you tomorrow."

"Maybe I don't want to be called the next day."

"Not my business." Scott snapped the phone shut and stared out the window. Peter Kindahl strolled out a couple of seconds later. He glanced up at the window, gave Scott a self-satisfied smile and wave, then climbed into his low-slung red sports car.

Scott watched him drive away.

I have no claim on her.

The prospect of supper at his empty apartment wasn't appealing, so he turned back to the computer. He tried to get a feel for Jeni Burgen's investments, but he guessed that he was just scratching the surface.

When he'd had enough, he leaned back in his chair. He took a hard-copy picture of the beastie in the mirror out of his briefcase and studied it. He thought about shredding the pictures but decided not to. "My ticket to the village."

Chad popped his head in. "What did you say?"

Scott slid the picture back in his briefcase, willing his hand not to shake. "Another obscure pop-culture reference."

"You look tired. Why are you still here?"

"Finding out that Darla is a bitch. I already kind of knew that, but it got confirmed."

Chad shook his head. "I'm so glad I'm not in the relationship market anymore. You've been married, haven't you? Still hate your ex?"

"I never did. I grew and she didn't."

Chad stood at the door as if reluctant to leave. "Did you see anything Indian-related in any of those pictures?"

Scott shook his head. "Nothing Indian. Nothing out of place except the scroll and that which must not be named, not that I have a name for it anyway. Why?"

"We can pick up the weak spots between the universes by satellite. There's nothing remotely weak in Europe. That means the murderer either smuggled the book through the Iceland portal or came in from somewhere else by sea, probably from North America. Indian stuff could narrow that down."

"North America's the best bet," Scott said. "There are marginal weak spots in southern Africa and deep in the Amazon, but it wouldn't be easy to get an ocean-going boat and a big power plant into either place. There are a couple of marginal weak spots in California near the coast and one in Northern Mexico."

Scott closed his briefcase, hoping the gesture looked casual, then brought up a map of the strength of the wall between the universes on his computer.

Chad looked over his shoulder. Scott said, "California or Northwestern Mexico would mean heading across the Pacific and going the long way around to Europe or going around the southern tip of South America. Not trivial without satellite navigation and weather satellites."

Chad nodded. "They either found a less energy intensive way of getting across or they're using a marginal weak spot in the interior of North America. Once they got across they could go downriver to the Gulf of Mexico."

Scott brought up a map with the fine-grained resolution of the wall strength in North America. "I've always thought this looks a lot like a map of European settlement. Very strong walls in Virginia and New England, even stronger ones in Florida around St. Augustine." He traced a path through the interior of the southeastern states. "And this looks a lot like DeSoto's path through the Southeast."

"Ah yes. The idea that the age and intensity of divergence determine the thickness of the wall between the universes. You aren't the first person to think that. No theoretical basis for it though."

"I bet they find one. The correlation isn't perfect, but it's too good to be a coincidence." Scott scrolled the map over to Europe. "And over here I would say the change started on this little island off the coast of Italy." He zoomed the map in. "Sardinia. So it started in Sardinia and spread to North Africa and Spain first, then southern Italy and the rest of the old Roman Empire."

"*If* the date of divergence and the strength of the wall between the timelines have anything to do with one another, which they probably don't."

"What, if anything, of significance happened in Sardinia in the first couple of centuries AD? Does whatever it was have anything to do with the Roman Empire freezing in place? And where does that which must not be mentioned, much less named, fit in?"

"I'd be more interested in finding out who killed and dismembered a young woman and brought a priceless Roman scroll over here if I were you. That is your job."

"Yeah, that would be good. Hey, I'm a history geek." Scott scrolled back to North America and pointed to an area not far from the Ohio River in eastern Ohio. "Maybe there, but our murderous friend would have to divert half the power of a nuclear power plant to keep the portal open."

"That we would notice. Plus buying that much power would quickly put a noticeable dent in even the biggest of fortunes."

Scott did a mental calculation and then whistled. "Wow. Yeah. Generally, only governments can waste money on that scale without someone noticing. So what are we missing?"

Chapter Twelve

DARLA STALKED INTO the conference room the next morning and sat at her computer without saying a word. Scott kept working. The silence deepened between them. Finally Darla said, "Jeni Burgen is mostly U.S.-based. I'm looking for connections to Iceland and seeing if her European subsidiaries are using too much power."

Scott didn't look up. "You're wasting your time."

Darla turned back to her computer and typed. The silence descended again. She finally asked, "Why? Because you think he's a pompous idiot? You should get to know him."

"No, because Europe is a dead end. Well, Petey's a dead end too."

"That's none of you business."

"Which is why I didn't bring it up."

Scott loaded the dimension-strength map and studied Europe, then scrolled across Asia. A few areas in far northern Asia were weaker, and some Arctic islands might even be feasible as portals, except for the logistics of getting power to the islands and getting anywhere useful from them on the other side. He repeated, "Europe is a dead end. Asia's a dead end."

Darla sighed. "Fine. Why are they dead ends?"

"Take a look."

Darla leaned over his shoulder. Her arm brushed Scott's. He pulled back from the contact and pointed. "The wall is too strong anywhere you could get power."

"How much too strong?"

"At the weakest points, more than ten times stronger than where we have portals."

"What if Burgen found a way of using less power? Or maybe they punch a hole with a burst of energy, let it close and punch through again to come back."

"That's been tried. If you let the hole close, the wall ends up stronger. It isn't practical to go back through anywhere near the hole you punched."

"So you set up a rendezvous a few miles away and punch an escape hole there. Or you do a smash and grab. Just punch a hole, reach through and grab stuff. So what if the hole closes in five minutes? You've got your scroll. You've got your mystery beastie. Who cares if you can't get through again?"

"Some of that could work, and as a matter of fact it has been done, but not in Europe or Asia. The walls are too thick there. If you tapped into the power grid, you'd bring it down. If you tried to store power, you'd need a fleet of eighteen-wheelers to carry batteries and another fleet to carry the portal. Anyway, most batteries couldn't release power fast enough. And the portal would burn out if you fed that much energy through it."

"Okay, so Europe's a dead end. What about the ocean? Put the equipment on a big ship, punch through and sail to Europe. When you're ready to come back, sail to a weak spot and punch through from the other side."

"Again, that's been thought of. The only part of the ocean where the wall is weak enough is near Antarctica. Good luck sailing from there to Europe and back without weather and navigation satellites. I know they used to do it before satellites, but sailors back then knew a lot of tricks we've forgotten, and they still lost a lot of ships."

"Okay." Darla turned away. "Anything new on the mystery

beastie?"

"Yeah. It was our imaginations. My brain formed a pattern out of random lights and shadows. Once I pointed it out, you saw it too."

"What? No. It was real. We both saw it."

"Apparently that's an opinion you need to keep to yourself."

"Why?"

"I don't know. National Security, I guess."

"I have a murder to investigate. There was a beastie in that mirror. I want to know what it was and how it tied in to the murder."

Scott shook his head. "I'm not your greatest fan at the moment, but fair warning: there are times to back off. This is one of them."

"That's not something I do well."

"Probably not." Scott turned back to the computer. He scrolled the map to Indonesia. The wall wasn't stronger in Flores than anywhere else in Asia. And that meant their light and shadows friend probably wasn't a hobbit, at least not from Flores.

Chapter Thirteen

JENI PULLED A cheap pay-as-you-go cellphone and a flowered dress out of the back of her wardrobe. She dropped the dress on the bed and packed several similar outfits in a scuffed blue suitcase. She dyed her auburn hair black, washed off her makeup and put the dress on. She divided a small wad of cash, a stash of gift cards from low-end department stores and refillable debit cards between a cheap black purse, her suitcase and the dress pocket. The cellphone and its charger went in her purse.

She went to the mirror and added a few touches using a cheap makeup kit. "Hi. I'm Jolene Beck." She went to the wardrobe and opened a panel on the side. A narrow stairway led down from the panel. She climbed down to a tunnel built around a drainpipe, barely tall enough for her to stand upright. She followed the tunnel, opening two doors on the way and carefully locking them behind her. She emerged in the basement of a nondescript ranch-style house two blocks from her compound. She made a rude gesture toward the compound. "Discreetly follow that, Bernhardt."

Dust lay thick in the house, and Jeni spent an hour cleaning before she went to the garage and disconnected a solar trickle charger from a five-year-old green sedan with a Green Party bumper sticker on the back.

The drive to Chicago took six hours. It was after four when she finally checked in to a moderately priced motel, using a refillable debit card and a college photo ID in the name of Jolene Beck. She flopped down on the bed and turned on the TV. In spite of the drive, her neck was no longer stiff. She curled up and felt the remaining tension of being Jeni Burgen fade away. She almost fell asleep, but forced herself to sit up and get out her cellphone.

"Hi, Dr. White? This is Jolene Beck from your summer class two years ago. I don't know if you remember me. I got caught in the rain and you loaned me a T-shirt."

And you didn't make a pass at me, which was the point of the exercise. You thought about it though.

"Yeah, I'm in town through the weekend and figured I'd say hi."

Jeni managed to get a dinner invitation from Dr. White. "Scott." She said his name aloud. She flipped through the TV channels until she found a distinctly low-brow talk show and watched a series of fat, pasty-looking women find out who the fathers of their children were. Maybe she should drink cheap beer and belch?

No. I'm going for working class, not trailer trash.

She turned the TV off when Scott knocked at the door. She gave him a *glad to see you hug*, slightly too long, but not too noticeably so. "How are your classes going?"

"I'm not teaching anymore."

Jeni feigned casual surprise. "I loved your Plains Indian summer course. Such a unique experience. Is somebody else teaching it this summer?"

Scott shook his head. "It was under a grant and the grant went away. Too expensive."

"Too bad. There's nothing like immersion to really understand a culture."

"What brings you into town?"

"Business, then a vacation." Jeni got ready to launch into her cover story, but Scott just nodded and walked her to his car.

They chatted casually through dinner. Jeni resisted the temptation to push the conversation toward Scott's work. Instead, she managed to get an invitation to run with him in the morning. When she got back to her hotel, she used the cellphone to check her email and voicemail and take care of the most urgent messages. Her neck stiffened as she worked. After she finished she went to the hotel pool and dodged rambunctious preteens to get in a few laps. By the time she finished, her eyes burned from too much chlorine and her muscles still felt stiff. A half hour of watching cage fighting on TV loosened her up, though probably at the cost of dozens of brain cells.

Scott picked Jolene up at her motel room early the next morning. She looked fresh and ready to run in a T-shirt and blue shorts. He smiled at her. "At least you're up. Are you sure you want to do this? I take my running seriously."

"So do I. I was wondering how I could get it in."

Scott had planned a light day of running—a slow six miles. He mentally prepared to pare that down if necessary. Jolene kept up the pace pretty well for four miles, chatting pleasantly, but Scott could see the pace starting to get to her after that. He slowed a little and she finished the six miles alongside him. She smiled at him. "You keep up a pretty good pace for an old guy."

"Hey, I'm not even thirty yet. Okay, I will be in a few months, but that's not that old. I'm not that much older than you."

"How old do you think I am?"

Scott grinned. "I never guess a woman's age."

"Smart man."

"I don't do 'does this make my butt look big' either."

"Again, smart man."

He drove her back to her hotel, then went to work. Darla came in a few minutes later, looking tired.

She said, "You look happy. Did you meet this ex-student?"

"We had dinner last night and went running this morning."

"Be careful. The timing on her showing up is weird."

Scott shrugged. "She's an ex-student. Quiet. Nice. Did well in the class. You're paranoid."

"I'm careful. And I don't believe in coincidences. Is she planning to be around long?"

"Through the end of the week."

"What kind of class did she take from you?"

"An immersion experience. We lived three months in a replica pre-contact Plains Indian village. It was a front to train BTI people for Dimension X, but they allowed real students in."

"And she shows up now."

"We all got pretty close. It was a bonding experience."

"How close did you get to this Jolene?'

Scott grinned. "None of your business. She's a smart one. She came up with a very sophisticated theory—sophisticated for an undergrad—on how European control of contact between cultures allowed them to...and you're hearing *blah blah* again."

"Have been for a while. Don't trust her."

He went to work on his computer. "I had a thought. Someone brought the scroll from Rome. If they started from North America, they had a ship."

"Or a plane."

"Or a plane. If they had a ship they probably started near one of the major rivers, but there are no weak spots right on a river. The only way they could get a ship over there would be bringing it through in pieces. That gives us a way of narrowing things down. If someone delivered a yacht in pieces to a good-sized facility, we've got a bingo."

"I already know where the portal is," Darla said. "Burgen has a data center in eastern Ohio, two miles from the Ohio River. It's perfect: remote, lots of power for the data center, and it's on one of the weakest spots east of the Mississippi. I saw the weak spot on your map yesterday and spotted the data center on a map last night."

"Show me."

Darla brought up a map and pointed out the data center. Scott superimposed it on the map of wall strength. He studied the strength level on the map and shook his head. "It would take a third of the power of a full-sized nuke plant to keep a portal there. Way too expensive and too hard to hide the power use."

Darla looked disappointed but turned back to her computer. "Got it. She has a windmill farm."

Scott glanced at her screen. "That's only a tenth of the power she'd need to keep the portal open, not reliable enough, and only half the turbines are up."

Darla went back to the computer. After a while, she added. "She's has a solar farm too. Not big enough though, I guess."

Scott glanced at the numbers. "Not even close, especially not in the Midwest. She'd need enough power for long winter nights."

Darla examined the map again and shook her head. "It would be perfect if she didn't need the power. Sure you aren't screwing up a decimal point?"

"Yep."

"Okay. Carry on with the yacht search. If she has anything else that could be a portal, she hid the links well."

They worked on their respective computers the rest of the morning. Close to noon, Darla asked, "Have lunch plans?"

"Yeah, with Jolene at the coffee shop across the street."

Darla didn't say anything. Peter Kindahl came in a little later. He sat by Scott. "What's new?"

Scott reluctantly filled him in, then glanced at his watch. "Got to go. Places to go, people to drink coffee with."

Jeni spent the morning catching up on voice and email messages.

The stiff neck returned as she worked. She ignored queries from Bernhardt. She almost ignored a voicemail message from Andy, but finally returned it. "What's up?"

"Why aren't you in the virtual presence room?"

"I'm taking a break."

"Where are you?"

"That would be telling. Anything new on the investigation?"

"The Boston detective is back in Chicago. Bernhardt is going crazy trying to find you. Dr. White seems to have picked up a girlfriend. We're trying to figure out if she has anything to do with the case."

Jeni grinned. "Let me know what you find out. I'll check in this evening."

"If you're outside the compound, be careful. A lot of people would love to get their hands on you."

"I know. I'll be okay. Taking a break clears my mind. By the way, has Bernhardt tried to find out what's going on with this investigation?"

"Not that I know of, unless he's behind the mystery watchers. Have you seen any sign of him keeping an eye on things? Hiring detectives?"

"Nothing in his budget," Jeni said. "No sign he's taking an interest. And that's odd, isn't it?"

"I hadn't thought of it that way, but yeah it is."

Someone knocked on the motel door. Jeni glanced at her watch. "Got to go."

She snapped the phone shut and greeted Scott at the door. "How was work this morning?"

His face grew guarded, and Jeni mentally kicked herself. *Too soon.* She smiled at him. "I bet you can't talk about it. That's okay. I don't want to hear about it. Work is work. I'm done with my work. I'm officially on vacation."

He laughed. "The lack of interest isn't real flattering, but work is confidential."

They drove to the coffee shop and chatted leisurely as they waited to be served. Jeni saw Scott stiffen when a tall twenty-something woman with purple hair walked in followed by a slender, impeccably dressed, waspishly handsome black-haired man in his early thirties. They both carefully avoided looking at Scott and Jeni. Jeni watched them sit at a table across the coffee shop. "Somebody you know?"

"Co-workers. I shouldn't have told them I was coming here."

"Enemies?"

"Not really."

"Are they curious about me?"

"Probably."

"Why don't you invite them over?"

Scott frowned, but led the two to their table. Jeni smiled and held out her hand. "Hi, I'm Jolene Beck."

The two introduced themselves. Jeni mentally dismissed Peter Kindahl as a lightweight. *Eye candy*. She studied Darla Smith and made a note to watch herself around the woman. *Very sharp*. She noticed indicators of current or past wealth in the woman's speech patterns and the way she moved. Jeni suddenly felt sorry that she'd asked the two over. What if she'd missed something in her disguise? What if Darla Smith figured out who she was? She steered the conversation to the summer immersion class.

"It was a life-changing experience," Jeni said. "There's nothing like it. We cooked like they did. We slept like they did. We literally walked in their shoes."

"And now you really understand them?" Darla smiled across at her with a smile that didn't approach her eyes.

Jeni matched the smile with one of equal warmth. "Yes, I think I do."

Chapter Fourteen

SCOTT DIDN'T LOOK up when Darla got back from lunch.

She said, "Don't trust her."

A little jealousy maybe?

Scott grinned. "Jolene? That's odd. She said there were some discordant things about you, too."

"Discordant?"

"Yeah, that's what she said."

"What did she mean by that?"

"I think I'll keep that to myself and see if she knew what she was talking about."

"She's not who she seems to be," Darla said. "Did you notice her shoes?"

"Nope." Scott glanced down at the black sneakers he wore in lieu of dress shoes. "I don't even notice my own shoes."

"Typical guy. The rest of her outfit says WalMart, but the shoes say a whole other economic class. And they weren't knockoffs."

"And you know that from a glance on the way to our table?"

"Yeah. I'm a detective. I notice these things. Oh, and she had an ink pen in her purse that cost a quarter of my monthly salary. She's a ringer."

"She was my student. We lived in close quarters for three months. Maybe she has money but wants to act normal."

"Or someone is using the connection to get close to you.

Burgen would have the resources to get your student list and bribe someone."

Scott thought about the class. Nothing there to suggest Jolene was all that interested in money. "You're being paranoid."

"Are you going to supper with her?"

"And running with her tomorrow morning. You aren't invited. And I'd prefer you didn't happen to show up where we go."

"You get supper to yourself, but I'm running with you tomorrow."

"Do you even run?"

"I'm in good shape."

Scott shook his head. "That's not the same thing. Why do you want to run with us?"

"Your Jolene Beck may be our tie to the other side. I'll find a way of using her. By the way, we're flying to Ohio tomorrow, you, me, and Peter Kindahl."

"Ohio and Peter Kindahl? That would be a no. I have things to do here. I can't take the time off."

Darla laughed. "I talked to Chad. He thought it was a wonderful idea. He even suggested that I allow time for you to see your mom and dad while you're out there. It would be a shame to be so close and not visit them."

"He's such a thoughtful guy. I suppose I could get deathly ill between now and then. Or I could just live the nightmare."

"Don't just live the nightmare, embrace the nightmare. And I get to meet your parents and your twin brother."

"How do you know I have a twin brother?"

Darla grinned. "I'm a detective. I have ways of finding things out. And now I get the scoop on your scandals."

"Maybe. Thanks so much for arranging this."

"Don't mention it. Next time don't stand me up for some piece of trailer trash."

"Next time don't stand me up for a Euro-trash wannabe."

Both Darla and Peter Kindahl showed up to run with Scott the next morning.

Great. What part of I run to relax didn't they get?

Scott glared at Peter. "What are you doing here?"

"I thought I'd have a spot of fun watching you try to be an athlete."

"There won't be much to see. We're running a route. If you sit here, you'll see nothing for forty-five minutes or so. If you run, you'll get all sweaty. How would that fit your image? Besides, if you tried to keep up with us, you'd probably have a heart attack."

"I'll run."

Scott grinned at Jolene. "Maybe we should take it easy on them."

"Why?" She frowned.

"Why indeed?" Scott started out at a moderate pace. Peter Kindahl pushed out ahead a few strides. Scott glanced at Jolene. "I'd love to pace you so we could chat, but a man's got to do what a man's got to do."

Jolene shrugged. "We can talk over breakfast."

"I'll buy. Sorry about this." He picked up the pace, staying one stride behind Peter. Jolene dropped back. Darla tried to keep up the pace, but quickly fell back too.

Peter increased the pace. Scott matched it. Whatever his faults, Scott had to admit that Peter wasn't a bad runner. He had a long smooth stride and somehow made running look sophisticated.

I'll fix that.

Scott ran faster, moving close but not passing. Peter increased his pace too, but the smooth stride became more forced. Scott grinned and held his position. They kept going at that speed for a couple of miles, as Peter's breathing grew labored.

Scott said, “We could slow down and keep the ladies company. Not everything has to be a competition.”

“Says the guy who can’t compete.”

Scott grinned. “Say again? Couldn’t quite catch that. You ‘re having a little trouble breathing.”

“You heard me.”

Scott glanced back. The women were almost out of sight on the path behind them, running several yards apart with Jolene ahead. Scott eased off the pace. Peter didn’t. Scott grinned and closed the distance, running beside Peter. “Nice day for a run. This is usually my fast day, but I guess I can do the fast stuff tomorrow.”

Peter didn’t say anything. His face was red and he’d stopped sweating. Scott said, “Buddy, you need to slow down or you’ll get heat stroke.”

“I’m fine. We’re probably pretty close to the six miles aren’t we?”

Scott shook his head. “Not even four miles yet. Look, so running isn’t your thing. No big deal. It’s like an Eskimo in a rainforest. He’s not going to do well, but that doesn’t make him a bad Eskimo.”

Peter’s face got redder and his breathing more labored. Finally Scott said, “I’m going back to talk to Jolene. Keep whatever pace you want. I’ll catch up when I’m done chatting.”

“No you won’t.”

Jolene looked surprised when Scott ran back and paced her. “I thought you were going to run his legs off. ‘A man’s got to do what a man’s got to do’ and all that macho crap.”

“Yeah, well, the guy’s pushing himself so hard he’ll stroke out if he keeps it up. It’s not worth it.”

“So he holds his breath until he turns blue and you let him win?”

“No. I still win. Over two miles to go. I’ll blow past him with half a mile left. That way I won’t have to carry him back.”

Darla caught up and ran beside them. She said, “Pretty cocky, aren’t you?”

“Not really. Running is my sport. I work at it. You can’t stop by and run like someone who does it every day.”

They ran on, not saying much. Finally Scott said, “About a mile to go, ladies. Off to humiliate a piece of wannabe Euro-trash.”

Darla said, “Don’t overdo it. Remember, you’re taking me home to meet your parents tonight.”

Chapter Fifteen

AT BREAKFAST, JENI smiled at Scott. She chose her words carefully. "Dr. White, I'm surprised you're working for BTI. You struck me as a free spirit. Now you're in an organization that's about keeping people from researching Timeline X."

"It's Scott, remember? That's not what we do. We study the world over there as much as we can without changing it."

"How much can you actually do, though? No computers over there, right?"

"True. And no books or knives or guns or glass bottles or bibles or pre-recorded music. It's a pain in the butt, but it's better than the alternative. We know what unrestricted access would do to the Indians. Look at what happened to them historically. Look what's still happening to tribes in the Amazon. Our kind of civilization comes and they die off in droves, even when nobody's trying to hurt them."

"Why can't you take prerecorded music?"

"Because people over there hear a song and it spreads. It influences their music. Maybe it doesn't change things much. Maybe it changes their music beyond recognition, and a piece of culture is lost before it can be recorded. Yeah, it doesn't seem like a big deal, but music is a huge part of culture." He sipped his coffee, looking mellow after the run. "The no-Bibles bit gets us the most flack."

"Well, yeah. To the religious, you're dooming millions of

souls by not letting missionaries in."

"But how do we study cultures when missionaries are trying to change the culture's most basic beliefs? A culture is a unit. If you change one thing, you can change *everything*. And how can we let one religion in without letting them all in? Then they bring diseases, and millions of Indians die."

He still sounded like a professor. And he still looked good. Jeni said, "That's not going to happen in this day and age. The big killers are gone. It would take a deliberate effort to spread them."

"Plenty of diseases would cause havoc over there: flu, even the common cold if everybody gets sick in the dead of winter. Everyone gets too sick to get firewood. Fire goes out. People freeze to death."

"Would you really get that sick from the flu or a cold?"

"The flu definitely. The common cold? Maybe. Our immune systems get toughened up by last year's version of these diseases, so even if they get us again, because the disease mutated, our immune systems can sort of tackle them. When we get a strain that's different enough to what our immune systems are used to, then they're deadly. Flu killed millions in nineteen-eighteen and nineteen-nineteen."

"True, but Europe with a fully functioning Roman Empire—we could learn so much about history and philosophy and literature and math. The old Greeks had a huge collection of great minds. They may have ninety percent of that literature over there. What percentage do we have?"

"A lot less than I wish we did," Scott said. "We've never sent people to Europe or Asia. Europe probably still has smallpox and measles and mumps and polio—all the childhood diseases we've knocked out. We can't risk bringing them back with us."

"Couldn't you just vaccinate against them? Aren't most people already vaccinated?"

"Not against smallpox."

Which is why we got the smallpox vaccine, in spite of the risks it took.

"So vaccinate anyone you sent over against smallpox."

"We can't even guarantee vaccines will work. Diseases shift over two thousand years. Their smallpox or measles may have changed enough to be like a completely new disease. And a huge reservoir of diseases that didn't jump from animals to people here could have over there. Going to Timeline X Europe, Asia or Africa is extremely dangerous."

Adam, come back safe. Don't die over there.

Jeni shook her head. "I understand that, but there ought to be some way to get at Timeline X. Make use of it. Get away from our screwed-up world for a while. How often have you been there?"

"Six times. All in the Great Plains around South Dakota."

"Didn't you love the freedom? Didn't you love knowing that you'd left all the problems of this world behind? Didn't you like the idea that you could go to a stream and drink without worrying about someone dumping toxic wastes into it? Didn't it feel good not to be part of a culture that slashes into the fabric of nature just to live?" Jeni stopped herself, surprised by the vehemence in her own voice.

"I enjoyed it, yeah. It's not a paradise over there. It's primitive and tiring and boring a lot of the time. It is good to get away from all of that stuff for a while, but you pay a price. I go into Internet withdrawal."

"We were isolated most of the immersion summer and I loved it," Jeni said.

"But you grabbed your phone and did your full hour of searching and texting and phoning when we let you."

Too true.

"Yeah I did. I'd miss it if I couldn't have it, but it would be worth it. I envy you. There's an unexplored, unspoiled world over there. You can get at it."

After breakfast Jeni took a quick shower, then watched TV. After a couple of hours she reluctantly got out her cellphone and worked through her messages, pacing as she went through them. Her neck had stiffened even before she got out the phone. She listened to several frantic voicemails from Bernhardt, then finally relented and called him back. "Hi. I'm fine. Chill. I'm on vacation, kicking back for a few days. I'll be back by the weekend."

"Where are you? Are you under duress? How did you get out of the compound?"

"How do you know I'm out of the compound?"

"Look, I'm your head of security. I can't ensure your security if I don't know where you are."

"And sometimes not even then."

There was a pause, then Bernhardt said, "I offered my resignation. Do you want it?"

"I'm not on a secure line, so be careful how you respond to this. I want a thorough review of security on the other side. I want a review on this side. How much could an investigator find given access to our facilities and records? I want contingency plans for a total shutdown. Could we maintain our *special* facilities over there for a year or two with no link? Could we reestablish contact close enough to be useful if we had to shut down?"

"Is this about the girl? We handled an unfortunate situation the only way it could be handled."

"An unfortunate situation? That's an understatement. Going to tell me what you did?"

"That would not be in your best interest."

"Why don't you let me be the judge of that?"

Bernhardt didn't say anything for an uncomfortably long time. Finally he said, "I'm sorry. I can't do that. Could you please let me protect you?"

"Just get those reviews done. Oh, and what did the Indian I caught in my room have to say?"

"Nothing useful. I let him go."

Jeni thought about protesting, then shrugged. "Did you get a video of the questioning?"

"Of course."

Jeni went on to the next voicemail. Eventually she got to Andy Hollsworth's message and called him back. "You were looking for me?"

"Yeah. I wanted to catch you up on the investigation. We found out that Darla Smith was adopted into a wealthy Virginia family. Old money types. Rumor has it that she rebelled, ran away twice, and had brushes with the law as a juvenile."

"Just rumors? She's a cop. She couldn't have gone too wild."

"Juvenile records are sealed. The grapevine can give you some of it, but I'm still piecing together what she did. She may be vulnerable if we need her to be."

"I don't think it will come to that. I talked to Scott under an assumed name."

"You what? Do you realize how dangerous it is to contact him?"

Jeni sprawled on the hotel room's bed, her hair still damp from the shower. "Yes, but we need someone inside the investigation."

"You need to get out of there, but if you insist on staying, I've heard a rumor that Darla seems inordinately interested in fire—like she's turned on by it."

"I'll check that out." Jeni thought about saying more, but couldn't figure out how to do it without giving away more than she wanted to share. "How are you doing on getting the other side ready to go it alone?"

"Slow. We need more workers. We're trying to get visas for more Guatemalans, but the paperwork takes forever. Are you sure we can't skip it?"

"No. We do this as aboveboard as we can." Workers for Timeline X were an ongoing problem. Locals would know they weren't in Ohio anymore and hiring Indians would cause no end of issues. Jeni pushed the problem out of her mind. "Any messages from the yacht?"

"No. I wouldn't worry too much about that yet though. It's not just that getting a signal across the Atlantic is tricky. Our friends with the Italian accents and togas do debauchery well. It's easy for the days to just slide by."

"Sounds like you wish you were there again."

"I do. It's seductive. Who knows? The crew could go native and never come back."

"They'd better come back. I took a lot of risks to get the yacht there. I should have put the money into taking care of the energy situation. Speaking of which, do what you can to speed up getting our energy secured."

She hung up and leaned back in bed.

Adam, I'll personally wring your neck if you don't come back or if I find out you did any debauching.

Chapter Sixteen

THE FLIGHT WAS quiet. Both Darla and Peter Kindahl moved stiffly. Darla winced a couple of times. She sat by Scott, but leaned back and chatted with Peter most of the flight. Scott closed his eyes and quietly dreaded the night to come.

Scott's dad met them at the airport, wearing his usual blue jeans and flannel shirt. Jim White had more of a gut than Scott remembered, and his hair was grayer, but he still looked solid, powerful, at fifty-five years old. He also looked disapproving, which was a practice Jim White had perfected: he looked at Scott disapprovingly; he looked at Darla's purple hair and East Asian features disapprovingly, though his eyes lingered on her chest; and he looked at Peter Kindahl with even more disapproval than he had at Scott.

Peter looked back with amused contempt. He said, "Is there room for four in the pickup truck?"

Scott's dad grinned and led them to a low-slung sports car. "Restored it myself. From back when we knew how to build cars. I've had it up to—" He lifted his eyebrows at Darla. "A little over sixty-five a time or two."

They crowded into the car and drove to the house where Scott grew up, a large brick ranch-style house in a neighborhood that had been upscale fifteen years ago, before the steel mills closed. Most of the young people left soon after the mills closed. Now elderly retired steel workers dominated the neighborhood.

Paint peeled or brickwork crumbled on most of the houses. Scrub trees grew in picket fences that had once been white. Grass grew eight inches high in the yards.

The White's house was well-kept, with lawn and fences carefully maintained and flowerbeds tastefully laid out. Jim frowned at Scott. "Still living in an apartment?"

"Yeah. You know that."

"You're pushing thirty, son. Time to get on with your life."

"It starts. We're not even in the house yet and it starts."

Darla smiled and brushed Scott's arm. "This is going to be fun. Like I said, don't stand me up for trailer trash."

Scott's mom, Stephanie, met them at the door. She stood almost a foot shorter than her husband's six feet, with hair dyed black. Her figure, makeup and nails were perfect. She smiled but made no move to hug Scott. She dismissed Darla with a glance, gave Peter Kindahl a longer glance, then dismissed him too. She led them to a supper table neatly laid out with plates loaded with steak and potatoes.

Scott counted seven plates at the table. He turned to his dad. "You didn't invite—"

"Your brother and his wife? Of course we did. First family meal in two years. They're out back."

Scott turned to Darla. "Congratulations. You're about to meet one of my scandals."

Jim White, Junior came in the back door, followed by his wife, Georgia. Scott nodded curtly. "Darla Smith, meet my twin brother Jim and my ex-wife. *His* current wife. Georgia."

Chapter Seventeen

THE SUPPER STARTED out even more nightmarish than Scott had expected. His mom seated him between Darla and Jim Junior. Darla and Georgia exchanged venomous glances, then smiled falsely at each other.

Scott told Darla, "We're obviously fraternal twins, not identical. We call Jim Junior L. J. Makes the conversation easier."

"Okay, he's Jim, but goes by L. J. Is there some logic to this?"

"It stands for Little Jim." Scott glanced at his brother, a taller, softer version of their father. "The 'little' part doesn't apply to the visible bits anymore. You'd have to ask Georgia about the non-public ones."

L. J. busied himself with a mouthful of steak.

Georgia said, "I'm satisfied. Which is a change."

Darla smiled at Georgia. "So you married one brother and then the other. Doesn't that make you feel—I don't know, like shopping for a double-wide?"

"That's the way I figured it," Scott said. "But the path of true love can be strange."

Scott's father shot him an angry glance, then said mildly, "At my table we mind our manners. Sometimes family doesn't act the way we would like them to, but they don't stop being family."

Scott relaxed a little. His dad turned to Peter. "Now, which are you, American or British?"

"A little of both actually. My mother is British. My father is a colonial, I'm sad to say. I was born in New York but grew up in London and of course went to Oxford."

"Oxford?"

"Oxford University."

"Universities. That's where people spend their parents' money learning how to look down their noses at them."

Peter smiled. "And by them, you mean..."

"Their parents. Didn't this Oxford teach you English?"

"Yes, but I'm not sure that what you speak out here in the flyover part of the colonies is English."

"Flyover, huh?"

"That's what the more civilized portions of the country call the parts where people play banjos and marry relatives. No offense intended."

Jim smiled. "Britain used to be a great country. Then all the Britishers with balls got them shot off in World War One. Plumb ruined the breed. They still have delusions they're a great country, even after we had to help them beat Argentina a while back. They still try to tell the world how to talk and how to act. In the real world, they're just a third-rate island with a third-rate economy. Don't even know how to raise their kids anymore. In ten years they'll be like those boys in *Lord of the Flies*. Sad end to what used to be a great country. No offense intended."

"British power has shifted from crudely military to financial and cultural, but I assure you—"

"British power has shifted from real to imaginary." Jim said. "Your British friends couldn't feed themselves without taxpayers out here in 'flyover country' footing the bill for aircraft carriers to keep your sea lanes open."

Scott glared at Darla. "And we're off to political diatribe land. Still think this is a good idea?"

"So far, yeah."

Scott's dad was saying, "When I was growing up, the U.S. was a great country. Yeah it had a flaw or two. It wasn't right the way they treated blacks some places, and if a guy liked other guys he had to do it on the quiet. The thing is, for most folks this was a land of opportunity. You didn't have to get a fancy degree to make it. Hell, you didn't even have to get through high school. You got a job and you worked hard and you could raise a family. The wife could stay home and raise the kids right and cook up proper meals instead of microwave crap." He gestured down the table. "We got raised up with real food like this, not fast food junk. You go out to a restaurant and you get the cheapest cut of meat they can buy, tarted up with grease and salt so you don't notice how bad it is. We went from the country I grew up in to one where you have to get some fancy degree just to get a job that pays half what a family needs. Then they work you and your wife enough hours you never see your kids when they aren't sleepy or in bed. You move away from your family and the people you grow up with. You work your butt off and eat crap—most people don't even know what real food tastes like anymore. Your kids grow up trying to be like the people they see on TV, which means they turn out worthless but they think they know so much more than we do. Anything we say about how things used to be is just old-fogey talk."

Peter laughed. "I don't quite know where to start on responding to that," he said. "Your good times were when your bunch of pig farmers came up from the south and made a decent living in the factories for a few years because Europe got shot to pieces in the last World War and there was no competition. They made enough to buy ticky-tacky houses, buy gas-hog pickup trucks and get roaring drunk, and they thought they were in paradise. But there are plenty of other pig farmers in the world, and factory owners figured out that they didn't have to spend a pile of money to have an ex-pig farmer tighten a screw. So pig-farmer paradise went away."

"Call it what you want. What we had was a time when a working man could make it. I've worked my butt off to keep a little piece of what we had and raise kids to appreciate it. Then one of them goes off to college at taxpayers' expense and becomes part of the decay."

"I earned a scholarship and worked to pay what it didn't cover," Scott said. "And last I heard, your other son was making minimum wage at a nursing home and living in a crappy one-bedroom apartment with his wife and a kid who may or may not be his."

L. J. shrugged. "I work for a living. I help dad for a little extra cash. When the mills reopen, I'll work there. The kid is family one way or the other. I'm doing fine."

"The steel mills are never going to reopen," Scott said. "That's over. Time to move on."

Scott's dad said, "Now one thing the British know how to do is television, especially comedy. I'll take PBS or BBC America over any of this local crap. American TV figured out that moving cameras around fast, showing boobs and blowing stuff up will keep people watching even if the writing and acting suck. And the people smart enough to not watch crap won't buy the junk they're selling anyway."

"And how do you finance this, shall we say, rather retro lifestyle and philosophy?" Peter asked.

"Now that, my friend, is none of your business."

"No big mystery," Scott said. "He restores classic cars and sells them on the Internet. He also does electric and hybrid conversions."

"Only on foreign cars and domestic ones from after Detroit forgot how to make real cars," Jim said. "I had a guy ask me to pull a working V8 and put in electric. That's like tearing out hardwood and subbing in drywall."

Jim White easily dominated the conversation through the rest of the meal. Scott said as little as he could. He glanced at Georgia. She hadn't changed much in the two years since he saw her last. Her blond hair was still cut short. Her face was unlined and her body was back to her pre-pregnancy shape. *The girl next door. The one I wanted to marry and did for a while. And that turned out well.* Georgia avoided looking at him and made a point of touching L. J. often through the meal. Over dessert she finally glanced at him. "Would you like to see your niece? She's at a babysitter's, but I could bring her over."

"That would be a tad awkward. I do look at the pictures you email me. She's pretty."

"Does she have your eyes or your chin?" Darla asked.

Georgia glared at her, then at Scott.

"There's a family resemblance," Scott said. "She's family. Her parents both love her, want to see her happy."

Surprisingly, Jim White and Peter seemed to warm up to one another as the meal progressed. Afterwards, they wandered out to the garage and drove off in a restored '57 Chevy. Scott's mom went out to build a fire in the firepit so they could roast marshmallows. Scott strolled out to a canopied swinging seat in the backyard near the fire. Darla followed him. "Mind if I join you?"

"A little. You were picking at old wounds during supper."

"Yeah. " Darla looked over at the fire. "Your family is more screwed up than mine, and that's saying something. I'm surprised your dad and Peter hit it off."

"A guy determined to stay a redneck and a blueblood snob. But they both like fast cars. Hobbies cut across class lines, I guess."

"You and your brother didn't say much to each other in there."

"L. J. and I have said everything we need to say."

"Really? Mind if I sit down?"

"Yeah, but I doubt if that will stop you."

"It won't." She sat in his lap and put an arm around his neck.

He sat stiffly. "What are you doing?"

"Sitting in your lap. Oh, and driving your ex-wife nuts."

"She's married. She's happy with L. J." He glanced at the door and saw Georgia turn away. "They're a better fit than we ever were."

"Maybe, but her claws came out whenever I looked at you or got close to you."

Scott frowned. "I didn't notice."

"You're a guy; of course you didn't notice. We do the claw thing subtly," Darla said. "So you have a dad who is living proof that you can still live like it's the 1950s—with a little help from the Internet—plus a brother, an ex-wife and a daughter you never told me about. You give good scandal. I bet your dad's even a Republican."

"You better be glad you didn't say that in front of him. He would've washed your mouth out with soap, policewoman or not. Dad's a diehard Democrat"

"So your *niece* really is your daughter?"

"Let's just say that the question of paternity is murky. L. J. may know. I don't speculate about it. Either way, she was conceived by the legal husband in a legal marriage."

"I'm not sure how that's possible. Sounds juicy though."

"And that's all you're ever going to know about it. Now are you going to share a scandal or two?"

Darla stared over at the fire, then kissed him hard on the lips.

"Yeah," she said. "I like playing with fire way too much."

Chapter Eighteen

JENI STROLLED TO the hotel dining room and ate supper alone, then went to the pool to swim laps. A couple of guys who were probably still in high school tried inept pickup lines on her. She fended them off as pleasantly as she could, half annoyed and half flattered. She glanced back as she left the pool.

Sorry kids, I'm old enough to be your mom.

On the way back to her room, the feeling of being watched returned. She made sure the boys from the pool weren't following her. Nobody was in the hall or in her hotel room, yet the feeling persisted. She checked under her bed and in the bathroom. Nothing. She pulled the drapes. The feeling didn't go away.

She watched TV for a while, then called Andy. "Do you or Bernhardt know where I am?"

"I have no idea and I don't think he has a clue. Why?"

"I have a feeling I'm being watched."

"Well, depending on where you are, it could be paparazzi trying to get a picture, Bernie could be a better actor than I think he is or it could be something more sinister. You might want to get back where your security can protect you. By the way, things are hopping on the investigation. The Boston PD detective flew out to Ohio with Dr. White and another BTI guy."

"Are they poking around the data center?"

"Not yet, but I suspect they will tomorrow."

"That wouldn't surprise me." Jeni sat up and rubbed her stiff muscles. "Any progress on the contingency plans?"

"We've moved solar panels, batteries and non-perishable food over there. The big bottleneck is workers to install the stuff. Are you sure you don't want me to use all means necessary to get the workers?"

"How much would that speed it up?"

"From months to weeks."

"I'll think about it. We would need deniability, and nobody new comes into the country."

"That's slower and drives costs up," Andy said. "I'll see what I can do. By the way, Bernhardt is looking into some of the same things. Did you authorize that?"

"I ordered it. I figured it would let us pick his brain and keep him busy."

"I would think seriously about cutting the vacation short and getting to a secure position."

"I'll think about it." Jeni snapped the cellphone shut and leaned back on her pillow.

The feeling of being watched didn't go away. Jeni tried to figure out when she first felt it. It had come to the fore in the hotel hallway, but now that she thought back, she remembered feeling traces of it on the run with Scott and his co-workers that morning. She shook her head.

No way of knowing when Scott will be back. I gambled that I could get close to him and came up empty. Which means there is no rational reason to stay.

Jeni buried her head in her pillow.

Sometimes rational isn't all it's cracked up to be.

Jim White drove Darla and Peter to a hotel. Scott didn't inquire about the sleeping arrangements when his dad came back but Jim said, "Well, they started out in separate rooms. I don't know if they'll end up that way. She's trouble and he likes trouble."

"You got along pretty well with him."

"I was being polite to company. He's okay for being half-British and stuck up. At least he knows cars, which I can't say about you."

"Sorry. Grease and busted knuckles never appealed to me."

"You never understood that there are things a man has to be good at. They come with the extra stuff in the genes and the extra stuff in the jeans."

"That was then. This is now," Scott said.

"Then was when this country was great and the average man could get ahead by working hard. Now is when the average man has to struggle every minute just to stay where he is."

"We got lucky for a while, Dad. Like Petey said, we were the only big industrialized country not smashed flat in World War Two. It took decades for the rest of the world to rebuild. That was your happy time. That's where you want to go back to, but you can't, and trying to just keeps you from dealing with reality."

"I'm doing fine."

"You are, but L. J. isn't. He's trying to be you, but he can't and trying traps him."

"I'm moving him into the business as I build it up. He'll be fine. He'll take good care of your daughter."

"We don't know for sure she's my daughter."

Jim shook his head. "You've seen pictures. You can't tell me you don't see it in her."

Scott closed his eyes.

This is why I don't come home.

"I don't want to see it in her. I want L. J. and Georgia and Sara to have a normal life—be a normal family. What would I do differently if I knew? Move back here and try to get Georgia to divorce him and marry me again? There's nothing for me here. Besides, that would be even more trailer trash than her divorcing me and marrying him."

"You should have kept your pants on."

"We were married. Married people have sex."

"You had to have been within a week of getting a divorce and it wasn't a friendly divorce either. What did you do? Go straight from telling a judge how much you hated her to spending the night in her apartment?"

"No. Actually she came to my apartment. There's a thin line between love and hate, Dad. We weaved across that line a few times. If she hadn't turned around and married L. J. less than a week later, things might have gotten less twisted."

"Don't screw anyone you aren't willing to raise a baby with."

"You've told me that a time or two."

"It didn't sink in though, did it?"

Scott grinned. "Life would be boring if everyone did what they were told."

"There would be a lot fewer screwed-up kids if everyone followed that little rule."

"Maybe. How is L. J. handling this?"

"He's still your brother," Jim said. "He feels guilty about marrying your ex-wife. He loves little Sara like she was his, which she might be. I doubt it, but it's possible. Are you going to talk to him?"

"Do you think I should?"

"Who are you and what have done with my son?"

"Huh?"

"Asking advice from the old man. Can't be the Scott White I tried to raise. I think you're old enough to make that decision for yourself. I'd give it more time. We still have your room set up for you."

"I can sleep on the couch."

"No need for that. As long as I'm alive, this will be your home."

Scott slept well that night. He woke up to the alarm with a half-remembered dream lingering in his head. It had something to do with Darla, and he felt disappointed when it ended.

Darla and Peter picked him up in a rental car. Darla got out and said, “Time to play native guide, O descendent of the Great Sun. In other words, you get to drive.” As Scott got in, she asked, “What happened to your grandma? The Natchez one?”

“She’s not really Natchez. At least I don’t think so. She’s in a nursing home.”

“Are you going to visit her before we go?”

“Probably. I’m not looking forward to it. Seeing her the way she was last time ate away at my memories of her.”

Peter said, “Preserve fond memories or give the person a little time of happiness with loved ones. Quite the dilemma.”

“You don’t need to be sarcastic.”

“I’m not. The only way we’re sure we live on after death is in the memories of those who knew us. Those memories are precious. They shouldn’t be thrown away lightly.”

Scott glanced over at Peter. “Well, aren’t we full of surprises this morning? A philosophical side. Who’d’ve thunk it?”

He settled into the seat and started the sixty-mile drive to the data center. Darla leaned forward from the back seat. “Have a nightmarish time?”

“Could have been worse. Dad is mellowing a bit.”

“That’s mellow?”

“A little mellower. Still a long ways from mellow. I’m sort of glad you pushed me into coming.”

“Geez, that takes the fun out of it.”

“I know. That’s why I said it.”

They didn’t talk much the rest of the way to the data center. The interstate took them past half-deserted malls, huge decaying hulks of factories and empty farmhouses surrounded by dense clusters of scrub trees. Scott said, “We’re seeing more gated communities hidden away from the main roads—hard to find if you don't know where to look."

"Most of the people who settled in flyover country were peasants and riffraff," Peter said. "Their descendants are going back to their roots, and quality people have to protect themselves."

"Well, so much for the interlude of civility."

The data center and warehouse complex didn't look very big from the main road, but as they approached along the access road, its scale became apparent. A field of wind turbines, most of them unfinished, towered over them on both sides of the road, with arrays of solar panels interspersed among them. A chain-link fence eight-feet tall and topped with barbed wire enclosed the turbines. Heavy construction equipment rumbled inside the fence, and the complex had a raw, under-construction look to it.

Scott counted the turbines and solar arrays as he drove. A lot fewer than half finished. Unless they had a dozen fields like this, they weren't getting enough power from wind and solar to run a portal. He looked up the road. "Gate ahead. This is as close as we should get on the first visit." He swung the car around.

"Well, that's one of the many reasons you're not a field agent." Peter gestured behind them. "We'll have a tail going back if their security is any good."

"What was I supposed to do? Go up to the gate and ask for directions to the portal?"

"No, but we could have gone up to the gate and asked for directions to the movie theater we passed. We would have seen more of the layout and put ourselves in a category—tourists asking for directions."

"Why doesn't turning around put us in that same category?"

"Because we're still an unknown. They'll want to know for sure what we are. Remember what you said about Eskimos and rainforests?"

"Yeah."

"Welcome to the Amazon. You might want to lose that parka."

"Someone knows we're here." Scott crouched in the woods behind the data center and scanned an area where he caught a glimpse of sunlight reflecting off metal.

"Been watching us for ten minutes," Peter said. "Now he knows we know he's there."

"I wasn't that obvious, was I?"

"As obvious as a four-alarm fire," Darla said. "Oh, well. Let's rattle their cage." She strolled out into the open. "Hey, you in the trees with the binoculars, let's talk."

Peter grabbed her shoulder. "What are you doing?"

"He knows we're here. He knows we know he's there. Why screw around?"

A tall, blond-haired, thirty-something man in a blue guard's uniform strode over to them. "I'm supposed to keep an eye on this field. Why are you here?"

"Scavenger hunt," Darla said. "We're looking for a wind turbine blade or a Roman scroll from Timeline X. Can you help us?"

"Uh, what?"

"A wind turbine blade. You know. Like the ones on those big whirly things out in front of the plant. We need one of those or a Roman scroll."

"Why?"

"I told you—a scavenger hunt. You don't have to give us a blade you're already using. I'm sure you have spares."

"I think I'd better call my boss. You aren't supposed to be here."

"Sure. I wouldn't want you to get in trouble. Be sure you mention the Roman scroll. You may not have a spare turbine blade."

"Why would we have a Roman scroll?"

"I don't know. Why don't you ask your supervisor? Remember, it has to be from Timeline X. We only get half points if it's from our reality."

"I definitely need to call my supervisor." The guard walked away, talking on his radio.

Peter glared at Darla. "Why did you do that? Unlike Scott, you're supposed to be a professional."

"It's amazing what kinds of things break loose when you screw with peoples' heads."

"It's amazing how easy it is to get buried in an unmarked grave if someone decides you're about to prove they killed someone."

Darla laughed. "It wouldn't be the first time someone tried to shoot me. I bite back."

The guard returned. "Would you mind waiting here? My boss wants to talk to you."

Darla smiled at him. "We have to get on with the scavenger hunt. We still have to find a rogue portal. Tell your boss that if he wants to help us out with the turbine blade or scroll, he can meet us at the restaurant down the road. Oh, and if he knows where to find a rogue portal he could help us with that too."

They walked back to the car. Scott glanced over his shoulder. "So, should we be running?"

"Probably not," Darla said. "They'll want to know how much we know, and they won't want to give whoever sent us an excuse for a search warrant."

"I'm not liking this probably stuff."

They hurried to the rental car. Scott saw the guard write something on his hand as he drove away. Probably the license number. He grinned at Peter as they turned onto the road in front of the data center.

"Why so glum, old boy? The game is afoot, as the British used to say back before they stopped mattering."

"No, as you Americans say, you two just stuck all four of your collective feet in it."

"That's not exactly what we say, but close enough."

"I hate working with amateurs. It's embarrassing and a good way to get killed."

Jeni woke at four in the morning. The TV and the lights were still on. She still wore her clothes from the night before. And she still had that *being watched* feeling. She searched the room for hidden cameras or microphones. She didn't find anything, but given her lack of expertise and equipment, that didn't mean anything. Finally she snapped open her phone and called Bernhardt Sloan. He sounded sleepy and irritated when he answered, but he perked up fast when he heard her voice.

"Bernhardt, do you know where I am?"

"No, and I wish you wouldn't disappear like this. I can't keep you safe if I don't know where you are."

"Look, I want to make this clear. If you figured out where I am, tell me. I'll be upset but I'll understand; you're just doing your job. I'll ask you again: do you know where I am?"

"No. What's wrong?"

"Over the years I've developed an instinct. I know when your people are watching me even if I don't spot them. My subconscious must pick up something I don't consciously see."

"You have good instincts for a non-professional."

"Those good instincts tell me I'm being watched. I wasn't for the first part of my vacation, but now I am. They're good enough I can't spot them, but they *are* there. Or maybe I'm just paranoid."

"Trust your instincts and get out of wherever you are. Better yet, I'll send a team to bring you back."

"I'm not quite ready to have you do that." Jeni sighed. "I don't know if I'd be safer if you did send people here."

"I'm going to be candid, boss lady. Your interests and mine may diverge at some point; I hope that doesn't happen. Even if it does, as long as I'm head of your security, your physical safety is my most important objective."

"And yet in the last month I've had a reporter in my library and an Indian in my bedroom."

"You have every right to be upset by those incidents." Bernhardt paused. "I've offered my resignation. Either accept it or let me do my job."

"Unless something comes up, I'll be back in my gilded cage later today. How are you doing on the contingency plans?"

"Not bad. I had some solar panels and wind turbines at the data center moved to the other side. I'm buying non-perishables in small quantities so it's not noticeable. It's more expensive that way though. You'll need to shuffle money around if I'm going to do much more."

"Done. Other bottlenecks?"

"Yeah. Labor and storage. I can't get enough people, and rechargeable-battery technology stinks. You can keep them going for years, but only if you know the black arts or sacrifice your first born. I would suggest small-scale hydro, but it's impossible to hide. I'm thinking about buying diesel generators for times when the sun doesn't shine and the wind doesn't blow."

"Great. So we repeat all the short-sighted, polluting, unsustainable decisions we made over here?"

"Give me enough people and enough money and I'll get you non-polluting and sustainable there—as long as the batteries hold out. If you want it fast and without a lot of people over there, we're talking diesel and some pollution. Your choice."

"I've been thinking about something. Why go through all of this fancy stuff with solar cells? Just concentrate the sun on water.

The water boils, expands, and steam pushes water on top of it up a tube. While it's going up, it drives a generator. When the water gets to the top, it runs down a tube on the other side, sort of like a waterfall. It drives a generator there too. Then you shift the concentrated solar to the other side, let that boil, and the water gets forced back where it started. You even get alternating current instead of DC."

Bernhardt laughed. "Congratulations. You just reinvented the steam engine—sort of."

"Oh. So I'm not a mechanical wizard."

"That's not a bad idea for a software kind of girl. I didn't know you thought that way."

"I don't usually. I used to hotrod cars in my misspent youth though."

"So you're definitely coming in today?"

"I'll be done with my vacation before sundown. No more reporters or Indians though."

"Sure you don't want a team? That feeling of yours worries me."

"It's not making me feel too good either. I'll be okay." Jeni hung up and frowned at the phone.

I hope.

She lay back in the bed and dozed fitfully as the morning's light tried to stab its way through the gap in the thin hotel drapes.

Chapter Nineteen

SCOTT DROVE THE rental car to the restaurant, a brown frame building with a thirties motif and a sign out front that said, "Rumble Seat." He didn't see anyone following them. He glanced back at Darla. "Sure you want to be here when their security shows up?"

"Oh yeah. Then again, I like playing with fire. Wait in the car if you want."

"I'll stick around—watch the fireworks, get caught in the crossfire, watch you flame out. I'm drawn to it like a moth to a flame. Help. I'm spouting fire clichés and I can't stop."

Peter got out and slammed the door. "I'll go in separately and sit at a different table. They probably have descriptions of all of us, but if not, maybe one of us can work without wearing a big flaming arrow that says, 'I'm investigating you.'"

As Peter stalked away, Scott glanced over at Darla. "See? Now I've got him doing it too—the fire cliché thing."

They waited a couple of minutes, then strolled in and sat at the opposite end of the restaurant from Peter. The Rumble Seat wasn't crowded, but two twenty-something women already hovered around Peter. Darla glared at them as she sat down. "Low-rent trailer trash."

Scott laughed. "I thought the claws coming out was supposed to be subtle—too subtle for a mere guy to notice. Is he really worth it? I doubt that he called you the next day."

"You really don't understand women, do you?"

"If I did, I'd understand why the Peter Kindahls of the world appeal to you strange and alien creatures. As it is, I haven't the slightest of clues."

"Here's one: we always want what we can't have."

"He doesn't seem particularly hard to have."

"There are levels of having. Sometimes you know you can't hold on to something, and that makes you want it even more. Like a rainbow or a thunderstorm. It's there and you enjoy it, but you know isn't yours."

"So Petey's like a thunderstorm or a rainbow, huh?"

"Except for the not living up to unreasonable expectations thing, yeah."

"And you like thunderstorms. That doesn't surprise me. Actually, I like them too. I go out on the balcony and watch them come in."

"That *does* surprise me. I bet you go in when they get close enough to be dangerous."

"Most of the time."

"I don't."

Scott and Darla nursed drinks and greasy burgers for an hour with no sign of anyone taking an interest in them. Three women were sitting with Peter by then, with a couple of others hovering nearby. Peter waggled his brows and grinned when Scott caught his attention.

Scott's phone rang. He glanced at the Caller ID. "And I get a call from my brother. That hasn't happened in—oh, since he got interested in Georgia."

He flipped open the phone. "What's up, brother?"

"Dad said you're looking into the Burgen data center—the one with the windmills."

"I didn't tell him that, but let's assume I am. What's up?"

"You'll want to be careful down there. Rumor has it that

they brought in a bunch of workers from Central America a while back."

"Illegals?"

"Most of them had work permits. They came in. They worked six months. They left. But another group of a couple dozen came in separately and people figured they were illegal. As far as anyone knows, they didn't leave. Nobody has seen them since they went into the data center. It's a small town and that data center is the biggest thing that's happened there in ten years, employment-wise. People keep an eye on who's coming or going. They may have slipped out, but chances are they're still in there. Either that or something bad happened to them."

"Like what?"

"I don't know. Maybe an industrial accident. Maybe they used people nobody would miss for something dangerous. All I know is that two dozen guys went in and probably didn't come back out. So be careful, bro. We may like each other's taste in wives too much, but we're still brothers."

"That we are. I'll watch my step."

Scott flipped the phone closed. "Well, that's interesting."

"Tell me later. We have company." Darla gestured toward the door. "Just one so far."

"That's probably a good thing." Scott looked over. A muscular blond-haired man with dark eyes and a face that looked cold even wearing a smile waved casually at him and marched over.

"Hi. Bernhardt Sloan. I'm with the security team at the Burgen data center. Were you over there earlier?"

Darla smiled. "Is that the big place with the windmills? We got lost, but the windmills looked really cool. Do you have like a postcard or something?"

"I'm a busy man, Ms. Smith. Or do you mind if I call you Darla?"

"Darla is fine."

"Good. And hopefully I can call your friend here Rob or Bob."

"I prefer Scott."

"Middle names are fine by me. Okay, Darla and Scott, you can call me Mr. Sloan."

Darla grinned. "Sure."

"Perhaps your other colleague, Peter Kindahl, would like to join us."

"I doubt it," Scott said. "He's busy sampling the local talent."

"Ah. He seems the type who would. Well, now that we've been properly introduced—"

"But we haven't," Darla said. "You're head of security for Burgen, not just part of the team."

Bernhardt grinned his cold grin. "I see you've done your homework. Now, what do the Boston Police Department and BTI want from my employer?"

"Nothing much," Darla said. "If you could tell us who murdered Samantha Murphy and show us where you're hiding the rogue portal, we could be on our way."

"Murder? Samantha Murphy? Portals? Sorry. We're a software company. I'll have to check our mission statement, but I don't think we're in any of those other businesses."

Darla smiled at him. "Maybe all the evidence is pointing the wrong way. Are you sure you guys aren't involved with those sorts of things?"

"We have some new acquisitions, so I suppose I could check." He pulled his phone halfway out of his pocket. "No, corporate would have filled me in on something like that. Anything else?"

Scott glanced at Darla. *I wish I'd gotten a chance to talk to her about this.* "Did you by any chance misplace a few dozen migrant workers? Central American types?"

Bernhardt Sloan's face went cold. "I'm afraid you'd have to talk to one of our lawyers about that. Oh, and if you do, you'll want to make the conversation brief. You'll want to head back to Scott's parents' house before dark."

"That sounds like a threat," Darla said.

"I get that a lot. It's the face. Makes the most innocent words sound sinister." Bernhardt smiled. "Do have a safe journey. See what I mean? A guy can't say anything less threatening than that. And yet you feel threatened, don't you?"

He got up and strolled out.

Scott turned to Darla. She smiled at him.

"He seems a might touchy about the Central American types. Where did that come from, by the way?"

"A rumor from my brother. I don't think I want Bernhardt Sloan touchy. As a matter of fact, I don't think having him touchy is healthy."

Darla shrugged. "He wants us jumping at shadows. He knows we can't prove anything yet, which means he probably won't do anything to gives us an excuse to go in and find proof."

"Again with the probably stuff. And if he wanted me jumping at shadows, he got what he wanted."

"Hopefully Jeni Burgen is doing the same thing."

Jeni jumped when housekeeping knocked on the door. "Sorry. I forgot to put out the 'Do Not Disturb' sign."

"We'll come back."

Jeni checked her watch. Nine A.M. She checked her messages, then had a sudden thought. "I'm an idiot." She dialed Andy. "Do you still have someone keeping an eye on the people in Chicago?"

"Yeah. We're watching a woman who Scott White spent some time with."

"Do you know her name?"

"Jolene Beck."

Jeni felt the tension flow out of her. "Why are you watching her?"

"We haven't been able to figure out who she is or how she fits in. Except I just did. I feel like an idiot. I should have figured it out from the timing. You didn't even change your initials. Oh, wait. If you happen to chat with Jolene Beck, tell her my people aren't the only ones watching her."

The tension flowed back in. "Any idea who else is?"

"Nobody my people recognize. They know a lot of tricks. You really do need to come home now."

"Soon. Anything new on the investigation?"

"They're on their way to a place we really don't want them right now. This is getting entirely too close. I say we go for broke on getting things ready over there, and be ready to shut the link down if we have to. Dismantle the equipment and lose it among boxes of miscellaneous parts in the warehouse."

"And which side would I be on when we did that?"

"Your call. My guy is looking at your security, by the way. Bernie isn't happy."

"We don't want him too unhappy, as you pointed out."

"I'll keep that in mind."

"Any word from the yacht?"

"No, and I don't expect any. I wish you had let me stay over there."

"I know you do. Actually, you seemed to like it a little too much across the pond. Can't have you going native. Besides, I need you to handle situations like this. Maybe next time."

"I'll hold you to that. So are you going to get out of there?"

"I promised Bernhardt I'd be back by sundown."

"Got you. What about the extra labor?"

"Sorry. Too risky. Find another way to get it done."

"I'll try. Got to go."

Jeni snapped the phone shut and sagged back onto the pillows. She said to the walls of the hotel room, "There goes the Jolene Beck thing. This has been a total waste of time. I didn't even get rid of the stiff neck, and now I go back to the gilded cage with a new set of stalkers. Adam, I need you back. And reasonably debauchery free."

After Bernhardt left, Peter ditched his entourage of women and joined Scott and Darla.

"So…Mr. Sloan doesn't like it when the conversation turns to migrant workers."

"How did you—"

"I read lips. Doesn't everybody? You know this trip has been totally counterproductive."

Scott shook his head. "Why?"

"He knows what we know and don't know. We gained nothing."

"We know migrant workers are a sore spot."

"Unless they're just a rumor and he decided to send us down a false trail."

"I don't believe that. Unless he's an awfully good actor—"

"Which of course he is," Peter said. "He's a professional. If he appears to give something away, maybe you caught him in an unguarded moment. More likely he's messing with your mind and diverting you from his real weaknesses."

"Which are?"

"That's what I'm going to find out. Go back to your cubicle and play with your computer. Tell Chad I'll be back when I get back."

Scott watched him stride away, then turned to Darla. "Are we really amateur screw-ups?"

"Well, I'm hardly an amateur at screwing up. I think we rattled Mr. Bernie, which was the point of the exercise. Now we'll let Petey see what he does next."

Her cellphone rang—a thunderclap followed by screams. She glanced at the ID. "Got to take it. Home office." She listened, asked a couple of cryptic questions, then hung up. "We got the Samantha Murphy autopsy results back. She died of a chemically induced heart attack."

"And her boyfriend died of a heart attack too. I wonder what his autopsy showed."

"That's the other news. There was no autopsy and his body was cremated without permission of the next of kin."

"How did that happen?"

"We need to figure that out. Could have been a screw-up. If it wasn't, it took a fair amount of money or power to pull off."

"Shouldn't we be able to trace it back to the money and power?"

"Maybe. It's something to look at." Darla stared out the restaurant window. "What do you think of Mr. Sloan?"

"Well…he's right about one thing. The face is scary. He could sing "Mary Had a Little Lamb" and scare the crap out of just about anyone."

Chapter Twenty

THE STRANGERS TORE Two Eagle's world apart just before dawn.

He woke up to dogs barking moments before lookouts sounded the alarm. The longhouse filled with quiet, well-practiced activity. Two Eagle strung his sinew-backed bow and put on his armor—wooden slats tied together by deer hide reinforced by precious bronze wire. He grabbed his stone ax and ten-inch bronze knife, the knife was a symbol of his authority as well as a potent weapon.

Around him, other Wenroh warriors hustled past sleepy chickens to their posts. Women positioned pots full of water to fight fires—and spare arrows for the warriors. They also checked the edges of their knives. Children too young to fight carried even younger siblings to a strong log house in the center of town, a fort within the fort. Runners sprinted out the gates to warn the rest of the Wenroh tribe.

Two Eagle strode to his position commanding a watchtower while his wife rushed their five–year-old daughter to the strong house.

Enemy warriors stomped through foot-tall corn, silhouetted against the early morning sky in the vast fields surrounding the palisaded town. There were maybe five hundred of them—mostly Erie, the Cat People, armed and painted for war. *But we have three times that many warriors here alone.* Two Eagle scanned the horizon, looking for more attackers.

The Erie stationed themselves around the palisade, barely out of bow range and not responding to challenges from Wenroh warriors. Two Eagle's senses sharpened as anticipation of battle flooded his veins. The warriors around him looked calm, even the younger ones preparing for their first engagement.

The enemy ranks opened. Five men stood in the open area, holding what appeared to be short spears or clubs. Suddenly those spears spewed flame. Snapping sounds, like giant kernels of corn popping, echoed across the cornfield. A warrior toppled against Two Eagle, blood pumping from a hole in his chest.

The popping sounds echoed again. More of Two Eagle's warriors fell around him. A tug at his left arm gashed a bloody line across his flesh. Pain jarred him out of his bewilderment and he yelled, "Down."

He ducked behind the waist-high log wall of the watchtower and hoped that the enemy's magic arrows couldn't go through it. Around him, most of his warriors bled, some from fatal wounds. One moaned. He closed his mind to the dishonoring sound, careful not to notice who made it. He whistled for the old men and women standing by to help the wounded, but similar whistles from every direction filled the air.

His warriors looked as dazed as Two Eagle felt. He poked his head above the wall for a heartbeat, catching a glimpse of the men standing in the field, as casual as women gossiping but with their fire-sticks poised. Wood splinters stung his forehead as he ducked. He caught a glimpse of Wenroh warriors falling from the palisade to lie unmoving on the ground.

Two Eagle felt fear growing in his men. The enemy stayed out of bow range, but the popping sounds kept echoing, almost continuous now, accompanied by thuds that vibrated the watchtower wall and sent splinters flying. The log walls shielded his men, but the warriors were useless cowering behind walls. He said, "Loose your arrows at my command." His warriors looked doubtful, but fitted arrows to their bows. Two Eagle waited a heartbeat, summoning his courage.

"Now." He hastily shot in the direction of the enemy. A pitiful handful of his warriors followed suit, their arrows falling pathetically short as they ducked back down. A barrage of pops and thuds came seconds later, but resulted only in more flying splinters. Two Eagle poked a stone ax head above the wall. It jerked, almost flying out of his grasp. A spray of stone chips stung his arm.

A white-haired Wenroh woman climbed stiffly up the watchtower ladder. She checked the wounded or dead warriors and pointed to several with severe wounds. Two Eagle helped her get them down the ladder. He pointed to others, but she shook her head.

The rising sun lit the eastern sky. Blood ran across the rough watchtower floor, making it slippery. Two Eagle jerked his leg back as an arrow hit and quivered inches from his knee. He peeked out through a gap in the logs. Erie bowmen strode toward the palisade, firing as they came. Behind them, a cluster of short, powerful-looking men in shiny armor marched toward the palisade, carrying crude ladders. A pitifully small and ragged volley spattered them. Two Eagle and his surviving warriors joined it, making themselves vulnerable to the firesticks. One of his men slumped, unmoving. Another rain of arrows arched over the wall and thudded into the floor.

For the first time since the fighting started, Two Eagle shifted his focus from his watchtower. He glimpsed the mounds of bodies below the palisade and knew fear for the town and the Wenroh people.

Chapter Twenty-One

JENI SAT IN the back seat of a four-year-old Buick as it drove west down the I-88 tollway. The man in the back seat with her didn't display his pistol, but she knew it was close at hand, as were the guns of the driver and the guy in the front passenger seat. The guy sitting next to her was young, probably no more than twenty-five, shorter than Jeni's five foot nine and of indeterminate race, with black hair cut close and spiked. He wore blue jeans and a tie-dyed shirt that said, "Turkey Testicle Festival 2009." The men in the front seat were taller, one well over six feet. They wore expensive but poorly matched dress pants and dress shirts. They were both Caucasians, probably Midwesterners, based on their accents.

The car rode smoothly down the toll road, with none of the men saying much. Jeni scanned their faces, memorizing details. She wondered if seeing the faces was an ominous sign.

The men had picked her up in the hotel room, a smooth, effortlessly professional operation. Dressed in hotel uniforms, they simply knocked, then displayed guns when she opened the door. They grabbed her suitcase and stashed the rest of her stuff in a duffle bag, with the exception of her cellphone, which she surreptitiously kicked under the bed. They marched her to the door. A car pulled up and they hustled her in.

The ride down the tollway gradually took them from the heavily trafficked suburbs, Oakbrook and then Naperville, to more sparsely traveled territory. They went through Aurora, and the landscape around them shifted from suburb to farm, with an occasional patch of urban sprawl reaching into cornfields in the form of a strip mall or housing development of cheaply made identical green or gray houses.

The guy in the back seat got noticeably uneasy as the cars and the houses thinned out along the tollway. Jeni glanced over at him and said, "I hear they have raccoons the size of bears out here in the sticks. And coyotes the size of wolves." The man didn't say anything, but looked even more uneasy.

They didn't respond to Jeni's attempts to get them to tell her why they had grabbed her or where they were taking her. They showed no sign of knowing who she really was, and she decided not to say anything that would tell them. As the traffic thinned, ironically they became more tense and more conscious of the cars around them. The driver kept the car at a steady 68, at least ten miles per hour slower than the cars and trucks around them. Twice they passed state troopers issuing speeding tickets. Other cars slowed briefly, but resumed their normal pace long before they were out of sight of the troopers.

Jeni looked for a way to escape or attract attention. That got harder as they drove into less populated areas. Her only weapon was a nail file stashed in the waistband of her sweatshirt—of little use against three armed opponents. She'd already tried one other use for the nail file, with no apparent success.

She despaired as the car continued on its way with no hint of unevenness in the ride, no sign that her desperate ploy would bear fruit. They raced past Orchard Road and on toward I-47, the fringe of expanding suburbia. Past that, they'd find twenty-five miles of cornfields occasionally broken up by farmhouses and electric lines. She remembered them from the trip in.

The vibration started a mile after they passed I-47. At first Jeni thought it was a product of hope and imagination. The shaking gradually got worse, and then the driver said, "Something doesn't feel right. I think a tire's about to blow."

The guy in the passenger seat swore and took out a GPS receiver. "We've got nothing but cornfield crap for fifteen miles. Can you nurse it?"

"Not fifteen miles if we're losing air. I'll slow it down a little, but—"

The front passenger side tire blew and shredded. The metal of the wheel hit pavement and the car slewed around, doing a 360. Jeni thought about grabbing the gun from the guy beside her, but she was too busy getting thrown against the side of the car to even try. The car tilted up on its side and threatened to flip, but it didn't. Finally it slid to a stop in the right lane, with traffic behind them frantically skidding to avoid them.

The driver took a deep breath and drove the car a limping few yards to get it the rest of the way onto the shoulder. The men looked at each other. One swore a long and obviously heartfelt string of words describing the car's checkered ancestry.

The driver said, "We've got to get the flat changed now. Out here we'll have a cop asking if we need help inside of fifteen minutes."

"Does this thing even have a spare?" That from the guy in the back seat.

"I think so. One of those donut things that let you drive fifty miles an hour. Okay"—the driver pointed to Jeni—"you stay in the car. Even roll down the window and we'll splatter your brains." He pointed to the others. "You two, get the car jacked up. I'll find the tire and keep an eye on the girl."

"How're you going to do both of those things?"

"Don't worry. I will."

They all got out. The driver reached back in and took his keys. "Not that this thing is going anywhere, but why tempt you? Oh, and don't toot the horn, don't wave to anybody. Don't do anything that attracts attention. Got it?"

"Yeah. I also get that if you shoot me now, you'll have a lot of explaining to do."

The driver leaned over the seat. "Thinking like that will get you killed. Got it?"

"Yes."

Jeni watched the men open the trunk and drag the jack out. The driver had the trunk lid up and fiddled with the fasteners on the spare tire, glancing at her through a gap where the trunk lid met the car body.

Got to do this before they take what's left of the tire off.

Jeni scooted forward, trying to stay upright, reached under the dashboard and used the fingernail file to strip the right wires, careful to keep her head in sight of the driver. She braced herself, waited until he glanced up and back at his work, then swung herself into the driver's seat. She hit the automatic door lock and held the stripped wires together. The car started, and she slammed it into reverse, sending men scrambling out of the way. She hit the brakes, slammed the car in gear and stomped the accelerator. The car struggled down the shoulder, steering wheel fighting to tear itself out of her fingers. The driver loomed in the mirror, sprinting, closing the gap. She accelerated and almost lost control, but gave it as much gas as she dared.

Not enough.

She felt a thud as he jumped into the trunk.

Jeni let the car jerk itself hard to the right and then to the left. She heard a curse from the trunk. The other men still chased the car, losing ground. She kept going, whipping the car back and forth to keep the man in the trunk off balance. That wasn't hard to do. The trick was keeping the car on the road. The jerking got worse as the last of the rubber flew off and hit the shoulder behind them. Drivers hit their brakes to avoid debris and gape at the strange activity on the shoulder. No one stopped though. Jeni saw the driver's angry face peering through the gap formed by the open trunk.

She didn't see a gun, but assumed the driver was trying to keep it out of sight of passersby. She figured someone would quickly report the bizarre altercation to the police. Just a matter of not getting shot in the meantime.

The driver must have figured that out too, because he started kicking the wall between the trunk and the back seat. It yielded and the seat pushed forward. Jeni watched as a hand gripping a pistol pushed through. She swerved the car, almost lost control, and heard a satisfyingly hard thump in the back.

The driver didn't lose his gun though. He yelled, "Stop. I can't miss at this range."

Jeni shook her head and slammed the car back and forth again. The motion took on a life of its own and a tire hit the outer edge of the shoulder. That threw the car into a spin, and Jeni lost control. The car tipped over and rolled down an embankment toward a fence. The roof collapsed toward Jeni. She slid down, more from the motion of the car than from any intent, and found herself being thrown around the interior. She hit something, actually several somethings, then the car landed upright with jolting force.

Jeni scrabbled for the door. It didn't open, and she could tell it was smashed in badly enough it was unlikely to open without mechanical cutters. The other doors were just as bad. She looked back at the trunk. The driver and his pistol were no longer in evidence, but she had no idea where he was.

She crawled over the back of the seat and pushed through the trunk. She saw no sign of the driver, but spotted the other two kidnappers running down the embankment toward her. She sprinted to the fence separating the tollway from the nearby field and climbed over it into ankle-high corn. She ran awkwardly across the plowed ground. The men behind her weren't doing much better, and as she thought about what she had seen of their physiques, she suspected they wouldn't be able to run for long.

Jeni considered trying to circle back to the highway. Police should be there soon, and that might make her pursuers think twice about shooting her. On the other hand, staying out of range was the only sure way to avoid getting shot, and she seemed to be doing that. She glanced back. The men were now walking. They went back to a trot, but couldn't maintain the speed.

The problem was that Jeni had no idea what was ahead of her. It would be easy to trap herself in the bend of a river or even a drainage ditch with steep sides. Even if nothing like that loomed, she couldn't run forever. She slowed to a jog and then a walk. She wasn't tired yet, but she didn't want to risk twisting an ankle.

As she walked, she began to realize how enormous an Illinois cornfield could be. It seemed to go on to the horizon. She heard the faint sound of sirens and thought again about circling back. The field had enough dips and rolling hills that she'd lost track of her pursuers, and that made turning back risky. She wondered what happened to the driver. She also wondered if the state police could see her from the road. Probably not.

She kept walking because she couldn't think of anything better to do. She slowed and her muscles grew stiff. Every article of clothing developed sharp edges. She lost track of time and of the road. She headed north, not because she had any destination in mind, but because it was the only direction she knew would take her away from the men behind her.

Jeni glanced at her watch. It was two in the afternoon, and the sun was at its hottest. She heard a high-pitched motor whine somewhere ahead. A twenty-something man in a hat, bib overalls and a pair of work boots drove a four-wheeler over a low hill and pulled alongside her. A shotgun sat in the back of the vehicle, within easy reach. A Rottweiler crouched in the seat next to the man. The dog jumped out when the four-wheeler stopped, but it stood in the shade and waited rather than approaching her.

The young man said, "Hi. A lot of city folks don't know this, but this field belongs to us. We don't mind visitors, but we like them to come in by the road and stop by the house."

Jeni sighed. "I understand. I had an incident back there."

"Have anything to do with the car that rolled over a couple of times?"

"Sort of. How did you know about that?"

"Police scanner. Now you're dinged up and you've been walking one hell of a long way. Is there a reason you're walking away from an accident?"

Jeni thought about telling him the truth, but realized that would bring a cascade of other questions. She said, "The guy I was with. My husband would kill me if he knew."

"A little messing around on the side? You don't look like the type, not that there is necessarily a type for that."

"No. I just accepted a ride. The guy tried to turn it into something else. I said no and he tried to get physical. I objected."

"Hmmm. Sounds like you objected a little too vigorously for your own good."

"Well, I didn't intend to cause him to roll the car, but I'm not sorry I did. He chased me for a while. He may still be out there."

The young man picked up a walkie-talkie from the seat beside him. "Dad, I'm going to give her a ride in. I'll let you sort it out."

The dog seemed to sense that the possibility of confrontation had subsided. It climbed back in the four-wheeler. The man gestured at the seat beside him. "It's a lot easier than walking, and I know how to not damage any more corn than I have to."

Jeni climbed in. The man said, "I'm Jordan. I didn't catch your name."

"Jolene."

Jordan turned the four-wheeler around and drove toward a farmhouse on the far side of the field. "Why did you need a ride from this jerk?"

"Car trouble."

"Where were you headed?"

Jolene tried to remember the nearby towns. She said the only name she remembered. "Cortland. I'm visiting a friend there."

"Where do you live?"

"I'd rather not say. I don't want this getting back to the wrong person there."

Jordan steered through the shallow water of a drainage ditch. "I don't mean to pry. I'm trying to figure out how we can help you if you decide we need to."

"I understand. I'm just being careful."

"You could tell your husband; keeping secrets eventually blows up on a person."

"You haven't been married long, have you?"

"I haven't been married at all. By the way, I can't help noticing you're not wearing a ring."

Jolene glanced at her bare finger. "The stone fell out of the setting. That's what the trip was about." The lie came smoothly and Jeni said a silent thanks for a whim that had led her to take college acting classes.

"What about the other guys in the car?"

Jeni glanced at Jordan as they pulled into the front yard of a brick ranch-style farmhouse. "They just sat there. His friends. They'll stick together. My mistake was getting in the car."

Jordan stopped the four-wheeler, stretched and climbed out. "The thing about dad, he likes it straight. Facts, not bullshit."

"You're acting like you don't believe me."

"I don't. You're not telling the whole story. Part of it may be true, but most of it isn't. They claim you were hitchhiking and acted nuts when they gave you a ride. They had a flat, got out to fix it and you went apeshit."

"And if you believe that, just take me to the other end of the property and drop me off."

"No need for that. Dad can help you. Just tell him the truth."

"I doubt that he would believe it, not now. I can't stay to satisfy your curiosity. Mr. 'won't accept no' has a gun. He was not a happy camper after I wrecked his car, which is why I ran."

"What's his name, by the way?"

Jeni glared at Jordan. "I'm done talking to you. Thanks for the ride." The dog stood as they stopped, watching Jeni intently, as though sensing the tension between her and his master.

"Okay. So I'm a crappy liar." Jeni got up from the four-wheeler, watching the dog warily.

"Actually you're a pretty good liar," Jordan said. "Why don't you just tell us the truth? We'll help you if you deserve it."

Jeni shook her head. "Sorry. I don't mean to sound ungrateful. Thanks for the ride, but we're done. The truth is complicated and messy enough you don't want to get into it. You really don't want to get pulled into my drama."

A taller, older version of Jordan strode out to the porch. He glared at Jeni. "Young lady, you need to chat with the police. A couple guys claim you wrecked their car. One of them is hurt bad. There may be another side to it, but you need to tell it if there is and you need to do it right away."

Jeni walked to the porch and plopped in the shade. "I screwed up pretty good here. I'll get it straightened out. Didn't the police find guns? All three of them had guns."

"Why don't you tell us what's going on. We'll get the state police over here and they can take it from there. If you don't want to talk to us, we can get you something to drink and you can wait here for the police."

Jeni thought about that. "I didn't do anything wrong. Three

guys grabbed me out of my hotel room this morning, pointed guns at me and put me in a car. When they had a flat, I tried to get away. The car rolled because of the bad tire. I couldn't control it. That's the truth."

"The police saw only two guys and they didn't mention anybody else." Jordan joined her on the porch. "So if this is true, why'd you give me the song and dance about your husband being mad and the guy coming onto you?"

"One of them is still out there. I'm sorry I lied. I didn't think you'd believe me and didn't want to get sucked into a big investigation. I want to walk away and go on with my life like this never happened."

"And then these guys just go and kidnap somebody else?"

"I don't know if they would bother anybody else. I think it may just be me they were after."

"Why?"

"I'm not going to lie, but I don't want to tell you that. As I said, you don't want to get mixed up in my drama."

Jordan bumped her from behind and nearly sent Jeni sprawling. She turned and started to push him away when she heard the gunshot. She grabbed him and tried to support him as blood poured out of his chest, but he slid out of her grasp. His father ducked for cover but fell clutching his thigh as Jeni heard the second gunshot and then the whiplash sound of a bullet coming close. She ran for the front door, saw it was closed, and ran back to the four-wheeler. She couldn't tell where the shots were coming from, but she ducked behind the inadequate shelter.

The Rottweiler growled and ran for a clump of trees near the house. It stumbled and plowed a furrow in the dirt with its muzzle, and Jeni heard another shot. She glanced up at the four-wheeler and saw the keys in the ignition. She glanced back toward the trees. The dog jumped up and limped on, still headed for the same clump of trees.

Jeni saw a glint of sunlight off metal among the trees. She jumped into the four-wheeler and headed for the far side of the house, swerving back and forth as she drove. She heard a shot spang against the vehicle, but she kept going. When she put the house between herself and the gunman, she paused, not sure if she should go on or help the two farmers. She glanced behind her. The shotgun was still in the back, but it wouldn't have enough range to get at the gunman if he had a rifle, which he apparently did, though she couldn't remember seeing one in the car. The radio was gone, either fallen out during her escape or removed by Jordan.

Jeni gunned the four-wheeler and drove off, trying to keep the house between her and the grove of trees. She heard a shout behind her, but didn't look back. She drove across the lawn at the back of the house, then back to the driveway. She couldn't tell if she was out of sight of the gunman, but no more shots followed her as she raced down the driveway. She came to an east/west road and mentally shrugged.

There had to be five or ten miles of farm country between her and the nearest town either way. East took her closer to the hotel and her car, but she figured someone would be watching that by now. She turned west, driving along the side of the road and veering onto the pavement to cross bridges and culverts.

The four-wheeler was unfamiliar to her, but she adapted easily enough. She had no idea what speed she was making, but cars passed, easily outpacing her. After a few minutes she heard sirens and four police cars zoomed past. None of the cars slowed, but if either of the farmers were still alive, the four-wheeler would soon be part of a search.

Jeni looked for side roads, or even paths that she could take with the four-wheeler, but she didn't see one for several miles. Finally she found a cross road and turned north on it. The road went to gravel after a few miles, but she kept going. All she could see were cornfields and pastureland, with occasional farmhouses and barns breaking up the monotony. She wondered how far she had gone and more importantly, how much farther she could go before she ran out of gas. She'd already searched for a gas gauge, but if the four-wheeler had one, she didn't recognize it.

The gravel road curved and then went back to blacktop. She soon came to a more substantial road. She turned west on it and soon saw a sign that said I-38. That didn't help at all since she had no idea where I-38 went. The sun started to go down, and the four-wheeler showed signs of giving up on her. In less than two minutes it sputtered and stopped, apparently out of gas. She let it coast as far she could, steering it to a low place hard to spot from the road, then hopped off and stared up and down the highway.

She saw nothing but road, shoulder and cornfield in either direction, though a sign to the west announced that Cortland was four miles away. She searched the back of the four-wheeler. The shotgun was still there, along with two warm cans of energy drink and a gym bag holding a man's shirt. The shotgun just fit in the bag if she broke it down. She stuffed it under the clothes and put the drinks at the top of the bag. She felt thirsty enough to drink them warm, but held off. She leaned against the four-wheeler, reluctant to leave the one semi-familiar thing in her world.

And I'm officially pathetic.

She half-hoped that Bernhardt would somehow track her down and swoop in to rescue her.

Which makes me doubly pathetic.

She pushed away from the four-wheeler and headed to Cortland, carrying the gym bag. By now her muscles had really stiffened and she had to push herself to keep moving.

Several cars slowed as they passed her, and one teenager leaned out to ask if she wanted a ride. She eyed the car full of teenage boys and reluctantly shook her head. She kept walking as the sun went low toward the horizon. It reflected off the clouds, making the west red, white and bluish purple. She finally reached a service station/mini-mart on the outskirts of Cortland. She strolled in and stared wistfully at the array of soft drinks and cold water in the cooler at the back wall. She opened the door to grab a water bottle, then realized her purse was back in the wrecked car. She stood with the door open for a second, hand poised, enjoying the cool air. Finally she sighed and closed the door.

The guy behind the cash register smiled at her. "You look like you really want that water."

Jeni nodded. "But I left my purse in the car, and it's far enough away that I don't want to walk back and get the money. I brought a couple of energy drinks with me, but they're hot. I'd probably get sick if I drank them."

"I could get you a cup of ice."

"Would you?"

He handed her a plastic cup full of ice. She let one cube dissolve in her mouth, savoring the coolness and the trickle of water down her throat. "Thank you so much. I owe you."

"Not a problem." His eyes lingered at her chest, and she thought he was about to make a pass at her, but he didn't. Jeni walked to the shade in the strip of grass between the crossroad and the station and poured one of the drinks over the ice. Most of the ice dissolved in the warm liquid, but the result was drinkable and she took a couple of quick gulps, then forced herself to sip.

A police car pulled into the station, and an officer went inside. Jeni didn't move and the officer didn't appear to see her. She thought about turning herself in. That struck her as a sensible idea, especially given the alternative of wandering aimlessly around rural Illinois. She got up to walk inside. As she did, a white van pulled into the parking lot. The rear door slid open and an Asian man in his late twenties pointed a revolver at her.

"Jolene Beck? Please get in the van."

Chapter Twenty-Two

SCOTT AND DARLA drove back to Scott's parents' house that evening. Scott's gaze flicked from the rearview mirror to Darla and then back to the road.

"I think we picked up a tail."

"We've had tails everywhere we've gone since I got to Chicago. Actually, long before that for me. My personal cloud again. We picked up a few more interested parties along the way. I'm guessing Bernhardt added a couple more after our conversation, if he didn't already have someone on us. It's a wonder they aren't tripping over one another."

"Your personal cloud, huh? From your police work before this case?"

"From playing with fire too many times."

"Is this cloud likely to rain on us?"

"It hasn't yet, but no promises."

Scott pulled into his parents' driveway shortly before dark. He turned to Darla. "Was Petey right? Was there really no point to this?"

Darla shrugged. "We saw the complex. We twisted their tail. We know the portal is inside that fence."

"There can't be a portal there. The power budget doesn't add up."

"Bernie's reaction to the missing workers says it's there," Darla said. "He wasn't worried about Samantha Murphy or the scroll; the workers worried him. Why? Where did they go? The complex is big enough they could be hiding in there somewhere, but not without the other workers figuring out where they are. So, where are they? For that matter, where were the other imported workers, the legal ones, working?"

Scott spotted his mom peeking out the upstairs window. "We might want to talk to my parents. They know we're out here."

"Welcome back to high school. We've been sitting out here long enough your parents probably think we're making out. We might as well let them think we've decided to go somewhere private."

"Dad already thinks you're trouble."

"He got that right. Smart guy in his own way. He just needs to figure out that the fifties are never coming back."

"He's making it work. L. J. never will." Scott sighed. "I'll call L. J. and ask him if he knows anything more about the workers."

"You really don't want to see your daughter?"

"She's happy. She has a dad and a mom and they both love her. This is a messed-up situation, but we have it handled. If I saw her and we bonded, the whole thing would come unglued. Now I'm the uncle who sends her nice toys and makes her life easier. That works."

He dialed L. J.'s number. "Those workers you talked about, what did they do at the data center?"

"Nothing. They came in. They disappeared. The legal ones came back out after three or four months. The illegals didn't. Nobody at the plant saw either bunch of them from the time they came in until the time the legal ones left."

"Now that's interesting. Who built the wind farms?"

"Locals."

Scott heard a little girl's voice in the background, asking for daddy to read her a story. "I'll let you go."

"You think they have a portal hidden in the data center," L. J. stated rather than asking. "Why else would you be interested?"

"Good point. You might want to keep that theory quiet. There are reasons having a portal there doesn't make sense."

"This stays with me. Actually, Dad figured it out too. I'll let you know if the missing workers show up or if they bring in more. Want to stop over before you go back?" L. J. didn't sound enthusiastic.

"That could get awkward."

"More awkward than dinner last night?"

Scott laughed. "That would be hard to top."

"That it would." L. J. paused. Finally he said, "Well, you're invited. Going back tomorrow?"

"Yeah. Back to my world."

"This is your world too."

"Not anymore. It never really was."

"It wasn't all bad growing up here, was it?"

Scott sighed. "Watching the town die? Watching families and neighborhoods break up and scatter to find jobs? I should never have come back after school. I was lucky to get out."

"Maybe. Maybe if I had known where things were going back in high school I would've done the same thing. But probably not. I am what I am and I was going where I was going," he said. "This is a tired land now. The best of the coal is gone and the best of the iron ore. Maybe we should open the gates to this other dimension. Go in and do mining and manufacturing there. Get us back to making things in this country."

"And how long would that last before TLX was as tired as this part of Ohio? Not long. We have to figure out some way of making a living that doesn't screw things up. The time of big manufacturing, of huge steel mills and mines, that's over. Time to move on."

"Maybe. Got to go. I have a little girl here who wants daddy time. Sara, say goodnight to your Uncle Scott."

A little girl's voice said, "Goodnight."

The phone went dead.

Darla reached over and took Scott's hand. "You look like something hit you between the eyes."

"Something like that." Scott sighed. "They love each other. They're a family and it works. I can't screw it up."

"You sound like you're working hard to convince yourself."

"Maybe. Probably." *And back to the job at hand.* He summarized L. J.'s part of the conversation for her.

When he finished, Darla said, "There's a portal. The legal workers built something in TLX. They had the illegal ones do something that could get them killed and maybe did."

"Or they wanted a permanent staff that couldn't be traced. Assuming that there *is* a portal there, which there can't be."

"Unless they know something you don't about how to make a portal. Did you tell L. J. there was a portal in the data center?"

"No, but he figured that's why we're here. Actually, dad did. *Works with his hands* doesn't equal stupid." Scott glanced at the window as his mom peeked out again. "I'd better go in. Sorry my parents didn't ask you to stay the night."

"That's okay." Darla leaned over and kissed him on the mouth, then worked her way down to his neck. "Sweet dreams."

"Thanks. I may have dreams. I'm not sure how sweet they'll be. Hmmm. No fire this time. What brought that on?"

"Your mom disapproves of me. When you go in and she's thinking about us, about me, I want her claws to come out. "

"Thanks. Now I feel like I'm sixteen again."

She scooted into the driver's seat and drove off. Scott started to wipe the lipstick off his neck before he went in, then shrugged.

I'm almost thirty. I can come home with lipstick on my collar.

Chapter Twenty-Three

JIM WHITE STOPPED by Scott's room the next morning and woke him up. "We didn't see much of you this weekend, but it wasn't all bad having you back."

"It wasn't all bad being back."

"You didn't see Sara, did you?"

"No. I want to, but that's a slippery slope. I know where it leads and I can't go there."

"She's going to be just like you," Jim said. "I can tell already. She'll have her nose in a book all the time and L. J. will never understand her. He'll try and she'll try, but they'll never quite mesh and they'll grow apart. That's tough enough, but you add in the fact he'll know she's your kid, and that'll make it ten times worse. L. J.'s a good man, but he'll resent it and that'll come out somehow. If they have other kids, it'll get worse for her."

Scott stared at his dad. "Who are you and where did you stash my dad's body?"

"Huh?"

"I don't remember you being insightful."

"That's because you were too busy being a smartass. She'll grow up book smart even though nobody encourages her. The other kids will think she's strange and she'll wonder if she's strange too. Being book smart when nobody around you is—that can be tough. You always have to watch what you say. You spend a lot of time doing stuff that bores the crap out of you so you can sort of fit in with people you have nothing in common with. You've been there. That's where she's headed."

"What do you want me to do? Try to break L. J. and Georgia up? Try to tear a little girl away from her mom and the only dad she knows?"

"No. Just be there for her. Be the uncle she can talk to. Help L. J. out when he doesn't understand her. Don't push your way into their lives, but be a part of them. You'll have to be smart and you'll have to be sensitive and it still may not work. But you have to do it."

"I'll try."

"I know you will. Are you going to shut down the portal?"

"We'll have to prove there's one there first."

"You guys can't screw around with this. One of the few things I remember from history class is how much disease messed up the American Indians when our ancestors came over. If somebody goes over there and brings something nasty back—"

"I know, dad."

"Well, do something about it then."

Darla picked Scott up a few minutes later. They drove to the airport quietly and flew back to Chicago. It was early evening by the time they got out of the airport. Scott drove Darla back to her hotel.

"In spite of a few tense moments, your evil plan failed," he told her.

"Aw, you and your dad bonded, didn't you?"

"Not really. We did get a few things sorted out. I still don't have a thing in common with him other than a few stray genes. And my life's not going to get any less complicated."

After Darla went inside, Scott sat in the parking lot and called Jolene Beck's cellphone. He didn't get any answer. He drove to his apartment, feeling sluggish from all the sitting, and did a brief calisthenics workout. When he finished, he paced, restless. He tried Jolene again, but didn't get an answer then or any time later that evening. Finally he drove to her hotel and talked to a desk clerk who told him that Jolene had checked out, but had left a message for him, a brief handwritten note.

Had to head home early. Nice seeing you again. Call me when you get a chance. Jolene.

Scott studied the note. It looked more masculine than he'd expected her handwriting to look, but then he didn't remember her handwriting from the class.

As he turned to leave, the clerk said, "The cleaning people found a cellphone under her bed. Only number she left was that cellphone. Her address is a post office box. We were going to send the phone to her, but if you know how to get in touch with her, maybe you could take care of it."

Scott shrugged. "The cell number and an email address are all I have. I can email her, I suppose." He took the phone back to his apartment and sent an email to the address she'd given him. As he waited for a reply, he checked the phone for an emergency contact. When he didn't find one, he scanned the numbers Jolene had called recently. The bulk of the calls were to three numbers, one of which was his. He hesitated a few minutes, reluctant to invade Jolene's privacy any more than he already had. Finally he dialed the one she'd called last.

Scott recognized the voice that answered.

Shit shit shit shit shit.

He finally said, "Hi, Bernhardt. I guess this means Jolene was a plant."

"What? Who is this? How did you get this number?" Scott heard the sounds of fumbling on the other end and then Bernhardt said, "Scott White. I recognize the voice, but I don't recall giving you this number."

"You didn't. Your Jolene Beck got sloppy."

"I don't have a Jolene Beck. Is a Jolene Beck is a person or something you put on a salad?"

"Why did she call you five or six times in the last couple of days?"

"You've got me. When was the last time she called me?"

Scott told him. Bernhardt didn't say anything. "Still there?"

"Yeah, just checking the time. I think I actually might have had a Jolene Beck call me then. Did she also call me around these times?" Bernhardt called out a few other times.

"So now you remember. How much did you pay her to get friendly with me again?"

"I'm afraid she did that on her own," Bernhardt said. "Do you know where she is now?"

"I have no clue. I was hoping you did."

"You're back in the Chicago area by now. I could tell from your voice that you didn't know who would answer when you called this number. That could mean you found the number on a scrap of paper and got curious. But that wouldn't explain how you knew the call times. I think you found our friend Jolene's cellphone. Would you mind telling me how that happened?"

"Yeah."

"You should understand that if you found her phone, Jolene Beck is in a great deal of danger. I'll find out everything you know whether or not you tell me, but that will take time and the trail will get cold."

"It's already cold. She checked out of her hotel room yesterday."

"Care to tell me which hotel? It'll save me five or ten minutes."

"No. I think any danger to her would come from you. Erasing the trail, punishing failure, that sort of thing."

"You'll want to hang on to Ms. Beck's phone until we get there to start our investigation. I don't suppose you thought to preserve fingerprints. Please don't handle it more than you already have. I'll be there in a couple of hours." Bernhardt hung up.

Scott sat and stared at Jolene's cellphone. That went well.

So I ended up getting some poor girl hunted by Bernhardt Sloan. Of course, she did betray our friendship. Maybe I should hope he finds her.

He thought about the grim-faced security man. No. Probably not.

He called Darla and told her what had happened. When he finished she said, "I told you she wasn't being straight with you. Remember, look at the shoes."

"I got that. Thanks. I'll notice the shoes next time. Shoes are the window to a woman's soul."

"Ha. A guy's soul too."

Scott glanced down at his sneakers. "I hope not. I won't have the slightest idea what I'm looking for, but I'll look at the shoes. Assuming Bernhardt Sloan doesn't put my head in a microwave tonight."

"He's probably just rattling your cage again, but it might be a good idea to be somewhere public. I'll let you pick me up at the hotel and take me out for a late-night coffee. Bring the phone. We'll see what kind of fun we can stir up by calling that second number Jolene Beck kept calling."

L. J. called Scott as Darla and Scott strolled into the coffee shop.

"Thought you'd want to know that dad's old union buddies say Burgen is hiring illegals, going for young singles with no attachments. They aren't making it obvious it's them, but they're going more for speed than for covering their tracks."

"Thanks. Somebody may be panicking, which isn't good because we aren't ready to take advantage of it. Thanks for the info, bro."

Scott hung up and turned to Darla. "We got our reaction. Burgen is scrambling for disposable workers. What do you think that means?"

"I don't know. We don't know why they're screwing around with a portal in the first place. They're spending a lot of money. What's their payback?"

Scott nodded. "It would help to know that. Maybe a place to run? But they wouldn't have to run if they weren't messing with a rogue portal. They may be planning to run there now, but it wasn't their initial motive."

"What's valuable over there?"

"Other than Roman books?" Scott shrugged. "The big diamonds would be priceless, but you couldn't legally sell them, and black market would be risky."

"Oil? Natural gas?"

Scott shook his head. "Portals require a lot of energy. It might be worth it if you happened to have an oil field within a few miles of the portal. None of them are. Actually, oil fields are the places with the strongest walls. Beyond that, there's the cost of building roads and pipelines. Add all that together and oil doesn't make economic sense. Believe me, we've looked at all this. Literature and art? That works. For natural resources, Timeline X is surprisingly hard to exploit. That makes our job much easier."

They took a booth in the corner and Scott dialed the second-most-often dialed number in Jolene's cellphone. An unfamiliar voice answered. Scott said, "Is Jolene Beck there?"

"You have the wrong number."

"No. I have exactly the number I want. Is Bernhardt Sloan there?"

"You really don't want to talk to Bernhardt Sloan. How did you get this number?"

"From Jolene Beck."

"Ah, from her cellphone. I'll take that off of your hands and get it to its rightful owner."

"Sorry. Bernhardt Sloan is already on his way to take care of it."

"You're more likely to keep your hands if you give it to me."

"And you are?"

"A friend of Jolene's."

"A friend with a name?" Scott asked.

"Yeah. I just don't give it out. So you found Jolene Beck's cellphone and chatted with Bernie. That would make you Scott White."

"Scott White, huh?" Scott kept his voice calm. "Are you sure?"

"Yeah. And I bet you're sitting in a back booth of a coffee shop in Oak Brook playing your little games with Darla Smith."

Scott put his hand over the receiver and whispered, "He knows where we are." He peeked around the coffee shop. Nobody seemed to be paying any attention to them. Scott said, "You have me at a slight disadvantage."

"The whole *you don't have the slightest idea who I am* bit? Or the *have no idea what's going on* bit? You're flailing in the dark. And you're putting a lot of people in danger."

"Like the latest batch of illegal workers you're collecting?"

"Well, Mr. White, you just promoted yourself from nuisance to problem. That's not a good thing from your point of view." The phone went dead.

Scott took a deep breath and turned to Darla. "That went stunningly well. At least we know the workers are a sore point with Mr. Anonymous too. I wonder where he fits in."

"Boston PD is tracking down the phone numbers. They're unlisted, but we'll get them."

"How did he know we were here?"

Darla shrugged. "We've known we were being followed since the beginning of the case. Mr. Anonymous must be behind one of the tails."

"How do you get so casual about something like that?"

"Long, long practice."

"What do you think Jolene Beck wanted?"

"Oh, come on. You know what she was after. Inside the investigation. She would have eventually tried to seduce you and hoped you got talkative afterwards. She may have already."

"No, she didn't try to seduce me. She didn't steer the conversation toward the investigation. She just seemed lonely."

"And then she reported back to both Bernhardt and Mr. Anonymous."

Scott nodded. "Seems like it. Mr. Anonymous doesn't appear to be a big fan of Bernhardt. Why was Jolene calling both of them? Who was she really working for?"

"Mr. Anonymous knew she was talking to Bernhardt. As to what that means, I don't know."

Chapter Twenty-Four

SCOTT AND DARLA lingered over their coffee. Finally, Scott drove Darla back to her hotel room. He left the cellphone with her and drove to his apartment. As he parked, a black SUV pulled behind his car, blocking him in. Bernhardt and a couple of other men got out. Bernhardt tapped on Scott's window. "We need to chat."

"Do you mind if the police sit in on the chat?"

"That wouldn't be helpful."

"Sorry. I have to disagree. I have nine-one-one on speed dial, not that the extra two digits would make much difference. I could also ram your SUV or see if I can drive over the curb. Maybe both. The apartment complex has video cameras to record the festivities. You need to back off."

Bernhardt put his hands up and backed up a step. "And you need to be less melodramatic. I'm here to talk. It's in both of our interests to find out what happened to Jolene Beck."

"Tell you what. You drive away. I go to my apartment. You call me there. Everyone's happy."

"And I'll tell you what. Give me Jolene Beck's phone. Tell me how and where you got it. Tell me everything that happened while you were with her. Tell me what she was wearing and what color her hair and eyes were. Then I drive away and you go on with your life."

"I left the cellphone with the police."

"Darla Smith, I assume. Did you know she had a nickname when she was a teenager?"

"A lot of people do."

"Hers was Dragon Lady," Bernhardt said. "She didn't get it because she was part Vietnamese; she got it because she liked burning things. She specialized in torching cars for insurance money. Amazing the things you can do as a juvenile and then go on to be a respectable citizen. Of course what the police knew and what they could prove when the juvenile had a high-priced lawyer courtesy of her adoptive parents were two different things. Even if they had convicted her, the records would've been sealed, her being a juvenile and all."

"Why are you telling me this?"

"Just to illustrate that the players in this aren't all clear-cut good guys and bad guys. How did you get the phone?"

"Jolene left it in her hotel room. The cleaning people found it. They gave it to me to give her. She left me a note saying that she had to go back to work early. We ran together, had supper together, talked a lot about not much, and then she went back and called you to report in."

"Did you notice anybody following you when you were with her?"

Scott shrugged. "I've thought I was being followed since Darla came to town. I didn't see anything special when I was with Jolene. Now tell *me* something. Who would I be talking to if I dialed this number?" He recited the number for Mr. Anonymous.

"That would be one of our corporate attorneys."

"Does he have a name?"

"Yeah."

"Not you too. Look, we'll find it by morning anyway."

"Give me the name of the hotel and the color of her hair."

"Sure. Her hair was black. What's the lawyer's name?"

"Andy Hollsworth."

Scott gave the name of the hotel. "By the way, Mr. Andy seems to have us under surveillance. He also knows a lot more about what your spy was up to than you do. That kind of sucks, doesn't it?"

"It's a little more complicated than that. You don't have any idea who Jolene Beck is, do you?"

"At this point, I don't care. I'm more interested in why Burgen is hiring illegal workers who wouldn't be missed. Is the same thing going to happen to them that happened to the others?"

Bernhardt stared at him for a couple of seconds without saying anything. Scott braced himself to throw the car in gear and ram the SUV if necessary.

Finally Bernhardt spoke. "How sure are you Burgen is doing that?"

"We can't prove it beyond a reasonable doubt yet, but you seem to be going more for speed than for concealment, so it should be easy to prove eventually."

"Thank you. You've been very helpful. Do be careful the rest of the evening. We wouldn't want you to go missing too." Bernhardt rushed back to the SUV and drove away.

Scott watched him go and then called Darla. "Hi. I just had a close encounter of the Bernhardt kind. He apparently only wanted to talk, but he gave me one of those 'be careful' kind of half-threats before he drove off."

"What did you talk about?"

"He asked a lot of questions about Jolene Beck. He did tell me that Mr. Anonymous is Burgen corporate attorney Andy Hollsworth. I don't know if we can believe him."

"Where are you now?"

"In the parking lot by my apartment building, kind of afraid to go in."

"Well, I would invite you over to my hotel, but you might read more into that than I want you to at the moment."

"It probably isn't much safer over there anyway. Bernhardt may stop by to pick up Jolene's phone. I said the police had it, but he immediately translated that to mean you." Scott peeked around and finally got out of his car. "I'm going in now. Keep talking."

"What else did you tell him?"

Scott sprinted the half block from his car to his apartment door, trying to look every direction at the same time. Darla asked her question again. Scott turned the lights on and went in. "I mentioned the Burgen new hires. Then he got very quiet and even more scary than usual. He thanked me and couldn't wait to get going. He did stop long enough to tell me to be careful so I didn't disappear like Jolene did. I'm searching my apartment right now. Oh, and he asked what color Jolene's hair was."

"Odd. I wonder if we'll discover that Jolene had herself a heart attack."

"Like the security guard who was dating Samantha Murphy?"

"Like him *and* Samantha Murphy."

Scott finished searching his apartment and checked the deadbolt. "Why make it look like Murphy died of natural causes, then hack off her head and her hands?"

"That's a very good question," Darla said. "Maybe I'll ask Bernhardt if he shows up here."

"I wonder if he'll bring up the Dragon Lady stuff to your face."

"Dragon Lady, huh? I assume Bernhardt told you a few things."

"That he did."

"And did you believe him?"

"Enough that I wouldn't mind hearing the rest of the story."

"Maybe someday."

Chapter Twenty-Five

SCOTT DIDN'T GET undressed that night. He stretched out on the bed, shoes on, a baseball bat within easy reach. He dozed off a few times through the night, but only for a few minutes at a time. Eventually the alarm jerked him fully awake. He decided not to go running that morning, so he dawdled around the apartment, then drove to work. Darla was already there. She glanced up when he came in.

"You survived."

"So far. Any sign of Sloan?"

"Nothing. You look, I don't know—not quite as energetic as usual."

"I didn't sleep last night," Scott said. "And I didn't run this morning. Either one would do it."

"Yeah, I can see *not* going out running on some isolated street at six in the morning with Mr. Stone-face Sloan lurking."

"I think that sentence would have driven my high school English teachers crazy, but yeah. I'll start again tomorrow, but vary my route," Scott said. "What are you doing?"

"While you were having fun with Bernhardt, I found something that doesn't make a whole lot of sense," Darla said. "Burgen is funneling money to a lot of non-profits. She's doing some of it through the company and some of it personally."

"So she's not all bad. Or maybe her conscience is bothering her."

"Maybe. Most of the money is easy to chart and it goes to typical charitable causes. Some of it goes to history and anthropology studies."

"Now it's starting to get interesting. Is this history and anthropology stuff centered on eastern Ohio?"

"No. That's what puzzles me. None of it is remotely connected to Ohio. It's all over the place *except* for the eastern United States. She's financing studies on the Pacific Northwest, Southern California, Siberia, the Ainu in northern Japan, Indians in Chile, the Khoisan cultures of southern Africa, and Australian aborigines or whatever they call them these days."

"What kind of studies is she funding?"

"Detailed reconstructions. How they built their shelters, chipped arrowheads, fired cooking pots, built canoes, grew plants. What plants they used. How they dressed. What their world views were."

"Wow. So is Ohio the tip of an iceberg, or is she trying to throw us off? Give me a detailed list of the cultures." Scott studied the list and tried to correlate it with relatively weak spots in the walls between the realities. Finally he shook his head. "In some cases there could be a place for a portal. In others there is no way. Not even remotely suitable."

"I looked for Burgen properties in the areas she targeted," Darla said. "That's a mixed bag too. There are Burgen properties near some of these places, but nothing where they could hide a power drain."

"Interesting. Could be a red herring. Could be a project she hasn't finished yet. Could be she's interested in history."

Darla shook her head. "She's doing something that will give her money or power. That's what she's about. You can't see it because it comes in a package that turns your brain off and sends the blood somewhere else."

"I've seen one picture of her from twenty years ago. Nothing to send the blood anywhere. Does Petey do that for you?"

"Not for long, unfortunately."

"Good." Scott turned back to his computer.

"Ever think about your little girl?"

"I try not to."

"Ah, so you *do* think she's yours. Does it bother you that someone else saw her crawl for the first time? Saw her take her first step? Heard her first word?"

Scott turned and glared at her. "That's vicious."

Darla walked over and put a hand on his shoulder. "I can be a bitch. It's part of who I am."

"Yeah? Sometimes you tear open things that should be left alone. Leave Sara out of it."

"Maybe I will. I'm curious though. I know you pretty well by now, and I can't see you letting this situation happen without it tearing you up."

"Maybe I spend a lot of time trying not to think about it. Maybe there are nights when that doesn't work and I don't get much sleep. Maybe you aren't helping much by tossing it in my face."

Scott got up. They stood uncomfortably, intimately close. He brushed past her.

"Wait. I'm doing an experiment." Darla brought a picture of Jolene Beck up on her computer. "I took it with my cellphone. I wonder what she would look like with different hair. What color do you think she would look good in?"

"Why?"

"She changed the color of her hair as part of her disguise, but from what? Hmmm. From her complexion she might be a blonde." Darla clicked on the hair and it turned blond. "Quite a change. I think I may have figured out who Jolene Beck really is, and why her shoes were expensive."

"Who?"

"It's easier to show you than to tell you." She clicked on Jolene's face. "Let's take away maybe twenty years."

"She looks twelve."

Darla nodded. "Yeah. She has good genes and takes care of herself. Let's make that ten years." She clicked again. "That's more like it. Now let's add in a few pounds." She clicked and leaned back in her chair. "And now who does Jolene Beck look like? Here's a hint: she didn't change her initials."

"Jeni Burgen? But that doesn't make any sense. Jolene Beck took my Plains Indian Immersion class. Why would Jeni Burgen do that? Why would she personally come back to try to get inside the investigation? And why would she disappear before she got anywhere with that?"

"All good questions. I don't know the answers to any of them. All I know is that Jolene Beck and Jeni Burgen are one and the same."

"And she's over forty," Scott said. "I thought she was younger than me."

"Wealth has its perks. Good diet. Good exercise equipment. Flexible schedule."

"Lots of stress though."

"And plastic surgery if she needs it."

Scott laughed. "If she's had plastic surgery, you would have noticed it and pointed it out to me. Your claws were out every time you were anywhere near her."

"Maybe. Unless the surgeon was really good, which he would be if she used one."

"So, what does this tell us? What do we know about Jeni Burgen that we didn't before?"

"Nothing. She was acting," Darla said. "We know she's a good enough actress to fool you, but not good enough to fool me. We know she has good taste in shoes. That's about it."

"I lived with her—well, in the same pseudo-Indian village

with her—for three months. We all got to know each other very well. I—"

"Didn't know her real name. Didn't notice the cellphone calls she made to keep her business going. Didn't notice the nice shoes she was wearing. Didn't notice she was running the village by the end of the summer. You didn't know her. Not at all."

"We had a phone hour. She took advantage of it like everybody else. She wore moccasins like everybody else. She didn't run the camp. Yeah, she worked hard. Yeah, she was a natural leader. She was a good student; loved learning all the details about the way Indians lived—even picked up quite a bit of Sioux, which wasn't required."

"Did you sleep with her?"

"I don't sleep with students. Ethical considerations, not that it's any of your business."

"Did she show off the sharp elbows she would need to control the likes of Bernhardt Sloan?"

"Not often. She seemed to be a good judge of character and you wouldn't want to try to walk over her, but she didn't throw elbows if she didn't need to. Competitive though. She never did understand why I didn't run Petey until he collapsed."

"Did you see any reason she would want a portal?"

Scott shook his head. "She enjoyed being away from the grind. She enjoyed nature. Maybe she got fascinated by the timeline and decided to go there."

"Out of the blue because she loved your class?" Darla laughed. "I don't think so. Not enough time between the class and when she had a working portal."

"True. So she took the class knowing she would have a portal or already had one."

"Yep. Learning as much as she could about what she would find over there. Would knowing Sioux help in eastern Ohio?"

"Some, maybe." Scott turned to his computer and brought

up a map of North America. He pointed to a large area of white centered on the Ohio River valley. "Nobody knows what language the Indians in this area spoke before the Europeans came. The only tribes there were recent immigrants."

"What happened to the Indians there?"

Scott shrugged. "Probably epidemics and raids by other tribes who got guns before the locals did. The thing is, we don't know what language they spoke, but it could have been a variation of Sioux. There were Siouan-speaking tribes to the east and west—different languages, but close enough that knowing one would help you learn the others."

"Which boils down to 'yeah, knowing Sioux might help.'"

"Hey, former professor here. That's a two-hour lecture in two minutes."

"So she used you and she used your class."

Chad strolled in. "What did you learn in Ohio?"

"That's where the portal is," Darla said. "Pretty much has to be."

"Except it can't be." Scott brought up the timeline wall-strength map, then plugged the numbers into a spreadsheet. "At best they'd have to have a nuclear power plant or two, even there at the weakest point."

Chad studied the numbers. "Divide by seven."

"About a fifth of a nuclear power plant. It wouldn't be impossible at that level. Expensive though, and hard to hide. Do you know something I don't about power requirements?"

"Not really. There's a theory that you could reduce the power requirement to about ten to fifteen percent of normal by feeding spikes of power into a portal and letting the power drop between spikes. It's not classified, but not proven either. It would take massive computer power to get the power spikes and valleys right, assuming it's possible. Even then it would be risky. You're flirting with the hole closing with every valley in the power, and the closer you get to ten percent, the riskier it is. Going to one-seventh is probably the best anyone could do."

"So nobody's trying this other than maybe Burgen?" Darla studied the map. "Why aren't the Europeans pushing it?"

"It wouldn't help enough over there. It would make a few weak spots feasible in North America and Australia, but the walls are still too thick in Europe and Asia."

"So the data center gives them the computer power to manage the portal's energy and a way of hiding the energy use," Scott said. "And the solar and wind farms make it even easier to hide energy use. So how do we prove it? And how do we keep them from shutting down the portal and hiding the pieces? And how do we nail whoever killed Samantha Murphy?"

Chad grinned. "Give me what you have. If it's enough that I'm sure the portal is at the data center, you'll win yourself a road trip."

Chapter Twenty-Six

PETER KINDAHL SHOWED up that afternoon. He poked his head into Scott and Darla's conference room and said, "If you want something done, ask a field agent." He sauntered on. Scott peeked out and watched him disappear into Chad's office.

"I'm sure he saved the day," Scott said. "And now he gets to brag about it."

"Found the portal. Solved the murder, got the girl. Time to move on." Darla shrugged. "He didn't need us at all. Well maybe me for the 'get the girl' part."

"Just one girl?" Scott said. "It's been almost a week."

His cellphone rang. He glanced at the Caller ID. "And we have Mr. Sloan calling. I wonder if this has anything to do with Petey getting back." He answered. "Hi, Bernhardt."

"I prefer Mr. Sloan. It keeps the relationship clear. We aren't friends."

"So why are you calling?"

"We may be able to help each other. And you still have something that belongs to my employee."

"I think you have the relationship wrong. You work for Jeni Burgen. At least that's what the organizational chart says. Which means you work for Jolene."

"So you know."

"That Jolene Beck is really Jeni Burgen? Yeah."

"That saves a little time then. Meet me at the coffee shop

down the street. We need to talk."

"I don't think so. Not after last night."

"Last night we chatted, then I left. Nothing else."

"You scared the crap out of me."

"I do that to people. Most of the time it's useful. In this case, maybe not. Bring your detective friend and guys with baseball bats if you feel like it. I will not harm you in any way. If I still scare the crap out of you, then so be it. It's urgent that we meet."

"Why?"

"I'd prefer not to say over a cellphone. What I have to tell you cannot go beyond you and your detective friend."

"I can't guarantee that." Scott glanced at his watch. "Okay. I'll take a fifteen-minute break in twenty minutes. That's all you get."

"You'll give me more when you hear what I have to say."

"I doubt it." Scott hung up and turned to Darla. "He wants to meet. In public and in broad daylight. You're invited too. He didn't say why."

Scott left a note on Chad's door and walked to the coffee shop with Darla. Bernhardt was sitting in a corner booth, expressionless as usual.

He said, "Have a seat. What are your feelings toward Jeni Burgen?"

Darla said, "She's a conniving bitch. She didn't fool me for two seconds."

"And you, Scott, what do you think of her?"

"Seemed like a decent enough sort until I found out she was using me, which killed the decent bit."

"Would you be willing to help her if she's in danger?"

"Why should we?" Darla glared at Bernhardt. "We have a murder to solve. She's a prime suspect. You're an even primer suspect."

That wrung a grin from the stone face. "A 'primer suspect,'

huh? And who is your primest suspect?"

"You're not my English teacher."

"Let's not digress. I'm going to tell you something I would rather not tell you. Jeni Burgen has been out of contact long enough that I think she's in a great deal of trouble."

"More trouble than a murder charge?" Darla asked.

"She won't be charged with murder; I can assure you of that," Bernhardt said.

"What kind of trouble could she be in?" Scott asked.

"Probably a kidnapping," Bernhardt said. "The last time we talked she said she was being followed. She said she was coming in that night, then nothing. No phone call. No email."

"You might want to chat with Andy Hollsworth," Scott said. "He knew exactly where we were and what we were doing. He probably knows what she was up to. Maybe she doesn't trust you anymore and cut you out of the loop."

"That's not what happened." Bernhardt's face revealed a hint of uncertainty. "That's not the way she would handle it."

"Maybe you scare the crap out of her too. It's not something you can turn on and off."

"I work for the brand. She knows that. I would never do anything against her interests."

"Loyal enough to kill for her? Loyal enough to cover up a murder?"

"This isn't about me," Bernhardt said. "This isn't about some unfortunate young lady who got herself killed. I need to know everything you know about who is following you. The trail is getting cold."

"If you think she was kidnapped, why not go to the police?" Darla asked. "And, by the way, if there hasn't been a ransom demand, she probably hasn't been kidnapped."

"You just answered your own question; there hasn't been a ransom demand. Whoever has her probably doesn't know who she is. Put the news out and they'll know. If she hasn't told them that she's Jeni Burgen, she probably thinks telling them would put her in more danger. Maybe she figures she can talk her way out of it if they don't know she's got money."

"Who would kidnap her if they didn't know she's rich?" Darla paused as the waitress took their orders. "And if you don't have contingency plans for a kidnapping you suck at security."

"She was a woman alone, not bad looking," Bernhardt said. "As to contingency plans, how can I plan for her deliberately ditching her security?"

"So what do you expect to learn from us? And why are you talking to us instead of Andy Hollsworth?"

Bernhardt glared at Darla. "You know who is following you, don't you? Somebody not involved in this case. Somebody from your past. Who?"

"You don't need to know. They watch. They haven't interfered with my life and I don't think they will."

"You're still in contact with the people you torched cars for, aren't you?"

"I haven't talked to them."

"But they're keeping an eye on you?"

"It's more complicated than that. They're not going to kidnap people because they come into contact with me. Kidnapping isn't their thing anyway."

"So you aren't their mole in the Boston PD?"

"They don't operate in Boston, so they don't need a mole there. This is personal."

Scott glanced at Darla. "Maybe it's time for you to tell me what's going on."

Bernhardt said, "It might be embarrassing for her to tell it, so I'll give you the gist of the story. Ms. Smith grew up in an upper class East Coast family. She ran away at fourteen to get in touch with her Vietnamese heritage, then ended up working for a

Vietnamese street gang in California. As I mentioned, she torched cars for them. I hear she enjoyed her work. She got in way over her head. The adoptive parents found her, dusted her off and sent her to boarding school until she turned eighteen. Didn't want the family name smudged, I assume."

"That's not quite the way it happened, but close enough," Darla said. "It has nothing to do with Jeni Burgen disappearing."

"You sure? They wouldn't take advantage if they found out who she is?"

"It's not the way they think. At least it wasn't the way they thought. If they changed enough to do that, I don't know them at all anymore."

"It's been nearly ten years. Maybe you *don't* know them anymore. But if that's true, why are they still following you?"

"That's not something you need to know."

"As you've noticed, I have ways of finding out things. We can talk when I uncover the rest of the story or I can concentrate my resources where they need to be. Convince me your past has nothing to do with this and as far as I'm concerned, it stays your past."

"How am I supposed to do that? I've already told you—"

"Nothing I didn't already know and nothing that explains what happened. Can you contact the people watching you or the people behind them?"

"Even if I could, I wouldn't. Talking to them lets them back into my life and makes my job with the Boston PD tenuous. I'm not going to try."

"A woman's life is at stake here."

"Maybe. But I have a murder investigation and my career to worry about. You're asking me to risk that career and you've told us nothing. Why was Jeni Burgen in Scott's class? Why did she try to get back into his life?"

"I have no idea," Bernhardt said. "I didn't know she was

going around as Jolene Beck until Scott called me. I didn't ask her to spy on you. She's too valuable. She didn't tell me she was going to do it."

"I don't believe that," Darla said. "How did she lose her security detail?"

Bernhardt closed his eyes. "I don't know."

"Then your security stinks. She was in his class for three months. Are you saying you had no idea where she was that entire time?"

"None. If I have gray hair, those three months gave it to me."

"I don't believe any of this," Darla said. "You aren't the type who would let that happen. Not once and certainly not twice. Even if she told you to take the security people off, they would still be there, just more discreetly."

"True, except she figured out some way of getting in and out without tipping off security. I don't know how she does it and that scares the crap out of me because if she can get out, somebody else could get in. There. I've been frank with you. I've even left myself vulnerable to you. I need something back. A name. You don't have to get involved with your Vietnamese friends. Tell me who I need to talk to and I'll do the rest."

"I might," Darla said. "These guys don't scare though. If they feel threatened, they'll kill you. No questions asked. No warnings. No posturing. No scary faces."

"That's fine. Give me a name. I'm not going to hurt them unless they kidnapped her. I just need to know if they were watching her and what they saw."

"Danny Minh. That's a name. It may or may not have anything to do with this, but it's a name."

"Thank you. Don't try to play me. I'm much scarier than I look and a lot scarier than your Vietnamese boyfriend."

Chapter Twenty-Seven

JENI THOUGHT ABOUT running or trying to get the police inside the service station involved. The hard faces behind the guns discouraged that. She stepped into the van and they drove away. Nobody said anything to her as they drove back into the suburbs. She glanced at the gym bag sitting between her feet on the floorboard. Ironically, the shotgun still sat in it, potent but useless. Finally she said, "How are your tires?"

One of the men grinned. The others stared ahead with no reaction. They drove along I-38 into Lombard, one of the western suburbs, and into a hotel parking lot, where they directed her to a room. A short, wiry East Asian man in his early thirties looked up from the desk as they entered. He wore an expensively tailored, tasteful suit. "Ah, Jolene Beck. You're hard to keep track of, but quite a few people are trying. I wonder why."

"Who are you, and why do you care?"

"Call me Danny. Why are people interested in you?"

"Why are you interested in me?"

"It's not polite to answer a question with a question."

"It's also not polite to point a gun at someone."

"The only thing that matters is what the person with the gun thinks is polite."

"Yeah. So I'll tell you everything I know, which is not much. I came to town on vacation, met a college professor from a few years back and some girl from Boston. She's a cop. He works for the Bureau of Timeline Integrity now. We ate dinner together a couple of times and ran together. Then I started feeling that I was being followed. It turns out I was right. Three guys broke into my hotel room and pointed guns at me. I don't know who they were. I don't know why they grabbed me. I don't know who you are or why *you're* interested in me."

"I have been reasonably successful in life. I have time, money and power to indulge my hobbies. One of my hobbies has gotten a lot of attention lately from certain business competitors of mine, and that attention started not long before she met you. I wonder why."

"Your hobby is a she? Darla Smith." Jeni shook her head. "So you think I attracted these business rivals of yours to Darla. It's more likely that whatever she's investigating drew the attention."

Danny sauntered over to her. "You don't seem as afraid of us as you should be. Do you need a reality check?"

"I told you the truth. I'm not sure what else you want from me."

"That's an interesting question. What use can I make of you? Hmmm. Decent body. Good bone structure. With a little work, you could look classy. I could find uses for a classy-looking Anglo woman. Hardly worth the bother though, and your escape from my competitors leads me to think you'd make it troublesome. That would be a bad thing from your point of view, but probably inevitable."

"So am I free to go?"

"You always have been. Of course, actions have consequences, sometimes severe ones. Leaving now would have consequences. What did your friends with guns ask you?"

"They didn't ask anything. They didn't tell me anything. They just pointed guns at me, forced me into a car and drove off."

"Okay. For the next two weeks, assume that my associates are watching you. Nobody else will be watching you or will bother you. In return, you will return to Oakbrook and find out what case Darla Smith is working on. While you're at it, you'll tell me anything else you find out about her and her friends."

"You want me to spy on them for you?"

Danny shrugged. "You don't have to. We can always try the alternative."

"So, two weeks. What happens then?"

"You go back to your life."

"I can't afford to take an extra two weeks off and live in a hotel. This trip left me tapped out," Jeni said. She didn't mention her total lack of money or identification.

"I didn't say you would be doing it for free," Danny said. He pulled out his wallet and started counting out hundred-dollar bills. "Tell them you got sick or a family member died. This will get you through the two weeks with a little to spare. Working for me isn't such a bad thing."

"They took my car keys."

"We'll loan you a car until you get new ones made. We trust your judgment. You won't do anything to irritate us."

"What about the guys who kidnapped me and whoever sent them?"

Danny grinned. "They won't bother you again unless the stakes are a lot higher than I think. We show respect for them and they show respect for us. It's much less messy that way."

"Who are they?"

"They're of eastern European affiliation. Not people to be messed with, but I see no reason they would have a vital interest in you."

"I hope you're right. How did they get interested in me?"

"I don't know. You know, you're a cool one. I tell you that the Russian mafia kidnapped you and that you can either work as a spy or as a high-class hooker and you don't blink. That's an odd reaction. Are you a cop?"

"No. I'm just numb. I've been shot at. I've been in a car wreck. I've run and walked through cornfields and gravel roads most of the day. I have two groups of guys with guns messing with me. I don't know how to react. I just want it to all go away. I'm not even sure I'm awake. I'm half hoping I'll wake up back in my hotel room."

Danny smiled. "You're a tough lady. I apologize for keeping you up. I'll tell you what: tonight you sleep in the other half of the suite on my dime."

"Does this offer come with strings?"

"A few. You'll formally agree to do the spying before you go in there. You'll get half the money for the two weeks in the morning. Just for tonight, we'll have a GPS wristband on you and an alarm if you wander too far from this room. Other than that, we'll respect your privacy and let you sleep."

"How can I be sure of that?"

"Ms. Beck, if we want to molest you, you are in no position to stop us. We choose not to at this point. As long as you uphold your part of any bargain we make, we will uphold ours and treat you as a valued employee. I demand loyalty, but I treat my employees well."

Jeni walked to the other room, then paused at the door. "How did you find me?"

Danny laughed. "A city is like a maze of streets you can lose yourself in. Out in the sticks you go miles between roads. Makes finding people a lot easier unless they go cross-country."

Jeni closed the door and manhandled the shotgun out of the gym bag. She stashed it under the bed covers. She laughed at the irony of being coerced into spying on Darla Smith, then winced as the laugh brought a sharp pain to her jaw. She staggered to the bathroom, glanced at the mirror and shook her head. Her makeup was smeared. One bruise was forming on her jaw and another on her shoulder. She washed her face and slumped into bed. She leaned back without undressing and pushed her hand under the cover so she could grip the shotgun.

I don't know if it's loaded, if the safety is on, or even if there is a safety.

In spite of that, the smooth feel of the stock under her hand felt reassuring. She tried to stay awake, but eventually dozed off. Nobody bothered her and when dawn brought sunlight through the curtains, she sat up, stiff and still tired. The reaction she'd been holding off finally overwhelmed her and she sat on the bed, trembling, as tears streamed down her face.

Scott and Darla got back to the office later in the afternoon.

Chad stopped them at the conference room door and said, "We're unofficially ninety-nine percent sure the data center is hiding the rogue portal."

Darla shrugged. "We've known that. What's new?"

"We really unofficially know the portal is there."

"Ah, Peter and his methods," Scott said. "Which would undoubtedly be frowned on by the courts. But he's that sure?"

"Yeah. Unofficially. Nothing we can take to court. That means we have two priorities. First is to capture the portal or plans for it intact, if at all possible. They have technology we want very badly. It would open up four locations in the eastern U.S. for portals and reduce energy costs enough on the existing portals to pay for the new ones. Second priority is to take control of the portal and keep anyone from screwing things up over in TLX."

"I didn't hear anything about solving a murder in there," Darla said.

"That's your job. If we get it done as part of our job, that's a bonus. It isn't a priority."

"It is for me."

Scott sat at his computer. "So the problem is proving to a court that the portal is there. Can we?"

"Not yet. Not well enough for a court to give us a search warrant, especially given the kind of lawyers Burgen could throw at us. Even if we got one, I doubt any evidence we found would be admissible."

"So we've still got nothing," Darla said.

Scott nodded. "Sounds like it." He turned to Chad. "How are we going to change that?"

"From the other side," Chad said. He glanced at his watch and clapped Scott on the shoulder. "That's where you come in. Wheels are already turning, and I need you for a job you'll enjoy. Come with me."

Darla started to get up, but Chad shook his head. "Sorry. *Need to know only* on this one." He escorted Scott to his office. Peter was already there. "Secure video link in here. I kept you insulated from the politics of this, but things are moving fast. You and I both know that contact with the Roman Empire is about the most dangerous thing that could happen short of a nuclear war."

"Yeah. I wondered why the investigation was so low-key. All it takes is one smallpox-type disease jumping the timeline and we have nuclear-war numbers of people dead."

"Until Peter confirmed where the portal was," Chad said, "this was in the same class as a couple hundred other cases where someone claimed Timeline X contacts, so yeah, it was low-key. It isn't anymore. Now it's real and we're scrambling. Have a seat."

A flat-screen display covered most of a wall. It came to life. "What you're seeing is the video feed from an Air Force unmanned aerial vehicle in Timeline X," Chad said. "It's flying south along the Mississippi river. We'll follow the Mississippi to the Ohio River and then follow that to the portal. If we get pictures of facilities on the other side, we can justify going in from this side to grab the portal intact."

"How are they flying that thing?" Scott asked. "Aren't long-range UAVs usually guided by a satellite uplink or GPS? No satellites up over there, so no uplinks and no GPS."

"We have a long endurance, high altitude UAV flying in circles over the portal and relaying signals," Chad said. "It's been having glitches, so cross your fingers. If we lose the signal, the UAV will fly straight and level for a while and search for a signal, but at some point we'll lose it."

The UAV flew over a fleet of several dozen huge canoes, almost big enough to be classed as ships. Scott studied the screen avidly. "Nice. This is our first real look at what's going on this far east. You're archiving this, of course. Can we control the cameras?"

"With a time lag," Chad said. "We'll be past that little fleet before we get them to zoom in on it. Maybe the guy at the controls will decide it's worth a look."

That didn't happen, and Scott had to be content with the high altitude shots. "We can clean up the stills and see more detail later. Frustrating though."

Chad typed a quick message on his keyboard. "I told the operator to zoom in next time he sees anything like that."

Peter laughed. "So you're a history geek too. I knew Scott was, but I didn't expect it from you."

"I don't know what Scott would be looking for, but I'm looking for trade goods from over here," Chad said. "I doubt that they would trade anything bulky enough to be seen from the air, but it's worth a shot. Plus science keeps people willing to pay your salary."

"I'll admit I'm psyched. I'm seeing this as a once-in-a-lifetime look at Indian life there," Scott said. "I'm a history geek. No mystery there."

The river seemed empty for the next several miles, then the UAV passed over two small fishing canoes. "We're getting close to where St. Louis is on this side," Chad said.

They started seeing farming hamlets along the river, with

canoes drawn up in front of them. A palisaded town sat near where East St. Louis grew up historically, with a set of flat-topped mounds scattered around it, each crowned by a building. Fields stretched for miles along the river.

"Looks like corn, beans, sunflowers and something else," Scott said. He counted houses in one section of the palisade and did a quick calculation. "Back-of-the-envelope wild guess: maybe fifteen thousand people. That's big for a North American Indian town, but not as big as Cahokia at its peak."

"We should be seeing Cahokia in a few minutes," Chad said.

The once great town disappointed Scott. A little village sat on top of Monks Mound and small fields were scattered around it. Most of the other Cahokia mounds were so overgrown that he couldn't even spot them.

"Probably Algonquians filtering in from the fringes," Scott said. "I'm surprised there aren't more of them. Cahokia was wonderful country for Indians."

"This might conceivably be mildly interesting if we didn't have anything else to do," Peter said. "It's an old Indian town or what's left of it after a couple of dozen years. So what?"

"Cahokia was the largest Indian settlement north of Mexico. Abandoned around six hundred years ago," Scott said. "Looks like it followed the same schedule here. Pity. I would love to see it when it was still alive."

The UAV headed up the Ohio River. Towns surrounded by wooden palisades dotted the lower part of the river, with flattop mounds near their centers. As the UAV headed east, the towns looked more Iroquois, without mounds and with longhouses. They stood farther from the river and came in pairs, with the two towns miles apart, each surrounded by vast cornfields.

Scott pointed down at the forest. "That's a managed forest. The Indians alter the mix of trees, encourage wild berries and keep the underbrush down to make hunting easier and increase deer populations. It may not support as big a population as our kind of agriculture, but it's sustainable. Well, not completely. They probably have to move every fifty to one hundred years when they run out of firewood and the soil needs to recover."

Scott's cellphone rang. He frowned when he saw the name on the display. "The hotel where Jeni was staying. They'll call back if it's important."

The picture on the video screen went blocky and froze. They stared at the screen as the cellphone kept ringing. Finally, the feed resumed. Chad settled back into his chair. "Thought we lost it. We tossed this mission together out of spare parts in a weekend, and I'm surprised it's working as well as it is."

As the UAV flew on, Scott pointed to columns of smoke rising ahead of it. "I'm surprised we haven't seen more smoke. Indians use fire to manage the forests." A few seconds later, he added, "But that isn't a forest."

A palisaded town was burning, with most of the longhouses destroyed. The UAV camera zoomed in on the town, revealing stacks of bodies, most of them near the palisades. Peter sat up. "Someone had a bad day. Looks like several hundred dead at least. How far are we from the portal?"

"A little over a hundred miles," Chad said. "Shouldn't be related."

"Unless Burgen and company are trading with the locals," Scott said. "If they are, they could easily set off wars for control of the trade hundreds of miles away,"

The video froze again. As they waited for it to come back, Scott's phone rang. "The hotel again."

The video came back as the UAV flew over another town. This one seemed intact, but deserted. The operator zoomed in on a hint of motion. They caught a glimpse of a man in armor, then the picture turned blocky again.

"Well, there's your smoking gun," Scott said. "No Indian

would that wear that kind of armor."

"Maybe." Chad stared at the screen as the video went to snow. "This is Jeni Burgen we're talking about—more resources than most governments. When we pull the trigger on her and her portal, we'll need the case to be airtight. She can toss the best lawyers in the world at us and if we leave the least bit of doubt, they'll crucify us politically and in court."

They waited fifteen minutes for the video to come back, then Peter said, "Time for Plan B."

Chad nodded. "Plan B is in the works, but won't come together until tomorrow. Scott, you're going to be in history-geek paradise. Sleep well and be ready to fly."

"Into Timeline X and without a quarantine? That breaks almost all our protocols."

"One plane only. Recon only. Don't have engine trouble or you'll walk back. I burned up a lot of political chips to get a UAV and a plane as a backup. If you get in trouble over there, you're on your own for at least a week or two."

"This is a tad urgent."

"Which is why I could do that much this fast."

As Scott walked back into the conference room, his phone rang again. "Hello."

"Hi. This is Jolene. I lost my cellphone and had some other adventures, but I'm still in town. Want to do supper?"

Chad stuck his head in.

"Hold on." Scott put his hand over the mouthpiece. "*Jolene*. She wants to do supper. What do I do?"

Darla laughed. "Play along. If she doesn't know we know who she is, we can play with her mind."

"Okay." Scott took his hand off the mouthpiece. "Sure. I was getting worried about you. You left the cellphone in your hotel room. The hotel people asked if I knew how to get it back to you, but I told them I didn't."

"I'll try to get that back. I'm calling from my new hotel room now. Can you pick me up? I'm having trouble with my car."

"Sure." They set a time.

"Oh, and if Darla wants to come along, bring her. She seemed nice."

"Okay. I'll ask." Scott hung up and turned to Darla and Chad. "So, what now? Do we feed her stuff about the investigation and see how she reacts?"

Darla shook her head. "Not yet. We make her work for it. And we don't panic her into shutting the portal down. Let her think she has things under control."

"Hmmm. Caution. That doesn't sound like your usual 'playing with fire' way of doing things," Scott said.

"It's probably a waste of time anyway. Bernhardt probably told her we're on to her. It's worth a shot though."

Scott turned to Chad. "Want us to play her?"

"Sure. Be careful though. If you decide to leak something, clear it with me first." Chad hurried away.

"Going to tell me what you did in there?" Darla asked.

"Sorry. Need to know only."

"And I don't need to know?" Darla turned to her computer. "Fine."

They spent the rest of the afternoon searching unsuccessfully for yacht manufacturers who might have built a ship in sections and shipped it to the data center.

When it was time to leave for his meet with Jeni, Scott stood and said to Darla, "About that time. Want to come?"

"I'm invited? I thought you were cutting me out."

"Only when I have to. I don't make the rules."

"No. But I can make you suffer for them."

They drove to the hotel. Jeni limped out as they drove up, looking tired. Scott noticed bruises on her face and upper arm. She sat heavily in the back seat.

"I don't know how to start telling you this," she said. "I wasn't entirely truthful with you on the phone. I'm in over my head and I need your help."

Chapter Twenty-Eight

SCOTT STUDIED JENI'S face. "What happened? How did you get the bruises?"

Jeni settled herself into the back seat. "You probably aren't going to believe this, but Russian mafia types kidnapped me. I got away by causing a car crash. I got chased, shot at and finally picked up at gunpoint by a scary Vietnamese guy named Danny. He didn't give me a last name, but I'm guessing Darla knows him. And how was your day?"

"You're right. I don't believe you," Darla said.

Jeni shrugged. "You asked. I told you. Can we head to supper?"

Scott pulled onto I-38. "Danny. I wonder if the last name was Minh. Darla, isn't that the—"

"Yeah. It is," Darla said. "A name from my scandalous past. How do you know about Danny Minh?"

"A van full of his guys pulled up, shoved guns in my face and took me to him. He offered me a choice. I could be a high-class prostitute for him—which I doubt I could pull off—or I could spy on Darla Smith for two weeks."

"So describe him."

Jeni did.

"Could be him," Darla said. "It's been quite a few years. Of course, your description is pretty generic. He called me his hobby, did he?"

"That he did."

"If you're planning on spying on me, shouldn't you keep that to yourself?"

"I can give him reports and hang around you whether or not you know what I'm doing. I've told enough lies. I'm not good at it and I don't like it."

"Could have fooled me," Darla said.

"Well, you can probably verify a good part of my story. Was there really an accident where and when I say there was? Did a woman matching my description leave the scene? Was there a shooting at a nearby farmhouse?" Jeni stopped and swore. "I left a couple of good guys lying there shot because I couldn't help them without getting shot myself. I hope the police got there in time to keep them from bleeding to death."

"Okay. Give me details." Darla glanced at Scott. "It should be easy to check on this. If it happened, the police will tell me, even if it didn't make the papers."

Jeni leaned back in her seat and closed her eyes. "Great. I get to relive that nightmarish day. I'll tell you everything I remember." She went over the sequence of events for the past twenty-four hours.

When she finished, Darla asked, "How do you know those guys were Russian mafia?"

"I don't. Danny Minh told me they were. I figure he knew what he was talking about."

Darla shook her head. "One thing to keep in mind about Danny Minh: he knows what he's talking about, but never trust anything he says unless you're on the inside, really on the inside. You aren't and never will be."

"Were you?"

"I don't know," Darla said. "I thought so at the time, but looking back, I doubt it."

Scott glanced at Jeni. "You're attracting a lot of attention, which puzzles me. Do you have any idea why that would be?"

"Because I'm in contact with you and Darla, I guess."

Scott said. "Two groups of people pointing guns at you."

"I don't want any of this. I want to wake up and realize that nothing happened yesterday, that it was all a nightmare." Jeni sighed. "Can we just go through a drive-thru and back to my hotel room?"

"Sure." Scott pulled into a fast food drive-thru. After they'd gotten their food, he asked, "Why the sudden change of plans?"

"I don't like being in public when I know people are watching me."

As they arrived at her hotel room, Jeni said. "I want my life back."

"Just click your slippers together three times and say 'There's no place like home,'" Darla said.

"Thanks. I may try that. Actually, what are you talking about?"

Darla laughed. "You need to get out more. Partake of the culture. I'm serious though. You probably have that option. Go home. Go back to your job. Don't hang around me. Don't hang around Scott. Send Danny his money back or better yet, give it to me and I'll throw it in his face. I'll tell him you're such a pathetic spy that I figured out what you were doing ten minutes after you tried to get into my life."

"Don't you want to try to play him? Feed him stuff that screws with his mind? He's stalking you and apparently has been for years. You can't just let that happen."

"Why not? I'm used to it. I ignore it. He doesn't mess with my life. Being followed bothers me, but I can live with that. I'm tough, and he knows me well enough to know that if he tried to push his way into my life again, he'd draw back a bloody stump. He knows things about my past that I would rather not have become common knowledge. I know a thing or two about him that he wouldn't want the police out in San Francisco to know. Balance of power. Eventually somebody will shoot him; bound to happen given the business he's in. You may get rich but you don't get old doing what he does. When that happens, it'll be like taking a pebble out of my shoe. I'll be a little more comfortable, but it won't make a lot of difference in my life."

Jeni shrugged. "It's your life. Do you know why you're his hobby?"

"I can guess. But like you said, it's my life."

Chapter Twenty-Nine

SCOTT AND DARLA headed back to her hotel as soon as they finished eating. They rode in silence for a couple of minutes, then Darla said, "So what do you think?"

"Well, it's getting a tad strange. Jeni Burgen is still trying to spy on us, but now she's letting us know she's spying."

"But not who she's spying for."

"Do you think Danny Minh really asked her to spy on us?

"I can find out right now." Darla had a couple of brief conversations on her cellphone. When she finished, she turned to Scott. "Accident happened the way she said it did. The guys involved said they picked up a hitchhiker and she wrecked their car, but they didn't want to press charges. The police didn't have any reason to hold them and they disappeared before anyone made the connection between the accident and the shooting at the farmhouse. The farmers are alive, but not in real good shape, by the way. She knew details the police kept out of the papers. So yeah, she was there and she probably got kidnapped. Was it by the Russian mafia or some random scumbags who saw a woman alone and took advantage? I don't know."

"Did the police get the guys' names and IDs?"

"Yeah, but they were phony. The state police are still looking for *Jolene*. They'll eventually find her from the hotel registration if they look hard enough. They may not. The farmers didn't claim she had anything to do with the shooting, but she did steal a shotgun and a four-wheeler."

"She told us about the four-wheeler but not the shotgun."

"I wonder if I should tip off the state police that she's staying at a hotel in Oakbrook. I am a police officer."

"Maybe eventually. We should play her a while longer. See what she wants. See if we can figure out what she knows."

"You like her, don't you?"

"You obviously don't. I did. I may still. Hard to know how to feel at the moment. She was a good student. It was a pleasure to have her in the class because she got into it—didn't just go through the motions. It carried over to the other students. I have good memories." Scott pulled into the hotel parking lot. "I hope she isn't a murderess."

"What do you think we'd find out if we keep playing along with her?"

"I don't know." He parked the car and turned to her. "I *would* like to know why she built a portal in the first place. Maybe we should ask her. We won't be able to play her long. She'll figure out I found her phone. Even if she doesn't, Bernhardt will tell her. He must know where she is by now. He probably already has security people shadowing her, which means we have Bernhardt, the Russians, and your Danny Minh all keeping track of one woman. How do they keep from tripping over each other?"

"We're not sure Danny Minh *is* involved. Bernhardt knew a lot about my teenage years; what he knows, Jeni Burgen knows. Maybe she's playing us. Another mind game."

"I knew her for three months—essentially lived with her. I can't see her killing anybody. I can't see her ordering anybody to kill anybody."

"You also couldn't see her making enough money to go from nothing to one of the richest people in the world."

"I don't know. Maybe. She's smart. If she had a good idea—"

"Lots of people have good ideas. It takes sharp elbows to end up with the money from a good idea instead of letting accountants and lawyers end up with it. At the very least, she is one tough lady."

"Which isn't illegal."

"No. The portal is though. And the murder. She'll call you again, after you drop me off. Watch it when she does."

As Darla predicted, Jeni called Scott a couple minutes after he dropped Darla off and asked him to take her clothes shopping. "All my clothes were in the car."

Scott groaned. "Clothes shopping with a woman. Not the fondest memory from my marriage."

"I promise I'll just pick up underwear, two pairs of jeans and maybe a shirt or two. I'll grab the first thing that fits, and I promise I won't ask if it makes my butt look big."

"It might be worth the price of admission to see if you can stick to that. Okay. I'll pick you up."

He drove back to the hotel. Jeni opened the door, wearing sweatpants and a man's tattered shirt. She still managed to look good. "Thanks for coming. Come in. I have to ask you something before we go."

Scott went in. Jeni said, "Have a seat." He sat in the chair by the desk. Jeni sat on the corner of the bed nearest him, with her hair still wet and water droplets running down her neck. She sighed. "Have you ever reread a favorite book from when you were a kid and it destroyed the memory?"

"A time or two."

"I wanted this to be like it was back in the class. I wanted to get away and enjoy doing things I wanted to do. That got thoroughly screwed up. I probably screwed up our friendship too. I talked to the hotel people. They told me they gave you my cellphone. I hoped they would. That's why I kicked it under the bed before the kidnappers took me. Then once I got away from them, I hoped I could get it back before you got it."

"You missed out on that."

"Yeah. I'm guessing you called the numbers I called, trying to track me down."

"I tried emailing you first. Have you checked your email? You'll find several messages from me. I'll probably sound worried."

"Thanks. And then you undoubtedly called the numbers. Even if the people at the other end didn't tell you who they were, you figured it out. If nothing else, Darla could have found out through her police connections. So you know I didn't just happen to take a vacation and realize you were in town."

"So why did you call me?"

"I'm not sure I know myself. I did enjoy your class. I did want to see you again. And I did think it would be fun."

"So now that I know what you're up to, you can go home."

"I could. I don't want to. I don't want to walk away with you thinking I'm—"

"A bitch? Someone who tried to take advantage of my friendship? Someone trying to cover up a murder? Someone playing around with technology that could get millions of people killed?"

"Okay. I can see the first two, but how am I risking millions of people?"

"You were in my class. You know what introducing new diseases across the timeline, going either direction, could do."

"You think I'm going to let diseases from here get loose over in Timeline X?"

"Yeah. Unless you're taking the same precautions we are, it's just a matter of time."

"If I did anything with Timeline X, I would do my homework. I would do everything reasonable to protect people over there."

"So are you going to put all the illegal workers your company is hiring through three weeks quarantine? Are you going to account for every piece of metal that goes over there so none of it gets to the Indians and starts wars over your garbage? If you don't, you're responsible for burned-out towns and piles of bodies."

The last sentence came out more vehemently than Scott intended. Jeni studied his face.

"There's a lot going on you don't understand," she said. "There's a lot going on I don't understand. I would love to start from scratch and tell you everything I know."

"So why don't you? We know most of it anyway."

"It's more complicated than that." Jeni sighed. "I suppose I should just make a call and go back to my life."

"Maybe you should."

"Do you want me to?"

Scott abruptly stood. "I don't know what I want. No, actually I do. I want to rewind these last few days and have you be honest with me. Decide whether you want to be Jeni the spy or Jeni my friend."

"You called me Jeni. So you know who I am, not just that I work for Burgen."

Scott shrugged. "I'm not cut out for spying and lying. Why don't you just tell me who you are and why you're here?"

"Okay. Cards on the table. As you probably know, my real name is Jeni Burgen. And yes, I'm that Jeni Burgen. I took your class partly because I had always been interested in Indians and partly because I needed to know stuff for a project. I took the class as Jolene Beck because I didn't want the kind of attention I get when I'm Jeni Burgen. I loved the class. I enjoyed doing what we did. I enjoyed being your friend."

"So you jumped at the chance to spy on me."

"I jumped at a chance to be Jolene Beck again. The spying was a long shot. I didn't try that hard. I mean, how many questions did I ask about BTI?"

"Almost none. Darla figured you'd try to seduce me and then get me on the pillow-talk thing."

Jeni grinned. "She figured that, huh? Well, if I tried to seduce you, it wouldn't be for pillow talk."

"What it would be for?"

Jeni walked over to him. "Maybe I had a schoolgirl crush on a teacher."

"I would be flattered except there's a headless body and a portal that makes you seducing me not an issue."

Jeni nodded. "I said 'cards on the table.' There are a few I can't put out there because I've gone down a path too far. I can tell you I didn't kill anyone. I didn't order anyone to kill anyone."

"And yet there's a body. If Samantha Murphy was alive, you'd have heavy duty explaining to do. You might even have been arrested already. Her being dead worked out well for you."

"Her being dead is a nightmare. Not knowing how she died is even worse."

Jeni sat back down on the bed, then flopped back to lie on it. She didn't say anything for a long time. Scott stood silently by the bed, staring at her. After a couple of minutes she pulled her legs up and rolled over so she was lying across the foot of the bed with her back to Scott.

Scott walked to the door. "I should go."

"Please don't. Sit with me."

Scott started to sit in the chair, but she pulled him onto the foot of the bed.

"I don't think this is a good idea."

"Just sit with me. Hold my hand and don't hate me."

Chapter Thirty

SCOTT WOKE AT two in the morning with his bicep and shoulder aching. He was slumped over in bed with Jeni's head on his shoulder. After a panicked moment he realized they were both fully clothed. He tried to pull his hand out from under her, but she sighed and gripped it without waking. She stirred and mumbled, "No way out."

Scott sighed and tried to pull his arm out again. Jeni woke up and grasped his hand more firmly.

"Sorry. I had a mind-blowingly bad day. Kind of did a meltdown, didn't I?"

"Yeah. Major meltdown actually."

She pulled away from him, sat up and laughed. "Well, you've now seen me in pathetic mode. At least our clothes stayed on. And my little vacation ended with you thinking I'm not just a bitch but a pathetic one."

"No. It left me confused. There's no reason for my opinion to matter to you anyway."

"Probably not. It seems to though."

"I'm flattered. Puzzled, but flattered."

"No need to be flattered. No need to be puzzled either. In your class, I enjoyed doing well at something new and being liked by people who didn't know me. I tried to come back and relive that, but I screwed it up. I got myself kidnapped and nearly killed in the process. Lesson learned. Time to move on. I have a life almost anyone would kill for; time to go salvage it."

"So you're going to make that call to your security people."

"Eventually. Still confused?"

"Yeah. Jolene Beck seemed like a lot of things Jeni Burgen can't possibly be. Are you really that good an actress?"

"Jeni Burgen is Jolene Beck with an opportunity. I saw a chance to make a little money. I hit the market with the right product at the right time and did well. Then I invested smart and got lucky. And after it was too late I realized that money frees you in some ways but imprisons you in others."

"So is this where you decide to give it all to charity?"

"No. I gave up too much to get where I am. I do the charity thing, but at the end of the day I'll still be basically where I am."

"What did you give up?"

"A normal life. A husband I can treat as an equal—who doesn't end up a trophy or a pet. Having kids."

"It might not be too late for children."

"I don't want to bring kids into my life. I live in a gilded cage and so would they."

"I liked Jolene Beck a lot. She was a friend. Jeni Burgen I don't like. At best she made a lot of bad choices. She's probably involved in illegal stuff, including murder."

"Jolene Beck isn't me acting. She's me being me for the first time in ten years. I like her too. I can't be her though, can I?"

"Not anymore. Too bad. As I said, I liked her. I even admired her."

"You kept her at arm's length."

"Yeah. One of those instructor-student things. Plus it was shortly after a painful and screwed-up divorce."

"Okay. I'm going to make that call, but first I'm going to make you follow up on your offer to take me shopping. I can't go back to my gilded cage in sweat pants, a farmer's shirt and no clean underwear."

"It's after two in the morning. I'll stop by after work."

"Let's do it tonight. A real city never sleeps."

"This is a suburb. The city is thirty miles away."

"Something will be open. Come on." She grabbed his hand, peeked in the mirror and said, "Eww. I'm surprised you didn't run away screaming when you woke up."

"Actually, you look good."

"I bet you say that to all the girls you wake up in bed with after discovering that they're rich as sin and haven't given you their real names."

"I'm not even going to try to sort that one out. So I'll just say 'Yeah. Probably.'"

She ran a comb through her hair and grabbed his hand again. "From now until the sun come up, I'm Jolene Beck. Sort of a reverse Cinderella. Okay?"

"Sure. One last time." Scott walked her to his car. "Climb into my pumpkin. It'll change back into a carriage when the sun comes up."

She sat beside him and said, "Thank you. I won't forget this." She leaned across the seat and kissed him on the cheek.

As they drove off, Scott said, "Ironic about this Cinderella thing. Your shoes gave you away as soon as you walked in the door. I didn't notice them, but Darla did. Way too expensive for the income bracket you were supposedly in."

She laughed. "I wasn't really into the spying part of this anyway."

"Good, because it didn't go too well for you."

"Yeah. Well, I'm Jolene Beck, remember. I don't even know who this Jeni Burgen person is until the sun comes up."

They drove past several closed malls and department stores before finally ending up at a Walmart. Jeni shrugged. "This is where Jolene would shop."

Scott and Jeni strolled in, drawing bored glances from a

couple of employees standing by the registers. Jeni surprised Scott by keeping her promise to be brief. She quickly collected a couple of outfits and a pair of flannel pajamas.

They drove back to the hotel. Scott turned to Jeni, leaned against the steering wheel and said, "We got it done. I hope that if I see you again I'm not a witness against you at a murder trial."

"Hold your horses, I'm not done with you yet. I'm still Jolene Beck for another two hours. Jolene Beck wants to spend a little time with you since it's probably the last time we'll see each other. Let's go back in."

"I'm not going to sleep with you."

"You already have, though in a disappointingly platonic way. How about a pizza and beer?"

"At almost three in the morning?"

"Why not? I think we can find a place to deliver the pizza. If we grease their palms with enough of Danny boy's money, they'll probably bring beer too. Come on. My Jolene time is wasting."

Jeni grabbed his hand and they strolled back in. She turned on the TV, flipped to a reality TV program with a lot of police chases and changed into flannel pajamas while Scott ordered the pizza. Jeni sat on the bed. "Jolene Beck wants to be held."

"That's not a good idea."

"You already slept with me. I just want to be held."

Scott sat beside her and slid his arm around her. "You smell good."

"For the first time in nearly two days. And I feel great: clean underwear, great company, lowbrow TV, and pizza and beer on the way. Plus a guy I like and respect holding me and caring about me. What more could a girl want in her last few hours of existence?"

"Yeah. The simple stuff."

The pizza and beer arrived. Scott reluctantly disentangled himself from Jeni and brought it in. They opened beers and Jeni held hers up. "To the simple stuff."

They touched bottles and Scott said, "Yep. To the simple stuff."

They ate pizza and drank for the next hour.

Jeni belched. "Excuse me. No, actually don't excuse me. This is lowbrow night." Her words slurred a little.

"Jolene Beck may not be rich, but she isn't lowbrow. She's classy and smart."

"Thank you." Jeni kissed him.

Scott shook his head. "No. Let's not go there."

"Oh, come on. You wouldn't kiss Jolene Beck? Don't tell me you never wanted to."

"Maybe I did. I'm not going to sleep with you though."

"I didn't ask you to. I am going to have one heck of a make-out session with you though."

She downed another gulp of her beer.

Scott grinned. "If you keep that up, you're going to pass out."

"Oh, well. There is no tomorrow."

"Don't say that."

"There isn't. Not for me."

"Why did you do it?"

Jeni stared at him. "Please don't ask that."

"You don't even know what I'm asking."

"I don't care. If it's the portal, don't ask. If it's the girl, don't ask."

"Okay. Tell me one thing and then I'll shut up."

"As long as it isn't about the portal or the girl."

"Okay. Are you keeping hobbits?"

Jeni gazed at him as soberly as she could after three beers. Her words slurred a little more. "No. One of my people is keeping pixies though. I wish he wasn't. They give me the creeps."

"Pixies, huh?"

"Yeah. Sort of like people only not really. I think the government knows about them. I don't know why they're keeping them a secret."

"That's an interesting question."

"But it's not what you want to know, is it? You want to know why someone with everything would risk it all." Jeni opened another beer. "I wonder if she knows herself. Maybe she looks at a world that will soon have nine billion people and not much nature left and wants somewhere to go when it falls apart."

"So Jeni Burgen is a survivalist? Or is she an ecologist?"

"Is there a difference?"

"Interesting question."

"Not to Jolene Beck." Jeni scooted over and climbed onto his lap. "Jolene Beck just wants to spend the next hour being held by a great guy and talking about nothing in particular." She leaned against him and took another sip of her beer. Her voice slurred more. "Maybe she wants to be Sky Queen of the Iroquois—the one who gives them fire."

"They already have fire."

She took another sip. "But they don't have beer, at least not cold beer." In a couple of minutes she was snoring gently. Scott carried her to the head of the bed and tried to put her down. She woke up. "Stay. I want my last hour."

"Okay." He sat her down on the bed and rubbed her back. She reached up and sleepily rubbed his neck, then pulled him down and kissed him again. "I don't want this to end."

Scott nodded. "I know."

"Do you want it to end?"

"No."

"Just hold me until I disappear and the cold, calculating bitch you hate is all that's left."

Scott held her gently. After a few minutes she fell asleep,

with one of Scott's hands firmly in hers. Scott tried to disentangle himself a couple of times, but she held tight. He finally fell asleep beside her and woke up with sunlight streaming in the window.

Jeni stirred and then sat up. She smiled at Scott. "My security guy is having a cow because I'm out here somewhere."

"Yeah, I can vouch for that."

"Look, Scott, thanks for being here for me. I can't tell you how much I appreciate it. And I guess Jolene Beck's gone. So, there's nothing left to say, is there?"

"No, but if you ever see Jolene Beck again, tell her I think I'm falling in love with her."

"I wish you had told her that last night."

"Yeah. That might have led to complications, but I sort of wish that too."

"I doubt if I'll see her, but if I do, I'll let her know."

Chapter Thirty-One

JENI FELL BACK asleep after Scott left and slept until just before noon. Her head ached and her stomach felt queasy. She forced herself to drink three glasses of cold water from the bathroom sink, then took a shower. She picked up her cellphone to call Bernhardt, but tossed it on the bed and sat down with a pillow behind her. "I'm pathetic."

She mentally reviewed what she could remember of the conversations with Scott last night and this morning. She couldn't remember anything incriminating, other than maybe the bit about the pixies.

The hotel room walls seemed to close in on her, and she finally dialed Bernhardt.

"Hi, boss lady. Try a little sleeping with the enemy last night?"

"You do have people watching me."

"Yeah, as of last night. Jolene Beck, huh? You didn't do a bad job of setting up the identity."

"Except for my shoes, or so I'm told. You're a security professional. Do *you* notice peoples' shoes and know how expensive they are?"

"I have to force myself to even look at a person's shoes, and I have no clue how much they cost. I bet you wore something expensive and Darla Smith noticed."

"Yeah."

"It goes with not having a Y chromosome. Hetero guys are genetically incapable of noticing anything specific about shoes. So, can I bring you in? Give you an escort?"

"You think that's necessary?"

"At least two groups of people other than ours are watching you, so that's a yes."

"Any idea who they are?"

"One of them is oriental. Not sure about the others. If BTI isn't already watching you, they soon will be."

"See what you can find out on Danny Minh. He probably has ties to a West Coast Vietnamese street gang."

"So Darla Smith got you involved with a street gang? Does he know who you are?"

"I don't think so."

"He doesn't need to then. If you can lose his people before we pick you up, that would be one less complication to deal with. I'll send you hair dye, business casual clothes and a low-end limo. Should be enough to get you out undetected. Then we pay for the room a few days and *poof*, Jolene Beck disappears without a trace."

"Maybe. Do the prep, but don't start it until I tell you to. In the meantime, look at our procedures again and make absolutely sure we're keeping our diseases over here and their diseases over there."

"We're covered as well as we can be without going totally paranoid about it like the BTI is."

"Yeah. I'm not sure that's good enough. If you see a way anything contagious could get over there, shut it down. Check our garbage disposal policies too. Nothing usable goes out."

"What brought this on?" Bernhardt sounded puzzled. "I thought the whole point was to get out from under the bureaucrats."

"What brought this on? Hopefully nothing. Give me a few hours to think about the extraction and I'll get back to you."

"There's a message from Europe for you."

Jeni sagged back against the pillow. "And I can only decrypt it if I go over there. That stinks."

"That's the way you set it up. Security. It's a short message—three or four sentences at most. One more reason to come in."

"I'll let you know."

Scott didn't have time to run that morning. He rushed to work and sagged into the chair in front of his computer. Darla glared at him. "You slept with her."

"In a way. Not the way you think."

"It's none of my business unless it messes with the investigation or unless she told you something useful."

"It won't and she didn't. Oh wait. She did say something about the things we've been calling hobbits. She called them pixies."

"Did she say anything we could use to get a search warrant?"

Scott replayed what he could remember of the conversation. "The bit about pixies is the only thing I can think of."

"If BTI doesn't want us to know about hobbits, they aren't going to take that in front of a judge to get a warrant."

"Would Boston PD?"

"If BTI won't admit these things exist, then what she said isn't evidence of anything."

Scott nodded. "So we have nothing. I don't think Jeni had anything to do with killing Samantha Murphy."

"Of course you don't. You're male."

"And you think she had Samantha killed?"

"I think she asked Bernhardt Sloan if anyone could rid her of that troublesome ex-cheerleader and didn't care how he managed it." Darla walked over and leaned against the back of his chair. "Sloan is the business end of the Burgen Empire. Jeni Burgen is the soft glove that usually hides him, but you don't have a Bernhardt Sloan on the payroll if you aren't willing to use him."

"Maybe." Scott sighed. "We need to shut her down anyway. She's going to kill millions of Indians over there if she keeps doing whatever she's doing to get those Roman books. She could even bring smallpox or something worse back to us."

"Does BTI have emergency powers to shut her down? Do you have to have proof that would hold up in a court of law?"

"That's classified. Let's just say things could happen if we have proof of imminent danger from an epidemic, but the decision would get made a lot higher up than this office. And if we were wrong everyone in BTI with their fingerprints on the decision would live to be very sorry they embarrassed whoever ultimately made the call."

"But you're already doing something."

Scott smiled. "We'll see."

Scott and Peter flew on a BTI jet to an airport near a portal in Northwestern Iowa. They landed near the smaller propeller-driven plane slated to take them through the portal.

The plane looked cramped, with barely enough room for the pilot and co-pilot, much less Scott and Peter. Peter looked it over as they arrived at the airport and nodded his approval. "Not fast, but it's reliable and it can land just about anywhere, including a cornfield."

"No quarantine time. Just a quick look in our ears, noses and throats, then breathe in and out and we're on our way. I'm the only one of the four of us who knows anything about Indian customs, plus all three of you are carrying firearms. We're breaking over half the rules in the BTI rulebook with this one."

"And you're bringing along your cute little Indian bow," Peter said. "It stays on your side of the seat. Do you even know how to use it?"

"Yep. I can use a sling and throw a spear too."

"But not shoot a gun, I bet."

"Not well."

The co-pilot leaned out and yelled, "Stow your gear. We're wasting daylight."

Scott glanced at his watch as they got in. It was still only ten in the morning. They took off and flew to a dirt field by the portal. They sat in the plane as a truck towed it carefully through the portal. Scott felt the nausea that usually rattled him as he went through, but it quickly passed as the plane made a bumpy takeoff from an improvised airfield on the other side.

"Sioux-speaking tribes down there," Scott said. "Mostly agricultural. Big towns along the rivers, but they abandon their towns for buffalo hunts part of the year."

Peter ignored him, staring out the window and cleaning his semi-automatic pistol. Scott pulled out a camera and an audio recorder and passed the time recording his observations. The summer day was cloudless and the flight effortless.

"Too easy," Peter said, "Going too well."

"What?"

"It's never this easy," Peter said. "When things go this smooth, the trouble is storing up—like a dam waiting to break."

"I take it you're a glass-half-empty type." Scott turned back to his window and his recorder. "Priceless stuff here. This will increase our knowledge of Indians east of the Mississippi exponentially."

Peter didn't respond, and Scott kept recording as miles of Timeline X territory passed by beneath them. Finally Scott recognized the Ohio River and a little later, the Indian town that had been burning.

The pilot circled, searching for hidden danger, then landed in the cornfield near the partially burned palisade. When the plane bumped to a stop, the pilot leaned back. "Our orders say we stay with the plane. They also say we take off without you if the locals attack."

"I'm pretty sure I can outrun most of the locals," Scott said. "Petey? Well, that's another story."

"Yeah, let's see how well that works for you," Peter said. "Don't fight them. Make them run until they keel over."

Scott stepped out of the plane into foot-high corn. The noon sun greeted him, along with too much silence and the odors of fire and battle. A dog howled in the distance. The breeze made small noises as it gently lifted and dropped the corn stalks. Scott turned his head slowly, surveying the ruined town. Part of the palisade had fallen outward, revealing piles of bodies and partially burned remnants of longhouses. The dog howled again. A large bird flew startlingly low overhead—a buzzard.

Much of the field had been trampled, but enough corn survived to ensure a good crop for—for who? For birds and raccoons and bears?

Peter stepped out behind him. "Got a strong stomach?"

Bodies of warriors—in armor made of wooden sticks tied together—lay in heaps as far as Scott could see into the town. None of them moved or groaned. Scott mentally calculated the toll and then pushed the thought to the back of his mind. A dog howled yet again.

The breeze brushed against Scott's face. "We're the first people from our timeline to set foot over here east of the Mississippi, at least officially. I should say something memorable, but it seems wrong—"

"Why? Because there are bodies over there? Here, I'll do it for you. That's one small step for Scott—"

"Into somebody's cornfield—"

"—one giant lurch for his stomach."

Scott looked across the town. The charred remnants of longhouses smoldered, with broken pots and half-burned bodies scattered among the ashes. A log strong-house near the center of town was burned too. Its charred logs lay in a pile. Other than the buzzards, nothing breathed inside the palisade. A buzzard eyed them and then the pile of bodies near it. It seemed torn between the feast of carcasses and ingrained fear of men. Other buzzards circled overhead, drawn by the feast, but more cautious.

Scott took pictures as they worked their way toward the destruction. The harsh odor of scorched chicken feathers mixed with the other smells, causing Scott to gag. The town's corn and bean storage sheds were charred ruins, though he couldn't tell if the corn had burned along with the sheds.

Few of the bodies had intact armor, moccasins or weapons.

"Some of them have gunshot wounds," Peter said as they reached a pile of bodies. He looked as shocked by the sights and smells as Scott felt.

"Some killed by arrows too." Scott took pictures of the bullet wounds. "I can't believe Jeni would let this happen. What would she gain from it?"

"Who cares why? People came through her portal and shot your precious Indians or Native Americans or whatever you call them. Those pictures should be enough to take Burgen down, especially when we show them a few bullets." He pried two out of the remnants of the palisade and put them in an envelope.

"Maybe. Then again, any good lawyer is going to ask for a link between this and Burgen. We don't have one yet. It'll help if we find survivors."

A dog squirmed in through the burned portion of the palisade, tail between its legs and hindquarters low in a submissive posture. It peered at them and whined, then slunk closer. An arrow with half the shaft broken off dangled from the fleshy part of its front leg. The dog licked the wound, then sat near them.

Scott held out his hand, careful to keep the back toward the dog. It sniffed him and then licked his hand. Scott patted the dog on the head until it relaxed, then he grabbed the arrowhead and yanked the shaft the rest of the way through the wound. The dog yelped and snapped at the wound, but then settled down to lick it.

Scott patted the dog. "Did they kill everybody?" The dog whined. "I doubt it. Not enough bodies for a town this size."

Peter found a shallow grave; he pointed out blood drops on the fresh dirt. "Someone must have survived."

"Unless the attackers buried this one."

"Why only one?"

"I hate to say this, but good point. Unless it's one of theirs." Scott dug into the grave until he exposed a strong middle-aged face framed in an elaborate feather headdress. "Nope. Same ornaments. He was a local. High ranking too, based on the headdress."

"What's this?" Peter drew a string out from under the man's deerskin tunic. "Roofing nail." He answered his own question. "Strung around his neck like it's gold."

"More valuable to them." Scott took a picture of the necklace.

They circled the town, finding only bodies and debris. Bodies of very young and very old Indians lay among the charred logs of the strong-house in the center of town. Scott closed his eyes. "We need to bury them. Not just the kids—all of them."

"We don't have time." Peter walked away from the bodies. "They took younger women and some men."

"Yeah, probably. But where?" Scott took more pictures of the bodies. He found a trail of trampled corn leading away from the town and toward the river. Most of the tracks were from moccasins, but with shoes and boots mixed in. "Half a dozen different shoes and twice that many boots."

"Not modern-style boots. Are they Roman?"

"Couldn't prove it by me."

They followed the trail of the departing attackers. Scott

spotted drag marks where a fleet of nearly a hundred large canoes had been beached.

"So they came in and left by canoe. Been gone for hours at least, probably over a day."

Peter turned and headed back toward the plane before Scott finished speaking. "Nothing we can do here."

The plane flew low up the river toward the next town. Scott saw no signs of the attackers or the locals along the river. The only sign of Indians or their possessions were two hogs that stared warily up at them before stalking off.

As they buzzed the second town, Scott saw drag marks where dozens of canoes landed and swaths of trampled corn. Nothing moved down there. The palisade seemed intact though, with no arrows embedded in it. The gate was closed. The pilot circled warily, through a scattering of buzzards.

Scott felt anger well up inside him, but he pushed the feeling aside. The canoes, trampled corn and buzzards all pointed to this town suffering the same fate as the other one, but the lack of battle signs puzzled him. Wary of a trap, he told the pilot to make another pass.

"I don't see the UAV," Peter said. "And nobody in armor down there."

The sun slipped toward the horizon. Scott sighed and motioned for the pilot to take them down. "I don't like this at all."

The plane bumped along the field before shuddering to a stop. Scott and Peter walked cautiously toward the palisade. The silence made Scott's skin crawl. They opened the gate and squeezed in.

The town appeared as intact inside the palisade as it did from the outside, and just as empty. Scott climbed a ladder to a watchtower and surveyed the town. Patches of dried blood caked the log floor of the watchtower, but he saw no bodies there or anywhere else. He did see a few signs of struggle—one end of a longhouse sagged; drops of half-dried blood seeped sluggishly from one of the other watchtowers.

Scott caught a hint of motion near a longhouse and then a flash of light against the packed dirt.

He started for the ladder, then stopped. Squinting, he carefully surveyed the town. *A trap?* Nothing else moved. He eased an arrow out of his quiver. He saw motion below him; Peter had his pistol out. Peter stared at Scott and held up his hand in a gesture Scott took as a command to stay put. Scott scanned the town again, his bow poised. Peter moved toward the longhouse, his weapon also ready. Scott saw a blur of motion and suddenly Peter was thrashing in the dirt and cursing.

Scott jumped to the ladder, climbed down the first two steps, then slid the rest of the way. He ran toward Peter, trying to look every direction at once. As he got closer, he saw that Peter was tangled in a net, his pistol in the dirt six feet in front of him.

Peter yelled, “Go. Run.”

“Which way? Where are they?”

Peter managed to raise an arm. Scott spun in the direction Peter pointed. He caught motion out of the corner of his eye and a quick glint of sunlight off something shiny, then nothing. Scott glanced back at Peter. “Who is it? How many are there?”

“Three.”

Scott lifted his head to see a figure in shiny metal armor seemingly materialize at the other end of the longhouse. Scott saw a flicker of motion to his left, and another of the figures appeared. He glanced behind him. Yet another figures stood there. To his right—nothing. The Romans were a foot shorter than Scott’s six feet, but massively muscular. They carried short swords and metal-studded shields. Helmets covered their faces, but the shape looked wrong—too low in the forehead. *Hobbits?*

The armored forms looked far more formidable than Scott

would have believed. Fear stabbed at his heart. He moved a step to the right, to his conveniently empty, inviting right, then stopped. "Three? Are you sure?"

Behind him, Peter said, "Just three. Don't fight them. Get out of here. Back to the plane."

The Roman to Scott's left took a step toward him, then another, each step crashing down and echoing in the empty town. Scott drew back the bowstring, but realized the Romans were too close. He ran to the right, trying to gain space to use his bow. He spotted a disturbed patch of earth and instinctively jumped over it. He tensed as he landed, half expecting to be caught in another net. When nothing happened, he sprinted toward the gate.

He heard footfalls behind him and to both sides. The ones behind got closer alarmingly fast. He felt thick fingers brush his back, reaching for his hair. Scott threw himself into a forward roll, slid sideways and used his legs to scissor the Roman's legs out from under him as his momentum carried the hobbit past Scott. The impact left Scott's legs feeling as though he'd tried to kick down an oak tree, but the Roman hit the ground hard and lost his sword. Scott picked it up and slashed, but the sword slid harmlessly off the Roman's shield. The Roman launched himself to his feet, yelled short guttural syllables and ran toward Scott, feinting with the shield.

Scott backed away, listening for the footfalls of the other Romans. The town, however, had gone silent again.

Don't fight them. Make them run.

He saw a droplet of sweat fly from under the Roman's armor, and for the first time since he saw them, he felt a glimmer of hope. Make them run. But how? Scott backed away, swinging the sword at the Roman's leg. His opponent casually batted the sword aside, almost knocking it out of Scott's hand, and charged, aiming his shield at Scott's face.

Scott dodged, grabbed the edge of the shield and tried to use his foe's momentum to slam him through the side of a longhouse. He would have had as much luck changing the course of a river with his fingers. The Roman swung his shield back toward Scott.

Don't fight them.

Scott pressed one hand to the shield and ran backwards as fast as he could—letting the Roman's momentum propel him—while he slashed at the short powerful legs. The Roman had an answer to that too. He changed the angle of the shield, causing Scott's hand to slide off, then he slammed the shield down on Scott's knee. It was a glancing blow, but the impact still left the knee numb and bleeding.

The fighting brought them close to the entrance of a longhouse facing away from the gate. Scott dodged into the building. His injured knee bumped the side of the entrance and he almost cried out, but he ran toward the entrance at the other end as quietly as he could. He heard heavy footsteps pacing him outside, then they abruptly fell quiet.

Does he think I'm doubling back? Or is he moving quietly to the same entrance I'm going to?

Scott kept moving to the far entrance. He dashed from the longhouse, headed left, and abruptly stopped as another Roman came around the corner. Scott caught a quick glimpse of a sword in the Roman's hand and ducked into another longhouse.

This Roman ran after Scott, shouting something in his guttural language, then tripped and went sprawling in the semi-darkness. Scott kept running.

Don't fight. Make them run.

He ran out of the longhouse and into another one and then another. The minutes blurred into a tapestry of running and dodging, like a deadly high-speed version of tag. His knee ached and his breath came harder.

Make them run.

Chapter Thirty-Two

JENI STARED AT her phone, then closed her eyes.

I don't trust them. I don't trust Bernhardt. I don't trust Andy.

She thought about the kidnappers. They came for her after Andy figured out she was Jolene but before Bernhardt knew. That didn't prove anything, but the fact sat in her mind and irritated her as a sore tooth would.

All this *and* the Russian mafia. She thought back to the meeting with Danny Minh. If the kidnappers really were Russians and associated with Andy...*no*. Background checks would have picked that up. She accessed the background files with her cellphone. Both his parents were third generation Americans from a mostly German background. Andy's mom was from an Indiana farming family. His dad worked in a factory. Both were now dead. She scanned a list of his cases from before his tenure at Burgen. No representation of organized crime figures.

"So Minh lied or the kidnappers had nothing to do with Andy. Or the background check screwed up."

She called Scott's cellphone but got no answer.

What was I going to say anyway?

She started to put the phone down, then impulsively called Darla Smith.

"Hi. Don't imagine you expected to hear from me."

"No. Main suspect in a murder investigation doesn't usually call the investigating officer. What's up?"

"Know where Scott is?"

"Nope. He left in a hurry and didn't say where to."

Jeni sighed. "I have issues I need to talk out with somebody."

"I hear Bernhardt Sloan's in town. He seems like the type you could pour your heart out to."

"I didn't hire him to pour my heart out to."

"No. You hired him to do the dirty stuff you didn't want to do yourself, like killing a harmless little fluff of an aging cheerleader and cutting off her head and hands."

"No. Look, it was obviously a mistake calling you."

"True. But if you want to pour your heart out to someone, I'm available after work. Feel free to bring a lawyer. I doubt we would need to appoint one for you, but if we do, let me know."

Jeni clinched her fists. *Bitch.* Out loud she said, "Stop by my hotel room after work. I won't pour my heart out, but I'll trade answers to a question or two."

"Are you kidding?"

"Actually, no. Do stop over. Maybe we can do each other some good."

After she hung up, Jeni called her technology chief and set up a dead-man procedure so that not calling in for twelve hours would trigger an existing plan to shut down the portal and hide the equipment in the warehouse.

If they're after the portal, they aren't going to get it.

She decided to take the process further. She set up a similar procedure to send out recorded voicemail and email messages suspending both Bernhardt and Andy and barring them from Burgen premises unless she acted to keep the messages from going out. Of course, that assumed people would believe the messages and act on them. She looked for anything else she could do to strengthen her position, but that seemed to cover it.

Scott tried to work his way around the Romans and reach one of the gates, but he barely kept enough distance to keep them from forcing combat on him. He uncomfortably realized the Romans were herding him toward a blank corner of the palisade. Finally he took the only option left to him. He sprinted for the nearest watchtower.

One of the Romans shouted. His pursuers converged on the tower, still moving fast. Scott swarmed up the ladder. A powerful hand grabbed his foot, but he slipped out of the grasp and climbed. He swung over the wall, hung and dropped the remaining six feet to the ground, then immediately sprinted across the field.

One of the Romans launched himself at Scott from the watchtower wall, arms outstretched. Scott saw his shadow and jumped aside. The short armored form smashed headfirst into the dirt, landing hard enough to kill or paralyze most men.

Scott kept running, cringing as he trampled foot-high corn. He glanced back to see all three Romans in the field, sprinting toward him with the speed of panicked deer. Despair welled up in him, but he kept running—his feet pounding ever faster—digging down for and recklessly using his reserves of strength. He stole another glance. The Romans still gained on him, no more than six yards behind, but they were slowing, and he saw sweat droplets spraying from them in the still-hot June sun.

Seeing his pursuers slowing gave Scott renewed strength, and he ran on with the speed of anger and desperation.

You've destroyed these people, but you won't catch me.

When he checked again, the three Romans were no longer gaining on him. He kept up the frantic pace a few heartbeats longer and then turned back to find the Romans had stumbled to a halt, chests heaving under the armor. Scott slowed to a more sustainable pace, putting distance between him and his pursuers. With the immediate crisis past, he realized that he was on the opposite side of the town from the plane. Not good. And his body screamed its urgent need for water.

He ran toward the river.

I've still lost. They'll recover and just keep coming, like creatures from a nightmare.

The thought snuck in, pushing triumph out of his mind.

Make them run. Make them keep *running. But how?*

Scott reached for his bow. Sometime during the fight the bowstring had been cut. He glanced back at the Romans. They ambled toward him. He took out his sling and picked up a rock from the riverbank. His first shot missed badly. His second bounced off a shield. He shot again and again, as fast as he could grab stones from the riverbank. Most of them missed or bounced off shields, but two hit the Romans. They did no visible damage, but the three spread out and trotted toward him, trying to trap him against the riverbank. Scott sprinted to the outside of the leftmost of the Romans and started slinging stones again.

Make them run.

Another stone hit one of his pursuers, bouncing off a shield and into the Roman's helmeted face. The Roman staggered, but kept coming with no change in speed. Another rock bounced off a shield and into an armored shin, again with no apparent effect. Like mosquito bites.

As the sun sank toward the horizon, Scott kept running and slinging rocks. He tried to work his way back to the plane, but the Romans kept herding him away from it. His arm grew tired and his knee swelled, making his body slower and less responsive. He thought about just running as fast as he could away from them, but that would take him farther from the plane and give the Romans time to rest and regain their speed.

Keep them moving.

The Romans tried to trap him against the riverbank. They weren't moving as fast as they had earlier. And then suddenly they were. The two outermost Romans put on a burst of speed and

Scott found himself trapped against the river with the three Romans closing in.

Danny Minh called Jeni on the cellphone he'd given her. "Why haven't I heard from you? Aren't thinking about backing out on your part of the bargain, are you?"

Jeni shook her head.

One more complication.

"I haven't found out much yet. I think Darla is suspicious of me. Are the Eastern European types out of the picture yet?"

"I won't let them bother you as long as you do your job. Why are you important?"

"I have no idea. Why do you think I am?"

"I'll figure it out. I need to be getting something useful from you for my money."

"She's coming over tonight. Is there anything specific you want me to find out?"

"Just tell me what she says. I'll figure out what's important. Give me something tonight."

Jeni spent the afternoon watching soap operas, then changed her hair and did what she could with the cheap makeup and clothes. She deliberately didn't go back completely to her usual style, going for a middle-manager look instead.

As she finished, Bernhardt called.

"Get out of the hotel now. You aren't protected and won't be for at least fifteen minutes. I'm on my way over, but you need to head somewhere public. Let me know where you're heading and I'll meet you there."

"What happened?

"Security failure. Get out, Jeni."

She hung up and gathered her things. She glanced at her watch. Almost 5:15.

She peeked out the hotel peephole just as Darla knocked on

the door.

Scott glared at the Romans. They spread out to keep him pinned against the river, not far enough apart he could run between them unless they were more tired than they looked. With Scott trapped against the river, they moved purposefully, converging on him with measured powerful strides. Walking, not running. Scott shot off rocks one after another as fast as he could, concentrating on the guy directly in front of him. His aim was more accurate now, and more of the stones zipped past the Roman's shield, but Scott was rapidly running out of suitable rocks.

Only a couple left.

In desperation, he picked up a fist-sized piece of dried mud and shot that. The mud hit the top of the Roman's shield, sending a spray of dirt into his face. He brought his hands up to his eyes, apparently blinded. That left his side unprotected, and Scott directed one of his two remaining rocks into that side at short range, aiming for the floating ribs. The Roman grunted, but showed no sign of damage.

Scott shook his head. Even with the armor, that shot should have broken ribs and left the Roman helpless.

Maybe it did.

Scott took his only chance. He ran toward the guy he'd just hit and then past him. The Roman moved toward him, then stopped, swaying and holding his side. The other two raced to cut him off, but the long game of cat and mouse slowed them just enough that Scott sprinted past them and back into the field. That left him with space to maneuver but also cut him off from the river with its supply of rocks and water.

He glanced back. The three Romans were still by the water, no longer moving toward him. They pointed at him, made a peculiar call, half growl and half yodel, then marched down the river bank. He followed carefully, keeping them in sight. They climbed into a canoe they pulled from the shallows and paddled downriver in it. Scott ran to the river bank and sent a shower of rocks after them, but they rowed the canoe toward the other side of the river without pausing. He kept up with them along the bank, grabbing more ammunition and slinging the stones as he went. He had to detour around a swampy area filled with a tangle of downed trees. When he got to the other side, the Romans and their canoe were no longer in sight in either direction. He did manage to get a couple of pictures of the Romans.

Scott thought about the opportunities for ambushes in the forest along the river. He avoided the path when he headed back toward town. When he reached the field, he searched for signs the Romans had circled back to ambush him, but found nothing.

It was almost twilight now. He filled his quiver with rocks for his sling and ran back to the town's main gate to search for Peter. The net was empty, with boot prints and drag marks leading away from it. Scott followed the trail to the river, where it ended. He ran to the plane. It appeared undamaged, but was empty. When he opened the door, a shell casing rolled out into the cornfield. A splatter of red glistened on the instrument panel.

Scott stood by the plane a few seconds. He felt vulnerable in the middle of the field. Lightning in the distance told of a thunderstorm coming. The plane wouldn't offer much shelter, but the silent town was eerie. He hesitated, not sure which alternative was worse.

The sky got darker. A breeze ruffled the corn. Wolves chorused in the distance. After scribbling a note in case Peter or the aircrew returned to the plane, and stashing the camera under a seat, Scott stumbled back to the deserted town, his legs and back aching from the chase, feeling spent, empty and lost.

Chapter Thirty-Three

THE THUNDERSTORM CAME in fast, bringing heavy, howling wind and rain. Scott stood guard near the dark entrance of a longhouse, his bow and the Roman's sword by his hand. He dug out his spare string and replaced the cut one. The longhouse was safe from the rain and all but the strongest winds, but the rain and wind together tested it that night. Scott did his best to stay alert, but he had pushed his body much too far, and now it demanded rest. The darkness and the rain combined with his fatigue to lull him into brief periods of slumber, from which he woke with a start.

If the Romans had returned that night, they would have found him sound asleep and defenseless. But they didn't come back, and he suffered through a restless sleep punctuated with nightmares and awakenings.

The thunderstorm ended in the early morning hours, and dawn came with the June sun bright in a cloudless sky.

Scott woke from the last of his brief intervals of slumber and blinked, disoriented. For a second he thought he was back in his apartment, but the longhouse and the silent town jarred him back to reality. He realized he was ravenous and extremely thirsty. He took care of the thirst by drinking rainwater from one of the pots he'd set outside the night before, hoping any intruder would blunder into them.

Then he began a search for food.

Most of the town's stores of corn, beans and dried meat were gone, but he found a small cache of parched corn. As he ate sparingly, he puzzled over some of the mysteries of yesterday's events. Why did they carry large numbers of people away? Why would Jeni or her people need the captives? Why would they travel over a hundred miles to attack these towns? Why the mix of Romans, men with guns and Indians? None of that fit Scott's picture of Jeni's operation.

The attacks themselves presented their own set of mysteries. Why were the attacks on the two towns carried out so differently? How did the attackers get into this town without the dogs giving the alarm? Why was one burned, while the other was left grotesquely intact, but with the hidden Romans? Why did a few Romans stay behind? Why did they suddenly leave, abandoning food and weapons? And what sheltered behind those armored masks?

Scott's memory gave an answer to that last question, but not one his mind accepted. The glimpses he caught of the armored Romans' faces when he got close to them during yesterday's fight told him they were more animal than man, with not enough forehead and too much jaw. The way they moved also suggested the animal. Before yesterday, Scott wouldn't have believed a man lived who could come close to chasing him down when he had a head start of over forty yards. Yet those men or animals had come very close to doing that in heavy armor, carrying heavy shields.

If they were animals, they were cunning ones. Scott thought about the way they reacted to his attempts to fight them. Those reactions weren't the ones most humans would've tried, but they were effective.

A dog solved some of the mysteries plaguing Scott.

He heard it barking in the distance, near the river. He warily worked his way down to where it stood several yards from what appeared to be a human body. As Scott got closer, he realized it was one of the Romans he fought the evening before, no longer armored. The man, if he could call it that, lay naked on a fallen log, his or its head cocked back at an angle no living man would maintain for more than a second or two, eyes open to the morning sun.

Wildflowers covered its torso.

Scott scanned the forest around him, alert for an ambush. He didn't see any sign of the others, so he found a long stick, approached the creature sprawled across the log and jabbed it twice in the groin. No response. Reassured, he moved closer. A glance told him why the Romans had fled: the body sported angry bruises where the rocks from Scott's sling had taken their toll. He couldn't tell which of the wounds had killed the Roman, but he suspected a broken rib had punctured an internal organ and the creature bled internally until it died and was deposited here by its companions.

The unburied body and the scattering of flowers emphasized the oddness of the creature for Scott. He hesitated, wondering if he should bury the body or take it back to the airplane and try to preserve it. He compromised by scooping out a shallow grave and covering it with rocks and brush. The creature's head and face made leaving the body more difficult for the anthropologist in him. It was even lower in the forehead and longer in the jaw than his earlier glimpses had led him to believe. Scott turned away from the grave and hiked back, once more, to the empty town.

Chapter Thirty-Four

JENI SAT ON the edge of the bed. "Bernhardt just called and told me I'm not safe here."

"You probably aren't," Darla said. "You've already been kidnapped once. Hotel's way under your income class. You need to stop slumming and go back to hiding behind Bernhardt."

"I don't trust him."

"Ah. Now I see why you asked me to come. Time to start tossing the hired help under the bus for the Samantha Murphy thing. Sorry. His scalp isn't big enough to save yours. I'm coming after you, and I'll keep coming until I get you."

"I didn't kill Samantha Murphy. I didn't tell anyone to."

"And you didn't tell anyone to take care of her or take care of it?"

"I—Whatever I said, I didn't tell anyone to kill her. And Bernhardt knows I don't operate that way. And we're deep in advice-of-an-attorney land. End of that conversation."

Darla headed for the door. "I'd say nice chatting with you, but actually you wasted five minutes of lifespan I'll never get back. If you decide to talk about something real, let me know."

"Wait. Have the police found anything about the guys who kidnapped me?"

"Nothing I want to tell you."

"I'm not the enemy here. Are the farmers okay? Is there anything I can do to help them?"

"I don't know. By the way, you did steal a four-wheeler and a shotgun. Most people would go to jail for that."

"No district attorney would bring that to trial, given the circumstances. And if they did they would lose." Jeni glanced at the gym bag. *If she leaves that comes out and gets loaded.* "Any link between Andy Hollsworth and the Russian mafia?"

"Your lawyer and organized crime? That's an interesting question. Why would there be?"

"Your gangster boyfriend—"

"Danny Minh was screwing with your mind. Count on that. Are you as bad a businesswoman as you are a spy?"

"I'm thirty-nine years old and—"

"Make that forty-one."

"Thirty-nine. You'll understand someday. I built a multi-billion dollar company and I kept control of it in spite of all the shark businessmen and lawyers who thought they could take it away from me."

"Yeah, you have claws. I figured that out. You hire people like Bernhardt Sloan, which means you use people like Bernhardt Sloan. If you ever really want to talk, you have my number." Darla opened the door, then backed into the room. "The cavalry arrives. Hi, Bernhardt."

Bernhardt pushed past her and closed the door. "You okay?" he asked Jeni. "Nobody bothered you?"

"Nope. Except for me, and I was just leaving." Darla grinned at Bernhardt. "Take care of her. We'll want her in good shape for the handcuffs."

Scott left notes in a couple of places in town in case something happened to the one in the airplane. Hunting and trading parties from the two towns would probably be trickling in. Scott hoped they would be too afraid of the unknown to tamper with the plane. He rummaged through it, taking the remaining stocks of food and water and as much of the emergency kit as he could carry, then locked the doors, not that doing so would stop anyone determined to break in.

He headed to the river. Could he walk fast enough to catch up to a group in canoes? He scouted along the river and decided he'd have to detour around too many swampy areas. He searched through the smaller damaged canoes until he found one that looked repairable.

Chewing gum and bailing wire time.

Fortunately, he actually had more than gum to work with. He patched the holes with super glue, birch bark from one of the other canoes and a waterproof sealant. He glued and splinted a couple of the broken paddles with sticks and wound duct tape around them, cut the top off a water jug so he could use the bottom half to bail water from the inevitable leaks, then stood back and studied his handiwork.

No real Indian would be caught dead in a canoe that fried.

He sat impatiently waiting for the glue in his improvised repairs to dry, knowing that every hour would reduce his already slim chances of rescuing Peter and the pilots.

Scott finally got the patched-together canoe in the water and headed east along the river, the way the two Romans had gone.

For many miles upriver he paddled through territory probably claimed by the people of the two towns, areas they used for hunting, fishing and gathering wild plants. Scott wondered how long neighboring tribes would respect the deserted territory. He suspected that human scavengers would visit the towns within a few days unless fear of the unknown enemy kept them out. Hunters would venture in, attracted by the relative abundance of deer and other game.

The animals already seemed bolder than anywhere else Scott had been in Timeline X. A deer stood at the edge of the forest and stared at Scott as though he was a strange interloper and not part of the dominant species of this world. A pack of wolves paced him along the riverbank for a time, blue eyes watching, evaluating. It wasn't unusual for wolves to follow lone hunters, though wolf attacks were extremely rare, if they occurred at all. These wolves seemed bold, as if they sensed Scott's vulnerability or the shift in power between man and animal in this deserted territory.

Scott also left messages in the burned-out shell of the first town they had visited as he passed it on his way upriver. He didn't approach the still unburied bodies, but they weighed on his mind. Giving them even the crudest of temporary burials would take days. He turned his back on them and paddled up the river, feeling like a traitor as the town receded in the distance behind him. He paddled on, stopping to nibble at the emergency food when his arms shook too hard for him to paddle. He ate sparingly, knowing that early summer was a lean time for food plants, too early in the growing season for most of them. He didn't have time to fish, let alone clean and cook any catch, so he endured the hunger and kept moving.

The trees were in full foliage, and visibility was low. Scott stayed alert for any sign of lurking enemies. He paddled until nightfall, then pulled the canoe ashore and holed up out of the reach of most animals. His night was full of startled awakenings and half-remembered dreams, but nothing bothered him. The next morning he continued his journey, the hours blurring as hunger, weariness and isolation pulled at him.

Scott kept an eye on the river as he struggled along in the patched canoe. He saw no traders with canoes full of goods going up or down the river; they seem to have cleared out entirely. He rowed past an intact town surrounded by cornfields and saw scouts watching him from the bank. They lurked on the bank for a mile before they turned back and gave him a chance to land briefly on the other side of the town to eat and see if he could spot signs of the Romans.

He scouted along the riverbank, searching for places where they might have landed. A few of them probably had; he saw signs that half a dozen canoes had pulled up onto the bank. A trail of moccasin tracks, mixed with the distinctive heavier marks of—he hesitated and then mentally labeled them *Jeni's people*—led inland for a short distance and then back to the tracks of the canoes. Scott saw a subtle mark on one of the trees, an arrow drawn in the dirt, and stones arranged precisely in a capital *P*.

Peter.

Scott followed the arrow and found a scribbled note under a rock: *A dozen Indians, five guys in armor, thirty captives, the pilot and co-pilot. Three guns. Ours. P*

Scott studied the tracks. He estimated that the Roman rearguard had stopped here sometime the previous evening. That meant that he was still nearly a day behind them. He reviewed his mental map of the river. It snaked back and forth across its floodplain, but trying to cut across the loops wouldn't help, especially since he would have to haul the canoe and his supplies with him.

At least he seemed to be moving faster than the group that stopped here—surprising given his improvised canoe. But they were probably stragglers. Too few to be the main body. He continued upriver, paddling as fast as his aching body allowed. No one greeted him from the towns he passed. Nobody challenged him or sent out canoes to catch him either, though scouts on the banks paced him as he passed through their territory. The lack of challenges and greetings struck Scott as ominous. Word of the earlier attacks must have spread, making the tribes wary.

Even the animals seemed more wary along this stretch of the river, bounding away sooner than normal as he approached. In every town he passed, dogs howled when they caught his scent, rather than gathering curiously near the bank. Smaller animals like squirrels seemed unaffected by the fear. They peeked at him, chattering and ducking behind tree trunks.

Scott kept the canoe moving as the sun gradually sank behind him, casting tall shadows on the river. In spite of his conditioning, his muscles trembled with fatigue. When the sun finally touched the horizon, he found a spot to make landfall in a buffer zone between towns. He scouted the area warily after he landed, not knowing how far ahead the Romans were or if they had a rearguard like the one that ambushed him earlier. He checked out as much of the shoreline as he could in the fading light, then pulled the canoe to a spot away from the river and hid it. He concealed his tracks as best he could and found a sheltered spot difficult for animals to approach. Eventually he slept, though not soundly.

He woke before dawn and eased the canoe into the river as soon as it grew light enough for him to see. He was already making good progress up the river by the time the sun rose above the horizon. Scott's morning became a blur of river and passing towns. The warming sun and his exertions sent drops of sweat down his tired back.

The sun reached its zenith, and still Scott paddled. He automatically guided the canoe out of the way of a log floating downriver. He watched it idly, then realized the *log* was a body, an Indian man. He steered the canoe over to it and pulled the body on board, nearly capsizing.

The man was young. He had three wounds, not one which alone would have been fatal. They looked no more than five or six hours old—probably from early that morning. Scott steered the canoe to shore, where he dragged rocks and branches over the young man's body. He stared at the partly exposed body and shook his head, but he didn't have time to do more. Another debt for Jeni to pay.

Scott thought about the freshness of the wounds. He'd probably escaped last night and they caught him around dawn.

The timing of the wounds gave Scott some idea how far ahead at least some of the Romans were. The man might have survived for an hour or two, in fact probably did, before the Romans threw him in the river because he was dead or too badly injured to be useful. A growl rose up in Scott's chest at the thought of the dead man's last struggles, whether with the attackers or with the river.

Scott kept an eye on the banks as best he could, searching for evidence of a landing site. The Romans would have stopped for the night somewhere nearby. He spotted an area that looked likely and steered the canoe to it. As he got closer, he saw marks where several canoes had beached. He studied the landing site, noticing faint scruff marks leading to a disturbed area in the weeds. He pulled his canoe ashore, put arrow to his bow and searched the area.

He stumbled across a canoe hidden in the weeds, pawed through it and appropriated a quiver full of arrows, plus the paddles. He hid the paddles in the nearby brush, then discovered a trail of blood drops leading inland. The drops led him to a large deserted campsite—big enough for a party the size Peter described. Patches of blood stained the grass near the camp and a pile of carelessly stacked Indian corpses among the trees, six of them, all young men. Bare footprints led into the forest, overlaid by the distinctive boot marks of the Romans. Scott figured that Indians—ten or twelve of them—tried to escape in the night. Some died immediately, but their deaths let others get away, at least for a while.

Scott studied the tracks. He spotted drag marks and footprints of returning Romans paralleling most of the outgoing bare footprints, but not all of them. *Are some of the Romans still here?* He scanned the forest, but saw no sign of them.

Then he heard a small unnatural sound ahead.

Unnatural for Timeline X.

The clash of metal on metal.

Chapter Thirty-Five

SCOTT CROUCHED BEHIND a tree and stared toward the sound. He didn't move for several minutes. Finally he crept forward, studying the forest ahead of him. The only other sounds were of small animals, and even they were silent in an area ahead of him. He tried to pinpoint the cause of the silence. A quiet male voice above him said, "Back away. If you go farther, they'll see you and get both of us." Peter's voice. Scott scanned the trees until he spotted the man. "How many?"

"Three. Not human."

Scott nodded. That fit the number of tracks. "You have weapons?"

"A sword."

"Know how to use it?"

Peter started to climb down. "Doesn't everybody?"

"Good luck fighting those things," Scott said. "I ran one to death. Know how to fly a plane?"

"That I don't. Co-pilot may be dead. Pilot escaped. We got separated."

A branch cracked and Peter fell the last ten feet. Scott caught him, then glanced around, uncomfortably aware of the racket in the quiet forest. There was no response for a heartbeat, then Romans burst out of the forest twenty or thirty yards ahead of them.

Scott sprinted back toward the canoe, with Peter close

behind. The thud of footsteps behind them got closer with frightening speed. Scott jumped over a fallen log and slewed around a bend in the trail as he calculated their chances. *Not enough time to get the canoe into the water.* He thought about trying to delay the Romans, but he knew an unarmored man would stand no chance of surviving a hand-to-hand fight.

Peter apparently came to the same conclusion. “Split up. Maybe one of us will make it.”

Scott heard a guttural shout behind them, then thrashing sounds in diverging directions. The sound of boot falls slowed for a heartbeat. Scott glanced back. The Romans were appallingly close but looking back toward the forest. Scott sprinted for the canoe. He yelled, “Grab a side and run into the water.”

They reached the canoe with the Romans no more than three or four yards behind them and grabbed the sides as they ran beside it. Scott tossed his bow and sword into the canoe as he pulled it into the water. The Romans ran into the water after them, and one got a hand on the canoe. Scott smashed a paddle down on the grasping hand. The hand didn't release its hold, but Scott jammed the butt of the paddle into the man's mouth, below the helmet. *That* got the hand off the canoe. Scott pushed further into the river until he had to tread water. The Romans followed, but turned back when the water reached their chests.

Scott braced his side of the canoe so Peter could get in, and then he hauled himself in.

“They have a canoe too,” Peter said. “So we don't have long.”

“But I hid their paddles.” Scott steered the canoe upstream, keeping an eye on the Romans. They headed toward their canoe, hesitated, then separated and ran toward a thrashing in the brush.

The pilot sprinted out of the woods downriver from the canoe, armed only with a club. One of the Romans ran toward him. Scott dropped the paddle to pick up his bow and shot one and then another arrow after the Roman. They both hit armor without apparent effect. The Roman covered the distance to the racing pilot with stunning speed.

Scott shot again and again without slowing his target. The Roman reached the pilot and beheaded him with a single slash of his sword. Scott seethed with anger. The arrows obviously couldn't pierce armor at that distance. He tried a couple of shots at the Roman's eyes when the man turned back toward him. The Roman ducked but marched on, still unscathed. Another arrow glanced off the armor, and Scott glanced back at Peter.

"Who shot that?"

"I don't know." Peter yelled. "Look out." He pointed to the other Roman. The canoe had drifted toward the bank and the Roman charged through the shallow water toward it. Scott grabbed the paddle and hastily moved the canoe into the center of the river. The Roman stopped when the water reached his neck, and he splashed back to the bank.

Puzzled, Scott watched the Romans. They headed upriver, pacing the canoe. "They have a canoe and they don't know I hid their paddles. Why aren't they going back to it?"

"There's one more guy back there. He looked Hispanic."

Scott pulled another arrow from his quiver. He fired it and hit one of the Romans, again without doing any damage. A man ran out of the forest and into the water upriver from them. Scott paddled upriver, then put down the paddles and again shot at the Romans.

"They'll catch him," he said to Peter.

They did. Their intent wasn't to capture the man; they hacked at him with their swords, ignoring the arrows Scott showered at them.

Peter yelled, "Go on. He's as good as dead. They'll come after us next."

Scott started to dig his paddle in, then paused, estimating speeds and distances. The man still struggled and dodged, trying to reach deep water. Scott yelled and sent the canoe leaping toward the Romans. The Romans turned toward the canoe, giving the man a precious few seconds. He splashed out to the center of the river. Scott backed the paddles and swung over to the man fighting to keep his head above water.

The Romans raced back toward their canoe. Fast.

Hope they don't have spare paddles.

Scott braced the canoe as Peter struggled to drag the wounded man over the side. He flopped into the bottom, gasped *gracias* and passed out.

Jeni insisted on going straight to the portal as soon as Bernhardt made sure they lost any followers. He drove without saying much for several hours. She remained tense, her hand on the gym bag with the shotgun. Finally, as they got close to the data center, she relaxed a little and settled back in the passenger seat.

"So I ask again, why the panic?"

"I lost touch with all the people I had watching you, all within a couple of minutes."

"What happened to them?"

"I'm trying to find out. I figured it was the first move in a kidnapping attempt."

"But nothing happened."

"Yeah. I don't understand that. Maybe I got the other two shifts in play before the kidnappers could make their move."

The cellphone from Danny Minh rang.

"This is interesting. Ever hear of Danny Minh?"

"I've heard the name," Bernhardt said. "Can't place it though. Who is he?"

"Tell you later." Jeni flipped open the phone. "Hi."

"Well played, Burgen. You had me believing you were just part of the scenery and even conned me into giving you money. You must have been laughing the whole time."

"You can have the money back. And no, I wasn't laughing. You aren't the type of guy I feel comfortable laughing at."

"Smart woman. Too smart and too rich to be playing the kind of games you're playing."

"Maybe. I'm back in my world now. I'll get your money back to you and as far as I'm concerned, none of this happened."

"Yeah, except it did," Danny said. "I could leave that alone, but I've been meaning to talk to you about your new line of business. I think we could work together."

"I'm not sure how."

"I could put a little distance between you and your sideline. It's chump-change to you and hardly worth the grief if they catch you. If I can trace it back to you, the cops eventually will too. Let's say you give me a decent discount and I do the retail work for you. I do the dirty work at this end and take all the risks. You get to be to Ms. Civic Responsibility and still get your tax-free money. I take a cut, but keeping your hands clean is worth it to you."

"I have no idea what you're talking about."

"Of course not. Kind of a ghoulish business if you ask me. We'd probably not want to talk about it on the phone. This business can generate a lot of power if you handle it right. But you already figured that out. You wouldn't be doing it if you hadn't. I'll be in touch."

Jeni flipped the phone shut. "What kind of business opportunity would a Vietnamese street gang see in me?"

"Vietnamese street gang?" Bernhardt stared at her. "What have you been up to?"

"You really don't want to know. I don't even want to think about it."

"A lot of illegal activities you could get involved in with a portal."

"You think he knows I have one? How could he know that?"

"You know more about that than I do. Going to tell me what happened while you were gone?"

"Not yet." She shifted uncomfortably, her feet brushing the gym bag on the floorboard. "How did things get this crazy?"

"You built a portal, committed a federal crime."

"Think I should get the people out and shut it down?"

"A lot of people would die if you tried that. Of course, people are going to die whatever you do."

"Why? What are you talking about?"

Bernhardt kept his eyes on the road. "You're far better off not knowing."

"I'll be the judge of that."

"Sorry. Not this time."

Jeni glared at him. "I've been way too patient and trusting with you."

"Probably." He concentrated on the road and didn't say anything more.

Jeni pushed her growing anger aside.

What was he talking about?

She thought about shutting the portal down immediately or letting the dead-man switch shut it down.

Finally she said, "Everyone I sent on the yacht would be trapped there forever. When the yacht gets back, I'll seriously consider closing it. But there's so much I could do over there."

"People on the yacht knew the risks. If you have to shut it down, you have to shut it down, Adam Stine or no Adam Stine. He's a good guy, but not worth losing everything over."

"I expect loyalty from my employees, but I also return it."

"Commendable, but also expensive."

"Maybe. Have I ever said anything that led you to believe I ordered you to kill someone or hurt someone?"

"Don't."

"Don't ask that question or don't ask you to kill anyone?"

"Both."

"When I hired you I wanted a cross between a soldier and a cop. I wasn't looking for a killer."

"Sometimes a soldier or a cop has to be a killer."

"I guess. Do you understand why I built the portal?"

"Not really."

"Any theories?"

"One or two." He turned the car down the access road to the data center. "You have world class business instincts—among the best in the world. Then you have an idealistic side. When you think with your heart, you're dangerous—to yourself, to anybody around you. Anybody you're trying to help. The portal is you thinking with your heart. It will end badly."

"Maybe. Maybe I want everything I gave up to get rich to mean more than it has so far. I'm sorry I asked." Jeni turned away.

They went through security. No one asked to look in the gym bag she carried. Bernhardt walked through the portal with her.

As they stepped out on the other side he said, "Hollsworth had people watching Darla Smith."

"I know. Do you have a problem with that?"

"You're the boss."

"Any reason I shouldn't trust him?"

Bernhardt shrugged. "You already know the answer. I'm going to review security over here."

Jeni rushed upstairs and decrypted the waiting message.

Hi Jeni.

This will be brief. Everyone on the crew is sick, including me. The doctor says it's probably a Timeline X flu, but it's a bad one, maybe even deadly. He's too weak to get out of bed, so I'm doing what I can to make people comfortable. That isn't much, and I feel my fever going up. There's a storm coming in, so I have to get the radio gear stowed while I still can.

This has been the adventure of a lifetime, and however it turns out, thank you for making it possible.

Adam

Jeni went through the standard routine to remove traces of the decrypted message from her computer. She pulled up a picture of Adam from before the trip, touched one finger to his face.

"Dangerous to everyone around me."

Chapter Thirty-Six

SCOTT KEPT PADDLING while Peter divided his attention between the three gashes on the Hispanic man's arms and back and bailing water from the canoe. Scott's patch job had finally failed and water spurted in from the side.

"Where did you get this canoe? It's a piece of crap."

Scott grinned. "I pieced it together with superglue. Used duct tape on the paddles. I couldn't find any chewing gum or baling wire." The grin faded. "Any idea where the co-pilot is?"

"Yeah. Burgen's crew has him."

"Still alive? He's our ticket back."

"I don't know." Peter finished binding the last of the wounds. "That won't hold. This guy needs stitches."

"Is it enough to keep him from bleeding to death?"

"Enough to slow it down. He'll have nasty scars if he makes it through, as well as a good chance of infection."

Scott looked downriver. The Romans had followed them along the riverbank for a mile or two, but had to stop on the other side of a large creek that ran into the river. "So now we're between their rearguard and the main group. Any ideas?"

"Why don't you just run home? It shouldn't take long."

"To the nearest portal?" Scott laughed. "Six hundred to eight hundred miles? Over rough ground, I might make twenty-five miles a day. I could get back in a month. The world gets a lot bigger without cars and airplanes."

"Speaking of airplanes, why didn't you stay with the plane? They'll eventually send help."

Scott guided the canoe around a partially submerged log. "I figured you needed rescuing, and even if you didn't, two towns full of Indians did. I left notes."

"How do you expect to do the rescuing?"

"Of the Indians? I don't know. Any ideas?"

"It would be a lot easier if I didn't have to nursemaid you and Mr. Gracias here."

"So who got trapped by a bunch of low-brows and who got away? I forget. Oh, and who rescued who back there?"

"The game's just getting started. I had already escaped anyway."

"Sort of. And there's a player in the game we haven't identified yet. Any idea who shot that other arrow?"

"My money is on survivors from the towns. If there are any, they'll be a tad irritated."

"These guys took several thousand people. What are they planning to do with them?"

"I don't know." Peter bailed furiously, then tossed the jug to the bottom of the canoe. "Is this thing going to hold together?"

"No guarantees. I have more glue if we can find a safe place to patch it."

The injured man groaned and tried to sit up. He didn't get far, but the effort opened up his wound. Peter went back to trying to stop the bleeding, but only partly succeeded. "You awake? Habla español?"

"I speak English."

"How did you end up out here?"

"I was looking for a job. I have a wife and three kids back in Guatemala."

Scott shipped the oars and leaned back to take over the bailing. "So you got a job with Burgen. Only it didn't work out too well for you. What happened?"

"They took us to a room in the basement and started shooting. I got away and kept running. They finally caught me on their way to raid the towns. Where is this place, and what are those things that chased me?"

"You may have noticed we're not in Kansas anymore," Scott said.

"What?"

"Never mind. What did you do before they started shooting?"

"Built a big building. Underground. A basement? And a big place to keep food cold."

"Why did they start shooting?"

"They wanted us to keep working after our contracts were up, but the men wanted to get their money and go home. They said okay and that they would get our stuff, but when we went down to the basement, they shot us."

"Sounds like the Burgen labor relations people need to work on their technique," Peter said. "Scott, I hear you and Jeni Burgen are close. Maybe you can chat with her about that."

"None of this sounds like her. She doesn't work this way. Doesn't have to. Why not pay them and send them back home? Less risky."

"Maybe something they saw told them they were in Timeline X. Maybe they saw something else she couldn't risk them talking about. Maybe she's running out of money. Bullets are a cheap way to pay off your workers."

"We would have picked up on it if she was short on cash. And why would they kill them at their base? Timeline X is a big place. Easy to lose bodies." Scott guided the canoe out of a current that pushed it too close to the bank. "They built a big basement and a freezer. Did they have you build anything else?"

"Big fences. Two of them. One inside the other. Tall with

barbed wire at the top. Like at a prison. Very big. It would hold thousands."

"A prison," Scott said. "Interesting, but not enough to get them killed. And it could be for keeping people out instead of keeping them in. Did they kill everybody?"

"Some they separated out. Mechanics and electricians. I don't know what happened to them."

"Can you get us back there?" Scott asked.

"Will you kill them?"

"We may have to try." Scott went back to paddling upriver. "I guess we have a destination."

Chapter Thirty-Seven

JENI SAT AT her desk, staring at a blank computer screen. Finally she pulled the shotgun out of the gym bag and examined it. It was loaded. She figured out how to fire it if she had to. She thought about going back through the portal, but decided she was as safe in Timeline X as she would be on the other side. She set the gun aside and brought up the results of the background checks for Andy and Bernhardt.

She studied Andy's background in depth, probing for anything she might have missed that would tie him to organized crime or give him a motive for dealing with them. When she finished, she called Bernhardt's office. "I've been looking at Andy's background checks."

"Did they do a good job? That was before my time."

"They didn't find much. There doesn't seem to be much to learn about the man. His parents were drones: worked all day, lived in the suburbs, solid working-class. Both dead now. The background check didn't find anything suspicious about the deaths."

"Doesn't mean there wasn't."

"Not likely. His dad died of a heart attack when Andy was ten, and his mom died of Alzheimer's in her early fifties. He was twenty-five."

"That's early onset," Bernhardt said. "It runs in families. Maybe it's starting early with him."

"Do you really think that?"

"No. He's just a psychopath."

"Why do you say that?"

"Because I know him. Other kids in the family?"

"And you won't tell me what you know, of course." Jeni scanned the file. "Two older sisters, both dead."

"Now *that's* suspicious."

"Pancreatic cancer and liver failure," Jeni said. "His mom's medical bills ate up most of what the family saved, so not much inheritance to fight over. Bad luck, bad genetics or maybe they lived on a toxic waste dump. He was a paramedic. Tried to get into med school. Couldn't handle the math. Then he switched to law school and found his niche. He started with criminal law, then went corporate. He did well, and we snapped him up. He didn't represent anybody with organized crime ties."

"What made you think he might have?"

"Long story. I don't have time for it now."

"What about women in his life?"

"I'll check." Jeni scanned the file again. "Short term only. Nobody lasted long enough to be a factor. I don't know about after we hired him. I suppose we could check for someone now."

"I checked into Danny Minh. You don't want anything to do with him."

"Tell me something I don't know."

"He was involved with Darla Smith when she was a runaway. He's the only reason she wasn't just a victim. Real street gangs normally just screw over slumming rich kid wannabes."

"Again with the 'tell me something I don't know.'"

"You've probably figured out that he's into smuggling just about anything—drugs, women, babies, stolen car parts, toxic waste, DDT, Freon, excess tires. He's a full-service slime-ball."

"I can attest to that. Is Darla Smith still part of his slime-ball service?"

"If she is, she's hiding it well enough to fool a very good police department. Danny Minh is going to be a problem. Unless he's an idiot, he'll figure out about the portal if he hasn't already. Why else would the BTI be interested in the Ohio compound? Once he figures it out, he'll think of a whole lot of uses for a private portal to Timeline X."

"He thinks we're already using it for something he could help us with. Any idea why he would think that?"

"I'll look into it."

"I took another look at your background too. You've had a family tragedy or two yourself."

"Yep. That I have. That was a long time ago though. It's not something I talk about."

"How did Samantha Murphy end up dead?"

"I think I just figured that out."

"So tell me."

"You're better off not knowing. Let me do my job."

Scott paddled by several riverside Indian towns as the sun gradually slid toward the treetops behind him. Armed Indians paced them along the riverbank at their closest approach to each of the towns, but didn't attempt to stop them or communicate with them. The river was empty of Indian canoes, and between towns it was silent in a way Scott had rarely encountered in the home dimension. No electric hums. No car noises. No distant trains. No buzz of conversation.

The silence seemed to bother Peter, and he filled it with uncharacteristic chatter. "Can you speak the language?"

"Maybe. There were Eastern Sioux tribes and maybe Iroquois speakers along the Ohio River back home. It would be like speaking Spanish to an Italian, but I could ask basic stuff."

"Why are they letting us float through their territories?"

"They're spooked and rightly so," Scott said. "Guns and wars that destroy whole towns are new concepts for them. They don't know where we fit in, so they watch us, but they don't do anything to set us off. Just hope nobody gets brave and stupid."

"Now tell me again why we're headed upriver toward a bunch of guys with guns instead of downriver to wait for help."

Scott stopped rowing. "As I said, you needed rescuing. I figured it would take a few hours with no radio contact for the powers-that-be to get worried, then another week to align the bureaucratic stars and organize another flight here."

"So we wait another five days and they come get us."

"I left a note saying I headed upriver," Scott said. "I also have a bad feeling about what's going to happen to the people they hauled off. I don't think they'll live long enough to get rescued."

"You think Burgen and company are going to kill them?" Peter repatched the wounds on the Hispanic man's back while he talked. "This needs stitches; it's getting worse. I don't want to think about how much blood he's losing. I think there may be internal bleeding too. Did your Indian immersion teach you how to handle people with big slashes in their backs?"

"Not enough to do better than you're doing."

"If they're planning to kill them, why didn't they just do it instead of hauling them hundreds of miles?"

"I don't know. I do know that they have too many prisoners. Those two towns had at least five thousand people between them, maybe more. Figure several hundred dead—no more than a thousand at most. Figure some escaped and others are out trading or hunting. Burgen still has three or four thousand what? Hostages? The Indians with them may take a share to adopt or torture, but we're still talking thousands of people."

"So they use them as slaves the same way they used Gracias guy's buddies."

"That's too many people. How many employees do you think came through Burgen's portal?"

"As many as she wanted."

"Come on; you're supposed to be a professional. She has a few dozen at most. Most of them probably don't know they're in Timeline X. And most will be spending their time keeping things from falling apart."

"That's about right," Peter said. "Any more and you couldn't keep it a secret. So like I said, she has as many as she wants—as long she doesn't want more than a couple dozen."

"And two dozen guards can't control that many people, not for long and not if they're trying to get work out of them."

"The Indians will be scared, unarmed and up against rifles. A lot of their men are dead. So Burgen and company separate out the kids and threaten to kill them if there's any trouble. They keep them terrorized. It's doable."

"Maybe. I don't think that's what they're planning though."

"So what are you saying? What are they going to do?"

"I don't know. This mass kidnapping doesn't make sense, and that worries me." Scott leaned back and nodded to the wounded man. "Is he awake?"

"No, and *that* worries *me.* What do we do with him?"

The man's eyes flickered open. "Give me a gun and let me avenge my brothers, my cousins and my childhood friends."

"We have a slight shortage of guns at the moment."

"It doesn't matter. I'm going to join them soon. Avenge them for me." His eyes drifted shut.

Peter said, "Speaking of vengeance, it would be nice to have a weapon other than a sword."

"I could make you a bow, but it would take a year for you to get any good with it. That does give me an idea though." Scott steered the canoe to a sandy beach in a buffer zone between two towns. "Keep an eye open for the locals, Peter, and see if you can patch the leaks. I'm going to get us some firepower."

"You're giving me orders?"

"Call them suggestions. Do you want to keep bailing? Do you want the canoe to sink? If not, patch it."

Scott scouted through the edge of the forest cutting half a dozen straight saplings off at their bases with his pocket knife. He returned to the canoe and stripped off the branches, then carved the thicker ends to a point. "Spears. They aren't much, but if you hit someone with them, he'll think twice about chasing you."

Peter hefted one of the crude spears. "Or you could make it a real weapon." He found a pair of scissors in the plane's emergency kit, carefully broke them and filed sharp points on the fragments. He super-glued the pieces to the points of spears. "Now we've got weapons; pathetic, but weapons."

They relaunched the canoe. Scott turned the radio on and scanned for signals. "Nothing yet, not that I expected anything. Our best bet is to catch up with them before they get back to the portal, do a night raid and rescue the co-pilot if he's still alive. Night-vision goggles will help. We can't be more than four or five hours behind them and the goggles should keep us moving longer than they can. We keep paddling, and raid their camp tonight."

"Tonight?"

"They'll be back to their base by tomorrow night. So we rescue the co-pilot, then make a dash downriver, fly back and hope Chad can light a fire under the powers that be. BTI raids the portal and rescues the Indians. You shack up with some random woman with a Barbie-doll figure and all is right with the world."

"Can we catch them in this leaky old tub? And even if we do, are we sure they don't have night-vision equipment? It's not that expensive. And the co-pilot is probably already dead."

"Okay. You're the field agent. Have any idea how to rescue a couple thousand Indians from guys with guns who outnumber us five to one, and have Indians and Roman pseudopeople as allies?"

"I think you had the right idea back there. Run."

Chapter Thirty-Eight

JENI WENT THROUGH the background checks again. I'm missing something important. She pushed away from her desk and thought about the message from Adam. I may have killed him. Why couldn't I be happy with what I have? Why do I have to change the world? I know what's going to happen over here though, and I can't let that happen.

She had a landline running through the portal, with only two points of access, one in her office and one in Bernhardt's. She impulsively dialed Danny's number.

"I've been thinking about your offer."

"Good. What do you have in mind?"

"There are some areas that would need to stay off-limits. Where do you think we can help each other?"

"Mostly in the medical area."

"We don't do anything medical, unless you count computer programming for hospitals and pharmaceuticals."

"Of course you don't. Maybe you can think of some other line you're overlooking. That's what I'm interested in. It doesn't fit your corporate image anyway and to be blunt, you're not doing it that well. I traced it back to you, no problem, which says you need a pro involved."

Jeni hesitated, not sure how to proceed without revealing her ignorance. "That does worry me, as you might imagine. Then there's the little matter of the guy who's handling this nonexistent business. He might get talkative."

"I have ways of making sure people don't get talkative. Or you can take care of him your way."

"You sure you can handle him?"

"Hollsworth? Not a problem. Him not getting talkative can be part of the deal if you say the word."

"I'll get back to you on that."

"Yeah, the thing is, I don't like to dance. If you're ready to do business, give me a call. Otherwise, don't waste my time."

He hung up. Jeni tossed the phone down and paced. What was he talking about? What was Andy up to? Drugs? A meth lab? A marijuana plantation?

That's not big enough to get Danny Minh interested.

Some kind of exotic drug the Romans or Indians developed? Something new and unknown that gave an exotic high? That sounded a little more reasonable.

Jeni called up the cargo list from the yacht's last trip. Nothing suspicious, but of course that didn't rule out something smuggled in the crew's personal affects or simply left off the cargo list. She also went back and decrypted the messages from both trips, reviewing them for signs of a candidate drug. The messages were frustratingly vague on Roman drug use. As far as she could tell, the Romans used alcohol as their drug of choice, and the alcohol didn't seem to have any unusual properties. She skimmed the detailed reports on local Indian life. They used mildly alcoholic drinks brewed from berries, but none of their drugs seemed particularly potent.

Jeni stood and stretched. She strolled to the balcony and let the sun and breeze play over her as she worked the stiffness out of her muscles. When she went back in, she searched the Internet for references to Roman drug use in the home timeline as well as drug use in ancient civilizations. After more than an hour, she leaned back. Nothing to write home about. Nothing that would have Danny Minh wanting in.

If it isn't drugs, what is it?

She turned back to her computer.

What if it's something else? Some kind of medicine? Why would it need to be smuggled? A poison?

Poison fit her image of the Romans, but she couldn't figure out any way to test the idea. "Mystery deaths? Convenient deaths? How do I research that?" She searched the Internet as best she could.

Frustrated, she called one of her security people, a man who predated Bernhardt and one she thought would be reasonably independent.

"Jeni here. I need to ask you a question totally off the record and totally confidential."

"Okay."

"Do you have your ear to the ground enough to know about any pattern of unexplained or unusual deaths, maybe of witnesses to crimes or people whose deaths would be convenient to someone else?"

"There are always unusual deaths in those kinds of circumstances. If a witness's testimony is about to put someone powerful in prison, the witness tends to end up dead."

"But anything unusual about the pattern or the causes?"

"Not that I know of, and I would probably know unless the police departments are playing it close to their chests. Does that help?"

"Some. Thanks." Jeni hung up and leaned back in her chair. She stared at the background file.

"Hollsworth, what are you up to?"

The Ohio River had been devoid of other canoes since Scott started out on it, but now river traffic cautiously came back to life. Canoes scuttled past in both directions, moving fast and avoiding Scott's little party. He grew arm-weary and his legs cramped, but he kept paddling against the current, scanning the river ahead for signs of the party they pursued. He saw no trace of the Romans or Burgen's people.

The sun sank in the sky, and the trees cast long shadows on the water. Scott's tired eyes kept seeing motions he at first interpreted as a fleet of canoes ahead of them. With each false alarm he pushed himself harder, digging into a dwindling reserve of stamina.

The patch held, but not completely. Peter spent most of his time bailing. That cut their speed almost in half. The Hispanic man never woke up again and died mid-afternoon. They hastily buried him and put a marker over the grave. They didn't find any form of identification or anything else personal on the body. Scott said, "He said he had a wife and kids. They'll never know what happened to him. We never asked him his name."

Scott went grimly back to paddling as the light dwindled. He studied the shore, making sure they didn't pass their quarry. Finally he put on the night-vision goggles and steered by the fuzzy green images. Only a sliver of moon lit the sky, and the night shift of the animal kingdom emerged from their dens. He saw a large cat lope across a clearing on the bank.

Peter said, "Mountain lion."

Scott's arms trembled with exhaustion, but he forced himself to keep paddling as the moon crossed the sky. He still saw no sign of the Romans. Without warning, he was dodging a floating log. A branch scraped the side of the canoe.

"Any damage?" he asked Peter. "I'm too tired. I didn't see it."

Peter examined the side. "It tore open one of your patches. You're supposed to dodge that stuff. We'll have to land."

"We can't. Tonight is our last shot."

"We have to." Peter bailed furiously. "I can't keep us afloat long."

"So we're giving up on rescuing the co-pilot?"

"Who is probably already dead. Does stopping make rescuing him impossible?"

Scott reviewed his mental calculations. "They'll get to the portal before nightfall tomorrow, so we have to catch them tonight."

"We don't have any choice. We either stop or sink."

They searched for a reasonable spot—one with banks low enough to ease the canoe out of the river without damaging it more, but far enough away from the nearest Indian town to keep from seeming a threat. They found a suitable spot and pulled the canoe up the bank, scraping the already battered hull.

They ate a meager supper of energy bars and used the night-vision goggles to patch the canoe as best they could. They purified water and refilled their water bottles. Scott felt despair course through his body, adding to the fatigue. He checked his watch. "It's close to one. If we rest a couple of hours while the glue sets, we may still be able to catch them before dawn."

Peter went still. Finally he said, "You're serious."

"It's our only shot."

"Will you be able to stand up in two hours? I'm not sure I will."

"We have to. We'll each grab an hour of sleep while the other stands guard."

Scott's eyes kept trying to close, but Peter didn't seem to be in much better shape, so he put on night-vision goggles and took the first shift. His hour passed uneventfully and Peter took the second shift. He shook Scott awake at four in the morning.

"Visitors."

"Why didn't you wake me?"

"A half hour won't make or break us. We needed the rest."

"A half hour might actually make or break us." Scott tried to keep his fury out of his voice. He put an arrow to his bow and goggles on, scanned the forest. "I see three, four, five of something. People?"

"Yeah. Do Indians really attack at dawn?"

"Sometimes. They don't like night attacks because of dew on their bows. A guard will be sleepiest just before dawn. Can you see them well enough to know they're Indians and not Romans?"

Peter shrugged. "I think so."

"They're probably a hunting party, trying to figure out if we're a threat. We have to get rid of them fast."

"And if they decide we aren't a threat?"

"Then they'll try to figure out if we're vulnerable and if attacking us is worth the hassle. If they're going to attack, they'll send for reinforcements. We need to get them talking." Scott stood and held his bow so he could quickly put an arrow to it if necessary. "Time to establish a psychological edge." He raised his arms to the sky and intoned, "London bridge's falling down, falling down," in a deep, slow voice. Then he held an arrow at arm's length and moved his arm slowly until the arrow pointed directly at one of the lurking Indians. Then he did the same with the next Indian, letting the arrow slide past, then angle back.

Peter snorted. "Can they even see this little charade?"

"Oh yeah. There's a moon. They see me."

"Are you sure this isn't going to get us burned at the stake?"

"Not really. The mythology may have changed enough to make this backfire. It's worth a shot though. We can't beat five of them, and even if we could, killing them would bring their tribe down on us. Now we see if we can learn anything from them." Scott switched to Sioux. "Lurkers in the dark, my arrow sees you. It sees your livers. We are strong, but seek only a night of rest."

Scott waited as the Indians silently moved closer together. "Looks like they're thinking about it." He switched to a simplified Iroquois and repeated the message.

The Indians responded to that. One of them stood, hands empty. "Are you of the firestick men?" The question came back in a barely recognizable Iroquois dialect.

Scott glanced at Peter. "He wants to know if we're firestick men." He switched back to Iroquois and lied. "We have firesticks, but we are not of the same people."

"Are you their friends or their enemies?"

"We neither fight for or against them."

The Indian asked a series of probing questions about the power and limitations of the firesticks. Scott kept his answers vague. He probed back, picking up a couple of interesting pieces of information. As near as he could figure, the Burgen party and their allies had passed by two hours before sunset. The Indian allies were an Iroquois-speaking group from near Lake Erie. He mentally named them Eries, though he had no evidence they descended from the historic tribe of that name. He also got a better idea of their number—around five hundred Erie, a dozen Romans and ten gunmen. He relayed that to Peter, then whispered, "This guy is sharp. He's asking all the right questions."

The Indian asked, "Do your people fight to destroy, like the firestick people?"

"What's he saying?"

Scott translated. Peter asked, "How else could you fight?"

"Small-scale raids to steal women or show off. Real wars don't usually start until there isn't enough farmland to go around. Population's getting dense enough here that they have real wars, but apparently not often." In Iroquois Scott said, "Only against enemies like the firestick men."

After a long pause the Indian asked, "Why have you come?"

Scott claimed they were searching for a lost friend and would leave at first light. The Indians wandered off as Scott and Peter paddled away, pushing desperately to make up the lost time.

Chapter Thirty-Nine

JENI TURNED ON the lights as the sun faded below the horizon. Her neck felt stiffer than ever. Bernhardt called her on the local line.

"Busy? I haven't seen you all day. I wanted to make sure you're still kicking."

"Yeah. And no Indians have bothered me."

"That won't happen again. It shouldn't have happened in the first place."

"That I'll buy."

"No. I mean the likelihood of all of the failures happening the way they did is so close to zero it nags at me. Something weird went on, and I'll have to take care of the source one of these days."

"You seem to be hinting that he had help from someone on the inside."

"If he did, I'll take care of it."

"So is Andy smuggling drugs or poison from over here?"

The line went silent for a very long time. Finally Bernhardt said, "No."

"Are you sure?"

"Yep. As sure as I am of anything in this life. "

"Excuse me if I check that myself. I'll be going through the videos of all the transits through the portal."

"I don't have you on the authorized list."

"Then you need to get me on it."

"That I can do. Give me a day or two to get the request through IT."

"No later than tomorrow morning at nine o'clock. I'm not a patient person."

"You won't find what you're looking for in the videos."

"And what do you think I'm looking for?"

"Andy hauling pot or cocaine through the portal. You won't see that. That's penny-ante stuff and if he wanted to do it, he could do it somewhere else a lot easier."

"No police with jurisdiction over here."

"Nobody's smuggling drugs or poison through the portal. I would find out, and I'd shut it down hard. Let me handle this. It'll work out much better that way."

"For who?"

"For everybody involved, including you. Well, not quite everyone."

"For Andy?"

"We'll have to see. Ultimately there's only one way to deal with a blackmailer."

"Andy's blackmailing you?"

"You don't want to know. By the way, I just found out Scott White's brother is working as a temp for Burgen."

Jeni put her hand over the phone's microphone and swore. She kept her voice calm when she turned back to the phone."That's interesting."

"Yeah. That's what we get for bringing in people we didn't have time to screen."

"Keep an eye on him, and have the temp agency move him somewhere else."

"Too late. He got halfway through the tunnel to the portal before security caught him."

"How did he get that far? Your security isn't looking good

these days."

"It seems to have developed holes. Maybe you'll know why when you look at the video tomorrow morning."

"Does he know what the portal is?"

"He's doing a good job of acting like he doesn't."

"What are you going to do with him?"

"Well, that's a buck-stops-at-your-desk decision. Unless you tell me to deal with it."

"What would you do if I did?"

"You won't."

"No. I won't. I don't operate that way. You know that, don't you?"

"I've had my doubts a time or two," Bernhardt said. "But yeah, I know."

"Where is he now?"

"Cooling his heels in the data center HR office. He never made it to Timeline X and he's seen nothing that would prove there's a portal here. We can't legally detain the guy. We could turn him over to the police for trespassing, but he works here. Hard to claim trespassing. Sometimes I wish corporations had dungeons, but he's among the least of my worries right now."

"You know everything that's going on here, don't you?"

"Maybe not everything, but a lot."

"So why not tell me? Are you a part of it?"

"A part of Andy's ghoulish little schemes? Not a chance. I looked the other way for a while, but that's over, and I would never have done even that if I'd known how far he would go. You really don't want to know what's going on. This needs to be handled without you ever finding out what you unleashed."

"I'll find out. You need to tell me."

"Legally and morally you don't want to know. You want to be the one who saves the Indians, the one who keeps them from getting screwed like they were back in real history. That won't work, even though it's a good goal, and your plans are going to get a lot of people killed. You're thinking with your heart again. The destruction your plans cause will be bad enough. It'll scar you. It'll haunt you. But it's nowhere near as bad as what I'm going to put a stop to."

"Where did that come from? It doesn't sound like you."

"What, I'm not smart enough? Boss lady, I've seen the world and know how it works. I do my job, and I scowl and I intimidate people, but I think too. You're unleashing a whirlwind with the best of intentions. Maybe it's worth it. Maybe it's the only way. I've held my tongue on that. I've also held my tongue on other things, for my own reasons. If you ever find out, you'll wonder how I slept at night. Remember though, I've never stopped trying to protect you. I'm not going to stop trying to protect you, no matter how much it costs me. I said I work for the brand, and I do. No matter what."

"I believe you, though it doesn't make a lot of sense to. But I'll still need access to those videos tomorrow morning."

Scott's muscles throbbed. He felt listless from not running. He wrapped pieces of cloth around his hands again to keep the blisters from popping and getting rubbed raw.

They moved upriver through the darkness. Peter did his share at the paddles, and his wiry strength had the canoe moving faster than Scott expected.

After less than an hour of paddling, the sky began to lighten. Scott saw no sign of their quarry. At a little after five, he had to admit defeat.

"They'll be up and getting ready to move by now. We might be able to jump in and grab the co-pilot if we catch them loading, but we can't outrun guns."

"No chance at another night? Are you sure?"

"I'll check again." Scott studied the map as Peter took his

turn at the paddle. "We're no more than twenty-five miles from the portal. That's maybe four hours. It's time to get our wits about us."

"And you have no idea what we're going to do when we get there, do you?"

"Not a clue now. I'm going to be a tad upset if we come to their campsite in the next half hour."

They paddled in silence for several minutes. Scott watched Peter. The agent was filthy and had to be exhausted, but he still managed to make paddling the canoe up a silent river look sophisticated.

Scott said, "You're the James Bond wannabe. What are you going to do? Here's an idea: get captured along with some random girl you had a one-night stand with—oh wait, a seven-minute stand—get suspended over a volcano or a nuclear waste dump by your toenails. And then, when the villainess turns her back, pull out some gizmo and do something improbable that causes everything to blow up. But escape and slide out the door to the portal with your bimbo just as it implodes and traps the villainess halfway through. There you go. Simple, but it should work."

Peter laughed. "Do I get to leave a geeky Indian wannabe behind?"

"That wouldn't be all bad. I could survive over here. Of course I'd be old by age forty, and I'd have to bite my tongue constantly to keep from changing the culture."

"Seriously, I have no idea what we're going to do. Hitting them at night probably wouldn't have worked, but it was worth a try. Now, I have no idea. Sneak close to their base, get pictures, then row back to the plane and wait to be rescued? Or do we just head back now? Your ideas any better?"

"I've been playing it by ear since you got trapped in the net. I'm pretty good at it."

"Until you hit the wall."

The sun rose and sweat beaded on Scott's forehead. It trickled down his aching arms and sore back. They saw no sign of Burgen's men. "They'll be back home behind all their defenses before we can do anything."

"All of them?"

"Probably not. If the Erie live the same place over here that they did back in our history, they should have already split off."

"So we only have to deal with a dozen or more guys with guns and some unknown number of Romans."

River traffic abruptly came to life. Dozens of canoes passed them, each canoe thirty to fifty feet long and crewed by a dozen or more Indians. The canoes were piled with cargo—mainly bales of fur, pottery and elaborately carved wooden statues.

Peter stared at the canoes and whispered, "Those things are huge."

Scott nodded. "Indians in the northwest had bigger ones—up to a hundred feet long and they held up to sixty people."

They eventually found the place where Burgen's people had spent the night. Scott waded in and examined the area. "Not many Indians. I think they split off and headed home. We're no more than an hour behind them. Definitely the guys we're after."

"So now you're a tracking guru," Peter said.

"Isn't everybody?" Scott stretched his legs and his back. "The tracking comes with the Indian immersion stuff. Unfortunately, it didn't include a rowing experience to get me in shape for this. I'm one solid mass of aches and cramps." He did a quick mental calculation. "We might catch them before they get home, but we won't catch them before they get close. We're making better time, but we would have to nearly double their speed to catch them and we aren't going to do that in this leaky, patched-up canoe."

They paddled on. A half hour later they rounded a bend and Scott shipped his paddle.

"Hang back. I was wrong." He pointed upriver. "We just caught up with them."

Jeni stayed in her office, the shotgun in easy reach. Andy called on her cellphone, but she didn't answer. She spent several hours catching up on routine business work. She reset her dead-man switches, made sure the door was locked and crawled into bed.

In the morning she checked for messages from the yacht. There weren't any, and that fact gnawed at her as she checked her email and voicemail. She took care of the most important of the messages, then brought up the video from the portal. She found numerous gaps in the records, going back several months.

She called Bernhardt. "Where are the rest of the videos?"

"You have all that I have."

"There are at least twenty gaps, some of them hours long. One of them covers the time when Scott's brother wandered in. So where's the video?"

"It didn't get made."

"The cameras were turned off? The only people who can authorize that are you and me, and I didn't, so you did and at least twenty times. Why?"

"I didn't have a choice. Self-preservation. It's not in your interests to know more. I'm trying to protect us both."

"Do you know what happened during those gaps?"

"I didn't at first, but I can guess most of it now."

"And you're not going to tell me."

"I'll take care of it. Trust me."

"I've done too much of that already."

"Yes, you have."

"And you want me to do more. I didn't get here by trusting people that much. When are you going to show me a reason to trust you?"

"Another couple of days. Maybe three at the most, and then

you'll be happy with what happens, at least for a while. I'll be happy with what happens. You'll get to go on with your plans and you'll get to find out where playing God leads. Then you'll be sorry you tried it."

"I'm not trying to play God. I'm doing what has to be done. I know it won't all be sweetness and light, but what I'm planning is the best way."

"You're going to get a lot of Indians killed."

"Most of them are as good as dead if I don't do anything. People from our timeline will come over for the natural resources or to convert them to the one true religion, and when we're done most of them will end up dead."

Scott let the current slow the canoe. He carefully made no abrupt moves.

Peter said, "They're looking us over from the back canoe."

"I know."

Scott made sure his bow and quiver were close at hand. "No abrupt changes. They'll probably notice we aren't Indians. If they do, we head for the bank. We can't outrun them on the river."

A tall man in western clothes stood partway up in the rear canoe and pointed binoculars at them.

"We're humped," Peter said.

They dug their paddles in and headed toward the nearest bank. Someone yelled from the canoes ahead of them. Scott felt the paddle jerk, then it broke in half in his hands as he dug in for the next stroke. He heard two quick rifle shots. The canoe glided sideways. "Paddle broke."

Scott grabbed his bow, let an arrow fly. A man in the nearest canoe stared down as the shaft sprouted from his chest. Scott cringed, but shot again. Several gunshots rang out and the canoe lurched. Scott glanced at the onrushing canoes, then at the bank.

"Too far."

Someone yelled, “Give it up. We can shoot you like fish in a barrel.” A man from the nearest canoe screamed and fell into the water with an arrow in his chest. Gunmen fired several shots at the riverbank, seemingly at random.

Peter shouted, “We’re giving up.”

“No we’re not.”

“Don’t be an idiot. No use getting shot when we don’t have a chance.”

Scott slowly put his bow down. “Okay. Fine.” He thought about diving overboard and swimming for the bank, but realized he’d have little chance of surviving with no food or weapons. He waited numbly as two canoes came close and a couple of scruffy-looking guys in western clothes pushed them into a canoe already crammed with disheveled Indian women and older children. None of the Indians looked at the new captives.

Their captors searched them and tied their hands and feet. A tall man with a bad comb-over flapping in the breeze stared at them from an adjacent canoe. “So, what have we here?”

Scott fluently insulted the man’s mother in an Iroquois dialect. The man laughed. “Okay, I don’t know what you said, but I got the spirit in which it was intended. Now, I know you’re not from over here, so the rest of this talk will be in English.”

“We’re on BTI business. Why did you shoot at us?”

“Hello. Because we’re *not* on BTI business, which means we’re here illegally and doing a whole bunch of illegal stuff, you moron. And I ask the questions.”

“You killed a whole bunch of people back there. How did you capture the one town almost without a shot fired?”

“We have people who do that kind of stuff. Well, sort of people.” Bad Comb-over glanced at half a dozen short, lithe figures in black tunics and hoods clustered at the other end of the canoe and muttered, “Creepy little pieces of crap, but they get the job done.”

"So why did you attack people who weren't doing you any harm?"

"Again, *I* ask the questions. Are you part of the batch that came in that plane the pixies told me about?"

"Nope. We're part of the rescue party. The scouts."

Bad Comb-over nodded and one of his men punched Scott in the gut. "Another rule: no lies."

Scott doubled over, miming more pain than he felt. "If you already know, why ask?"

"Good point. Any reason we shouldn't shoot you and dump your bodies?"

"You might want to ask Jeni Burgen about that one."

The man shrugged. "Why? I don't take orders from her."

"Really? She's somewhere in your chain of command," Scott said.

"Nope. But I do think I'll kick the decision upstairs."

Chapter Forty

JENI RAN UPSTAIRS. She pulled up the code for the security system and patched the portal security subroutine so Bernhardt could no longer turn it off or access it. She grinned.

"Try messing with that, Bernie."

She brought up the messages on the deadman switch and stared at them.

I should send them now, but that was the nuclear option. Not unless I have to or someone's keeping me from deactivating them.

She added several other subroutines to the security code, enjoying the hands-on feel of writing computer code.

She tore herself away from the code and called Darla.

"Heard anything from Scott?"

"Why are you asking? You're not his friend."

"Neither are you. You're just a cop on a case. Have you heard from him or not?"

"No, I haven't. Doesn't Bernhardt have somebody watching him?"

"Not at the moment, apparently."

"What kind of security operation is he running?"

"I wish I knew."

"Back to the 'throw a hired hand under the bus' routine, I see. I'm still not buying it."

"Why would Danny Minh be interested in something medical he thinks I can get him?"

"Medical? Are you making meth or growing opium poppies?"

"I'm not, and it doesn't make sense that anyone I hired would either. It's not that hard to smuggle that sort of thing using normal channels."

"Instead of a portal?"

"You'll have to ask Scott about that." Jeni felt her neck stiffening. *This is pointless. She isn't going to tell me anything useful.* "Something ghoulish."

Jeni didn't realize she'd used Bernhardt's word until Darla asked, "Do you have someone robbing graves over there? Could be a market for grave offerings—arrowheads and the like. That doesn't sound like something Danny would be interested in though, and it isn't medical."

Call waiting beeped on Jeni's phone. She glanced at the ID. *Bernhardt.* "Can you hold? I'll just be a couple of seconds." She clicked over without waiting for Darla to respond.

"Hi."

"Did you take control of portal security away from me and close the emergency doors?"

"Yep."

"You need to open the gates and give control back now—within the next thirty seconds."

"Or what?"

"Or a whole lot of people get killed, probably including both of us. Let me do my job."

"Sorry. I'm through trusting you."

"You need to get out of there then. Get out of the house. Go to the woods and hide. Get out of the compound if you can."

"Why?"

"If I don't have control of security inside of—fifteen seconds now—all hell will break loose and I can't protect you."

"Is that really what you're trying to do?"

"Believe it or not, yes. You need to get out of there."

Jeni pulled the shotgun out from under the blanket on her bed. She held it in one hand and flipped the safety off. She moved to a corner where she could keep an eye on both the windows and the door. "So protect me."

"I'll try."

The line went dead. Jeni flipped back to Darla. "Bernhardt tells me that all hell is going to break loose in a minute or two. Somehow I don't think he's kidding. Stay on the line and don't say anything. I'm going to speakerphone. If I end up dead, I want whoever kills me to fry."

"This is getting melodramatic."

Jeni heard faint, unfamiliar sounds in the hallway. "Just stay on the line and don't make any noise. Please."

Jeni turned on the speakerphone and hung up the receiver. She kept the shotgun aimed at the door. The knob rattled. She focused on it, then glanced at the balcony window in case the noise at the door was intended to distract her. She heard a wisp of sound outside the door, what might have been snatches of whispered conversation. Something slammed against the door. The lock held. Jeni thought about the door in her closet. Not enough time. She watched in helpless fascination as the wood around the reinforced steel cracked under one blow and then splintered under the next.

The door slammed open and short armored figures poured into the room. Jeni fired the shotgun and one of them slammed against the wall. The sound blasted into her ears with a wave of pressure, and the stock of the weapon drove into her shoulder. Then the armored figures poured over her and tore the shotgun away. Someone yelled, "Don't kill her." She recognized Andy's voice. He came in and smiled at her.

"Hi. You think you could do me a little favor? Open up the portal gates. I'm doing business on the side and you're getting in the way."

Jeni tried to jerk her arms away from the armored pixies who were holding her. One of them handed Andy the shotgun. He levered another shell into it. "Nice. I wasn't expecting this. Maybe a pistol, but not a shotgun. How's your shoulder feeling?"

"You're fired, in case you're wondering."

"I wasn't really wondering. Knocking down your boss's door and having a bunch of armed guys—or whatever these things are—grab her is generally considered a firing offense. Not that it happens real often. This is an old-style corporate takeover. The kind where blood gets spilled and people get tortured until they turn over the keys to the kingdom. I wonder why that sort of thing doesn't happen more often."

"Because it doesn't work. People with enough money to make it worthwhile are too smart to let it work."

"Yet here you are and here I am. Maybe we should say *most* people with enough money to make it worthwhile are too smart."

"Where's Bernhardt? I thought he would be here to gloat. You two had me fooled. What an acting job! I thought I had duties divided up between rivals and neither would be able to do anything without the other finding out and telling me."

"Bernie's occupied at the moment. He's dodging bullets. The rest of your security people on this side of the portal are dead."

"So he wasn't in on your penny-ante scheme."

"Nope. Didn't have the stomach for it. I knew he wouldn't. That's why I let the Indian into your room, to make sure you didn't trust him. Big husky guy like that, with a face that scares babies, but it turns out he's soft."

"He did call your little scheme ghoulish."

"So he did tell you what I'm doing. I figured he might. I thought I had enough leverage to keep him looking the other way, but I guess not." Andy stared at her. Then he smiled. "You have no idea what I'm doing. You are an idiot."

"So tell me your genius plan."

"I'll give you a hint. It might give you incentive to cooperate."

"It's too late for that. You could have just asked for a raise."

"I'll have all the money I need. Here's your hint: Some things are much more valuable in pieces."

"Pieces?" Something ghoulish and medical and valuable in pieces? Jeni frowned. Then she glared at Andy. "Organ smuggling. You're going to chop them up and sell their organs? You smarmy little bitch! And you used my portal."

"Yeah, I used your portal and yeah, I'm cutting up your precious Indians for spare parts. They're marvelously healthy in Timeline X. No AIDS. No herpes. No mercury buildup in their cells. Totally free of the contamination every human being in our reality carries around. And no government to protect them, no reporters to put the operation on the evening news."

"That's part of the reason I did the portal. I'm trying to keep them healthy. I'm trying to make them strong enough to keep out psychopaths like you."

"Yeah, that isn't going to work out for you. I have another use for those bodies. They're far more valuable in pieces than digging in the dirt or sitting in a mud hut."

"You are so going down." Jeni tried to jerk her hands free again, but the pixies held her effortlessly. "What are you doing? Starting tribal wars and harvesting organs?"

"Actually, I'm going a step beyond that," Andy said. "I'm bringing back the product, processing it in an area I had built under your nose—in the basement of your wonderful Indian college—and keeping a supply on ice until wealthy, desperate buyers come along. They'll pay for and get quality parts."

Jeni felt anger push her fear aside, but reined it in, focused it.

I've been swimming with sharks for years and beating them.

"When did you turn into a monster?"

"I haven't changed. I'm a lawyer and a good one. That means I can be whatever the jury or the boss wants to see. So, I want the portal gates open now. I'm not a nice person. If using people as spare parts is my business plan, you don't want to make me angry. It would be bad for you and for anyone you care about."

"I don't have anyone you can threaten me with."

"Sure you do. Scott White." He grinned. "Or Adam Stine."

"Good luck getting Scott White or Adam."

"I already have Mr. White. If he doesn't give me enough leverage, I can probably get Adam." He glanced at her desk and then swore. "Who do you have on the line?"

Jeni didn't respond. The dial tone came through the speaker. Andy rushed to the phone and redialed. He wrote the number down. "Darla Smith. Well, I don't have a lot of choice." He dialed a number. "Pick up Darla Smith right now. I know she's a cop. Just do it. Alive would be better but do what you have to."

He slammed the phone down and glared at Jeni. "You won't stop me. You're just dragging more people down with you."

"You're going to kidnap a policewoman who probably already told somebody what she heard you say, probably recorded every word and forwarded the recording to law enforcement?" Jeni forced a laugh. "Talk about painting a target on yourself."

"I'll take my chances. She'll disappear. Boston PD will get info I dug up about her gang years. A Vietnamese gangbanger by the name of Danny Minh will get a lot of heat. He's been having her followed. So she was a mole. Or maybe she left the gang and the gang decided they didn't want her running around with what she knew. It can be handled."

"How did our background checks miss the fact that we were hiring a psychopath?"

Andy grinned. "You knew you were hiring a lawyer. Doesn't that kind of follow?"

Chapter Forty-One

SCOTT WATCHED A spider cross an eight-inch-square window set six feet high in the cement wall. Sunlight caught the spider's web and cast a faint shadow on the concrete floor of the small room Peter and Scott shared. There was no furniture, no cot or chair, just an ugly, poorly formed clay pot in the corner. The window stood open a few inches, and a little air seeped in, not cool, but not as warm as the stagnant air in the room.

The concrete floor felt warm against Scott's bare feet. He felt the added heat from the patch of sun when he crossed it in his pacing. He stood on tiptoe and peered out the window. Two layers of fence topped with barbed wire separated them from a field about the size of two city blocks. Thousands of Indians were crowded into the field, standing or sitting in mown grass five or six inches high. The fences the Guatemalan worker had described stretched around the field. Unpainted concrete blockhouses stood twelve feet high at each corner of the field, outside the fences, each with a high, small window like the one he looked out. More of the ugly clay pots lined the fences, their roughly formed sides making them gratuitously hard to use for their intended purpose. The wind blew gently across the field toward them, carrying the stench of too many people and too little sanitation.

"This isn't intended to be a long-term holding area."

Peter sat in the corner opposite the clay pot. "We knew that. They aren't planning to keep most of these people."

"So they're going to kill them. But why?"

"We'll probably find out. Then again, if the guy in charge is smart, we may not."

"The guy in charge? So you think it isn't Jeni Burgen?"

"There's no way a woman set this camp up. It isn't done the way a woman would do it."

"That sounds sexist."

"It is sexist, but it's also true. This place is totally practical. No aesthetics at all. No woman could bring herself to build something like this even if she tried. She couldn't even let someone else build something this ugly if she had a say in it."

"Bernhardt?"

"No. He's a ruthless bastard, but he has style. Whoever designed this has no style." Peter shifted his weight and a grimace flitted across his face. "Why do you keep pacing? You have to be falling down tired."

"My arms and shoulders are. My legs need a run."

"You'll get all the running you want when we get out."

"So you have a plan?"

"I'm working on it."

"How are we going to get out of this room?"

"That's the part I haven't figured out yet."

"Shaken-Not-Stirred wouldn't let a foot of concrete and a steel door stop him. You don't have a plan. You're just hoping some random bimbo will come along and—" Scott heard the electric whine of a golf cart engine. "Someone's coming."

A face showed briefly at the five-inch-square hole crudely cut in the metal door. The door swung open and Jeni and Darla staggered into the cell. The door slammed shut behind them.

Jeni smoothed her disheveled hair and leaned back against the door.

"Well, I screwed up big time."

Chapter Forty-Two

"I SUPPOSE THIS could be another try at spying on us," Scott said.

Darla shook her head. "Not this time. I wish it was."

"So who was it?" Scott asked. "Bernhardt or the lawyer?"

"Our genius businesswoman here hired a psychopath as her lawyer," Darla said. "I guess the psychopath bit is a given, but more psycho-pathetic than usual. He's planning to cut up the people out there for spare parts—kidneys, corneas, livers, hearts. He says he'll back off on the organ trade if our genius here lets him play puppet-master for her business empire. I figure he'll do everything he planned to do anyway because that's the kind of screwed-up bastard he is. Which leads to an obvious question: don't you do background checks on these guys?"

"Didn't you investigate him when he showed up on your radar?" Jeni shot back. "What did you find?"

"Not much."

Scott turned to Jeni. "Is this all true?"

"Most of it," Jeni said.

"Is Bernhardt Sloan in on it?" Scott asked.

"Apparently not. He mentioned blackmail. He claimed to have a plan that would make it all better." Jeni tiptoed gingerly across the concrete in her bare feet. "They took my shoes. And that sounds so vapid, doesn't it?"

"Yeah, it does. They took ours too," Scott said. "You didn't keep your feet tough after the immersion experience."

"No. I guess that's the least of our problems."

"Not really." Scott felt the rough cement under his feet and wished he had done more to maintain his calluses. "Try running away in bare feet. Unless you're used to it, it'll cut your speed in half. How did Darla get here?"

"He had people watching her. They grabbed her when he figured out he'd confessed with her on speakerphone."

"And then she wimped out—let his people bring me over here," Darla said.

Jeni sighed. "He found leverage that worked."

"What keeps him from using it again?" Scott asked. "Where are you going to draw the line?"

"I have a card or two I can still play. I'm buying time. I bought a couple hundred of those people out there two days."

"But he's still planning to kill them eventually."

"So I buy them another two days some other way and then another two days after that."

"And he gets stronger while you get weaker," Darla said. "Eventually you run out of things he wants and then he goes ahead and does what he planned to anyway."

"Or I outmaneuver him and they all go home alive. Plus Scott walks away with his legs still attached." Jeni grabbed Scott's hand. "Bernhardt is still out there, and he can handle himself. So can I. I've dealt with sharks before. I wouldn't have gotten as far as I have if I was the victim type. I can handle this and I will handle this."

"Oh, you've really handled it well so far," Darla said. "You're locked up in your own compound with no shoes, in a room with three other people, no place to sit or sleep except a concrete floor and—let's just say the sanitation facilities leave something to be desired."

"This isn't over; it's just getting started. And before it's over my psychopath ex-lawyer will get a lesson in why I got to the top and why I stayed there."

As the afternoon went on, the little concrete room got hotter. Scott paced restlessly. He stared out the window. Some of the Indian women pulled the five-inch-high grass from the field and wove it into ingenious but hopelessly inadequate sun shields. Others dug holes with their fingers, apparently trying to burrow to cooler dirt.

Scott studied the door. It fit snuggly against the wall with the hinges on the outside. Whatever locking mechanism it used was entirely on the outside too, with no keyhole on the inside.

Peter said, "I've already checked it out. There's nothing you can do to get it open. I have a few ideas I may try tonight."

The door didn't move when Scott tried to jiggle it. He wandered back and sat along the wall away from the sun. At some point he stopped noticing body odors and the increasing stench from outside. They all sat on the hard cement floor with their backs to the wall, avoiding the sliver of sunlight from the window. Darla claimed a place near Scott. Both Jeni and Peter glared at her.

"Your brother got caught wandering around in the portal tunnel," Jeni said to Scott.

"Great. What did you do with him?"

"I told Bernhardt to find out what he knew and then escort him from the premises. Did you send him?"

"No. I don't get family involved in my business. And L. J. is even less suited to snooping than I am."

The air grew humid, hinting of rain to come. When clouds covered the sun, the temperature became a little more bearable. No one used the clay pot in the corner, though Scott felt an urgent need to do so. "Just another way to humiliate us."

"Talking to yourself?" Darla sounded amused.

"Mixed sexes. No privacy for"—he gestured to the corner—"sanitation. It's a way to humiliate us. He's messing with our minds."

"He's more likely to mess with my kidneys," Darla said. "I'm not putting my butt on that thing. I don't care if my eyebrows are floating."

"We'll eventually have to use it," Scott said. "I'm more worried about something to drink."

Drinks didn't seem to be forthcoming, either for the people inside the room or for the throngs of Indians outside in the field. Scott tried not to think about the Indian kids sitting in the heat with no water.

Peter sat uncharacteristically quiet, but with his face calm. Thunder rumbled in the distance. Scott strolled to the window. "Definitely a storm coming in. Well, at least that'll cool things down. But I wouldn't want to be sitting out in the field when it hits."

Clouds covered the sun and the room abruptly darkened. Darla said, "I haven't seen much evidence of your uber-plan, Miss Has Everything Under Control."

"He's trying to soften us up. He'll stop by when we're hungry and thirsty and hot, and then he'll take me into my office and drink a big glass of water in front of me. Then he'll offer me a deal."

"And what are you going to do about that?" Darla asked. "It looks to me like you're not in the greatest of negotiating positions. All he has to do is wait, and eventually we die of thirst. We're at his mercy. He can starve us. He can beat us up. He can cut us up for dogfood. Anybody have a plan to change this before I bust a kidney? Time is not on our side here."

"Actually, time is on my side," Jeni said. "My ex-lawyer will be back to chat with me in two hours. I hope it's in the middle of this thunderstorm. Thunderstorm or not, he'll be back."

"Then what?"

"Then we'll just have to see."

Thunder rumbled again, much closer this time. Scott asked, "Why did you do it? The portal, I mean."

"Sorry. Not something I want to talk about."

"Why not? We obviously know you built it, since we're on the other side. What are you trying to do? Why did you risk everything on this?"

"You should be able to figure that out. I pretty much told you what I was going to do back in the immersion class."

"You didn't say anything. You only—"

"Yeah. I'm trying to implement the theory I told you about back then." She glanced at the others and then focused on Scott. "On our side of the portal, five or six hundred years ago there were hundreds of very different human cultures, each one of them a natural experiment. How can humans take what they need from nature without destroying it? How can we live together without killing each other as technology makes each of us more powerful? We like to pretend all those other cultures were primitive, unchanging, waiting for our cultural ancestors to come along and lift them out their superstitions—to turn them into parts of modern civilization."

"First, leave me out of the *us* stuff," Darla said. "Half of my ancestry had nothing to do with any of that, and the Irish half was too busy fighting off the British to do anything to anybody else."

"The point is that all of those cultures were changing, developing, each at its own pace and each in its own path. Then our culture spread over the world. We assimilated the pieces of all of those other cultures that fit into ours and discarded the rest. A few places like China and Japan kept to their own path to some extent, but over most of the world, over hundreds of cultures, our ancestors imposed this composite of what fit our current tastes. In much of the rest of the world, knowledge—ways of dealing with nature and other human beings—got lost if it wasn't valuable to us."

"Okay. I'm hot and hungry and thirsty, and I need to pee," Darla said. "And now I'm getting a history lesson. Can plagues of locusts or boils be far behind?"

"Scott asked why I did this. I'm telling him."

"Fine. Get to the point."

"The point is that all of that hasn't happened over here yet, but it will unless somebody stops it. Something stopped technology advances in Europe and Asia, and so far the BTI and its Australian and European equivalents have stopped people from our timeline from coming over here and screwing things up. That won't last. We figured out how to keep a portal open with a fraction of the energy BTI uses. That means people can open portals a lot more places. So what happens when someone can get over here who doesn't care what happens to all of these cultures, all that knowledge?"

"They cut up people for their organs after they capture the overconfident bitch who set up the portal," Darla said.

Jeni glowered at her. "Shut up. I'm tired of trying to make nice with you."

"You were trying to be nice? I didn't notice."

"Eventually the culture that destroyed so much in our history will come here and do the same thing. And if anyone over here has the answers to our problems, that knowledge will be gone. I built the portal so I could stop that destruction from happening again."

"And how did you plan to do that?" Scott asked.

"I plan to do it the same way I talked about in class. I'm going to give hundreds of cultures the ability to take what fits from other cultures and put it into theirs, just as the Europeans did back in our world. I'm starting with the cultures around here—Iroquois, Eastern Sioux and some Algonquin."

"And how is it different when *you* do it from the way the Europeans created their mishmash of cultures?" Darla asked.

"It's voluntary and it's hundreds of cultures both contributing and learning, not just one taking what suits it."

Scott tried to loosen back and shoulder muscles cramped from rowing. Darla reached over and rubbed his back, earning another glare from Jeni. Scott said, "That's why you were researching all of those cultures. And what do you expect to accomplish by all of this?"

"Progress, but not what we typically think of progress. Not more and bigger, but better and more satisfying. I want to see cultures advance in their own way, not our way. I want to harden them against the time when our world seeps over here in earnest. I want them to find solutions we never found and never will because our culture put blinders on us."

"The Sky Queen of the Iroquois," Scott said. "That's what you said when you were drunk and playing Jolene. You're going to bring them today's *fire*—knowledge. You realize they'll burn themselves with it? Knowledge is a magnificent gift, but it's dangerous."

"Which is why we're not sharing knowledge of weapons or how to fight wars."

"You can't separate technology that way. No matter how carefully you choose what you give them, their wars will get deadlier. The cultures that adapt fast will overwhelm the ones that don't and if cultures advance, they'll invent their own weapons. They'll have to if they're going to compete with us. Knowledge is inherently dangerous."

"So is playing God," Darla said. "Even if you didn't have a psychopathic lawyer trying to kidnap people and *process* them for their kidneys, you'd still get a lot of people killed."

"That's what Bernhardt told me. I told him the people are already going to die if I don't do anything. I have a chance of saving them and I'm going to do it."

"Speaking of Bernhardt, what happened to him?" Peter asked.

"Andy hasn't said anything about him since he captured me, which I think means he's still running around loose," Jeni said. "That's one of the reasons I'm not panicking yet."

Scott jerked as lightning flashed and the accompanying thunder cracked almost simultaneously. Rain pelted the concrete roof. He hurried to the window. Indians were leaning back and letting rain fall into their parched mouths. Scott reached out with a cupped hand and let runoff from the partly open window trickle into it. The water soaked into his dry throat without making it feel any wetter. He scooted to one side of the window, cupped both hands under the trickle and said, "Get it while you can."

The others crowded around him, catching rainwater and downing it. The lightning flashed continuously, with thunder following it too close and too loud for Scott's comfort. He kept drinking until he felt bloated. "I wish we had a way to store it."

Peter took his shirt off and held it under the trickle. Scott followed suit. After a couple of seconds, Darla did too.

She asked, "Why are we doing this, other than to show off our finely sculpted bodies?"

"It's the only way I can think of to store any of it," Peter said. "Soak it now. Wring it out and get a few drops in an hour or two when the sun comes out and you'd kill for those few drops."

The rain went on. Scott's bladder berated him for taking on the additional water. He grabbed the clay pot, diverted the trickle of water into it and rinsed it thoroughly. Then he let it fill up.

Darla said, "I'm not drinking out of that thing."

"Wait a few hours or a day and you might."

Scott saw movement out the window.

"Well, Jeni, you were right about one thing. Your lawyer is about to make a visit."

Chapter Forty-Three

JENI GOT A better idea of the lay of the land as they took her from the prison back to her compound. She saw a couple of pixies with short swords and two men with guns, including one of the guys who had kidnapped her from the hotel. He glared at her. The prison was half a mile from her still empty Indian college. That in turn was about a mile west of her main compound.

He had this built under my nose, maybe with my money.

A surge of anger pushed up inside her.

Andy's men drove through the rain in an electric golf cart. They made a point of forcing Jeni to wade through a puddle as she got in the cart. Her soaked clothes stuck to her skin and her feet and legs were cold and muddy by the time they got to her house. They didn't tie her hands, and Jeni thought briefly of making a dash for the woods, but realized that without shoes she wouldn't get far.

Andy sat at her desk when they led her in, his feet on her in-box and her computer keyboard in his lap. He was smoking a cigar, but he coughed as she entered the room, and it took him several seconds to get his breath. He flicked ashes into an ashtray on the desk, cleared his throat and said, "Filthy habit. I'm not sure why people use them to celebrate. It'll take weeks to get the smell out of my office."

He glared at her, challenging her to dispute his claim of ownership.

She wasn't sure she wanted to face that challenge. Her wet shirt and pants clung to her body and the air conditioning chilled her. She fought to keep her teeth from chattering. Her voice sounded weaker and less confident than she intended when she said, "So, are you getting much use out of *your* computer?"

"The previous owner encrypted a bunch of stuff. I'll get that straightened out though; you don't have to worry yourself about that. Do you want to get out of those wet clothes?"

"I'm fine. So, to what do I owe this honor?"

"It seems that the previous owner sent instructions to employees saying I'm fired and should be removed from the premises. You need to rescind that statement."

"I'm afraid I'm going to have to say no."

"And I'm afraid you aren't in a position to say no. How did you send those messages out anyway?"

"Dead-man switch. They would have gone out any time in the last several days if I hadn't kept it from happening."

"When did you set that up?"

"After you had me kidnapped from the hotel."

"Are you sure that was me?"

"I wasn't at the time, but I am now. Were you planning on kidnapping me all along or did you just grab the opportunity?"

"There was always going to be a hostile takeover," Andy said. "I hoped the Murphy investigation would scare you into making this place more self-sufficient and moving money where it would be easier for me to get at, but that wasn't vital. Once we built the prison we had plans to collect you any time if you stumbled across it. We almost got you again at the hotel, but the Boston cop and then Bernie showed up."

"By the way, how is the hunt for Bernhardt coming?"

"He'll turn up. Do you have any more little surprises lined up?"

"One or two. Well, maybe more than that. I guess we'll

have to see."

Andy smiled and strolled up to her. "Make sure you've got a good grip on her hands." His two men grabbed her arms. Andy blew cigar smoke at her and then slapped her across the face. She immediately kneed him in the groin. He doubled over, then toppled to his hands and knees. One of the men punched her in the stomach. Andy struggled to his feet. "No. I'll handle that part of it."

He stood and staggered, then straightened up. "That was just a shot across the bow, to let you know we're not playing by boardroom rules. Your face is not off limits."

"And what I did was a shot to the balls. Your balls are not off limits."

"But the reality is, when it comes to force, if I choose to escalate, I win."

"But what exactly do you win? Can you run my company without me? You're fired. Until I personally tell people otherwise, that's the way it stands. Can you use the portal without me? Good luck going back and forth across company property. Can you access company money without me? Not a cent. You need me."

"But you're only useful to me if you cooperate. If you don't, I'm better off killing you, killing Scott, the policewoman and the other BTI guy. I get rid of witnesses that way. So if you don't cooperate, I will kill you. I can and will kill you painfully by taking off a piece here and a piece there. I may stop a time or two and let you watch my people dismantle one of your friends or one of your precious Indians. At some point, you'll cooperate. That won't give you or your friends back any missing pieces; it'll just keep you from losing more. Your little trick gained you nothing. You still have the same weak hand you had before and just as few options."

"What do you want from me?" She kept her face impassive.

No fear. He'll smell it, like a shark.

"The keys to your kingdom. I'm now CEO. You're Chairman of the Board, but you have no real power. I have free access to the portal and control of security for it."

"And I would have no bargaining chips left. Sorry. That's a *no*."

"For now. I can go slow and give you a lot of chances to change your mind before you're permanently maimed."

"And if I don't change my mind you end up with nothing." Jeni's voice got stronger, filled with a confidence she didn't feel. "So we negotiate. I give you something you want. You give me something in return. Power is only meaningful if it can be used—sort of like the old Soviet and U.S. nuclear standoff."

"You'll see how meaningful my power is."

"And you'll see how meaningful mine is. This is a kidnapping situation. You and your men succeeded in kidnapping me. Now you want to get the most out of that situation. I want to give you as little as I can to get out of this alive. So, there are really only a few questions to negotiate. How much is the ransom going to be? How will I be sure you'll release me once the ransom is paid? And, of course, how do you know that I'll let you get away with whatever ransom I pay?"

"Simple as that, huh?"

"Pretty much. Time isn't on your side. The longer you wait, the more of my booby traps go off and the weaker your position will be. It's in my interest to get this done fast because the BTI is entirely too close. I didn't ask him, but I'm guessing Scott and the other BTI guy got here from one of their portals."

Andy shrugged. "My guys picked them up about twenty miles downriver in a patched canoe. They didn't come through my portal, so they had to come through somewhere else."

"As soon as they linked the portal to my data center, they came through to check it out." Jeni glared at the Romans standing beside her like statues, still gripping her wrists. "The BTI wasn't going to get a search warrant based on what they had, not with the kind of lawyers I can throw at them. And yeah, I still have plenty of good lawyers without you."

"Why does that matter?"

"When Scott and friend or friends don't check in, they'll send somebody else. Neither of us can stop that. Both of us together can't stop that. You didn't even try to camouflage your prison. If they show up and find crimes against humanity, we're both through. There's no place on either version of Earth where we could hide, and no place where we wouldn't die shortly after we got caught. My money couldn't save me and your tongue couldn't save you. You may be a psychopath, but you're a logical man. You know I'm right."

Jeni paused and let the words sink in, studying Andy's face without making a point of it.

I'm right, but how rational a man am I talking to here? He's planning to process *a couple thousand people. Rational may not cut it.*

"If the BTI shows up here, it's your problem," Andy said. "I found out about your operation. You fired me. And maybe you killed yourself when you realized they were closing in on you. That would work."

"But it doesn't give you anything, and it doesn't even necessarily save you." Jeni caught a glimpse of herself in the mirror by the closet and her hand automatically tried to smooth her damp, disheveled hair. She suddenly felt as small and weak and vulnerable as the figure in the mirror, but she didn't let any of those feelings show on her face. "So the issue is, how can we both get out of this with as little damage as possible?"

"And I suppose you have an answer to that."

"I'm willing to listen to reasonable ideas."

"Which means you don't have any."

"Actually I pretty much know what's going to have to

happen."

"Which is?"

"You take your human friends and get all the evidence of your ghoulish hobby out of my compound. You let the Indians in your prison field go. You leave and forget there was ever a portal."

"And what would I get out of it?"

"A generous severance package, including enough money to live comfortably the rest of your life, plus all of the benefits, including free legal services, which you'll need."

"Sorry. I'm a greedy bastard. I'll take three-quarters of everything you own. You can have the portal. I'll take the proceeds of my little operation, process as many more as I can in three days while you're transferring the money and stock, then when the money transfers, I leave."

"And you have no incentive to keep me alive and a lot of incentive to kill me. No thanks."

"Think about the offer while you're lying there in that hot cement blockhouse. You may find it more appealing after a few days without water or food."

"Sorry. No guarantees means no deal."

The storm passed and the sun came out faintly, low in the west. Scott heard the electric whine of the golf cart. The door slammed open a couple of minutes later. Jeni staggered in and flopped down in the corner opposite the pot. She didn't say anything. Her knees drifted up toward her stomach.

Darla broke the silence. "So how did the negotiation go? I see you have a new bruise on your cheek."

Scott stared at Jeni in the fading light. "He hit you." He jumped up. "Are you okay?"

"He slapped me. And then I nailed him where it hurts the most. It was just a little posturing before we got down to business."

The words were strong, confident. Her voice wasn't. A tremor shook the last word.

"One of his guys hit me in the stomach. It hurts, but nothing serious. I'm wet, cold, tired and hungry. What's a little bruise among all that?"

Scott sat beside her. Darla scooted over to his other side and asked. "What kind of business did you set up with a mass murderer?"

"I'm trying to get us all out of here alive." Jeni rolled over so her head rested on Scott's knee. She gazed up at him. "Bernhardt says that when I think with my heart, I'm dangerous to everyone around me. Right now I'm in business mode. Think like a shark, only smarter. Why is it good for him to do what I want him to? Why would killing us hurt him? Will it work? I don't know. I'm not out of cards though, and I gave it my best shot."

The sun set, bringing deep shadows to their prison. Peter moved to the door.

"You might not want to look over here," he said. "You might even want to close your eyes."

Scott saw a brief flash of intense light even through his closed eyelids.

Peter said, "Okay. I'm done."

A hot, harsh smell filled the room.

Darla said, "Cool. I knew you were good at something."

"I cut through the concrete so I can get through to the lowest hinge. If I calculated it right and guards didn't see the flash, I should be able to pry the hinge pin out."

"So when are you going to do the other hinges?" Scott asked.

"When I figure out some way to do it."

Scott snorted. "So you had enough of whatever you used to get to one hinge. That's useful."

"It can be. You just have to know what you're doing."

They waited as the room got darker. Finally Peter said, "Okay. They didn't see it. Let's see if I can get the pin out." He worked at that, then finally said, "Got it."

"I like the flash, but what does breaking one hinge pin do?" Darla asked. "Even if you get the door open, we would still have to cross a football field worth of bare ground guarded by guys with rifles and night-vision scopes."

"It gives us options if things get desperate or if the Indians try to make a break for it."

They sat in the darkness. Scott tried to gauge how much time passed, but without a watch, he couldn't tell. The moon came up and cast a faint light through the window. Jeni shifted her head on his knee and reached up to put her hand on his arm. She said softly, "I'll get us out of here. All of us, including the Indians."

Scott didn't say anything. He didn't move his arm, but he didn't look down at her. He kept peering through the window at the distorted glimpse it gave him of the night sky. The sky went dark for a fraction of a second, and then a thump sounded outside the concrete room, followed by a yell from the watchtower above them. A spotlight snapped on. It was focused lower than the window, but the edge of the light cast a net-like set of triangular shadows over the room. Scott disentangled himself from Jeni, threaded his way to the window and peeked out. One of the guards lay on the ground beneath the window, an arrow through his chest. He thrashed and breathed shallowly, then apparently saw Scott's face through the window. His eyes stared into Scott's until they glazed over and his body grew still.

Peter joined him at the window. "What is it?"

Scott tore his gaze away from the dead guard. "Our mystery bowman shot a guard." He tried to make the words come out casually, but they sounded high and nervous.

Peter glanced at him with an amused grin. "You aren't used to seeing people die up close, are you?"

"Are you? Is anybody?"

"I've seen a thing or two. Get away from the window and act like you don't know what's happening. Other guards will be nervous and they may lash out."

Scott nodded.

They heard shots a few seconds later. "I really hope he figures out about night scopes," Scott said. More shots sounded. "Maybe we should take advantage of the distraction."

"No. If anything, they'll be more alert now," Peter said.

The shots died away. The guards played their flashlights through the window. Scott tried to look harmless.

Which I am at the moment, unfortunately.

The flashlight snapped off and the guards' footsteps receded. "They probably didn't get him," Scott said. "They're too jumpy. So we have a wild card."

"That we don't need," Peter said. "We need them complacent, not scared."

"Dead works too," Darla said.

The night settled into silence. Scott put his head against the wall and closed his eyes. He tried to doze and did manage to seize fragments of sleep. Deep in the night he heard an electric whine and a shouted conversation outside. The door opened and Hollsworth came in, backed by three guards with flashlights and drawn guns.

He gestured to Jeni. "Get out here."

"Why?"

"You know why."

Jeni smiled. "Oh, dear. Did one of the other shoes fall?"

"I'm through messing with you."

"Let me guess. This would be when the emergency gates to the portal close and you can't get them to open. Right?"

"You'll want to open those gates now and disable any other logic bombs you set up."

Jeni stood. "No. You'll want to start the cleanup now. Release the Indians. Give them food and canoes and send them on their way."

"You aren't in a position to make demands. One wave of my hand—"

"And you're trapped here with thousands of kidnapped Indians, probably the remnants of bodies, and the BTI gearing up to come in. I offered you a deal. You need to take it."

Scott stood quietly near the corner, studying the lawyer's face. The flashlights made seeing his expression difficult, but Scott thought he saw desperation in the man's eyes.

Cornered rat. No way out without losing the prey he thought he already possessed. Totally unpredictable. We may have less than a minute to live.

Scott glanced at Peter. Peter shook his head slightly.

Darla cleared her throat. "I'm not sure you want that gate opened. I assume you've heard of Danny Minh."

Andy turned to her. "Stay out of this."

"Just a word of advice. You may think you're tough and ruthless and cynical. To Danny Minh, you're a rich Anglo slumming."

"And what would Danny Minh want with me?"

Darla shrugged. "The real question is what he wants with me. He's had somebody following me for eight years, in every town I've been in. Now I'm somewhere he can't follow, as long as the gate's closed."

"We have security."

"How late is it?" Jeni asked.

"Who cares?"

"As of three a.m., you don't have security in the main compound. The electricity won't work. The computers won't turn on even if you get electricity to them. And electronic locks won't work, so to get back in to my property, you'll have to break in like the common criminal you are."

"I don't believe you."

"Hey. Paranoid gal who started out as a programmer here. I could reverse it, but you'll never know if the reversal is temporary or permanent. When I realized someone inside the company was playing for his own team, I didn't screw around. You literally can't go to the bathroom in this compound unless I let it happen. Now, what are you going to give me so I'll let it happen?"

"Your life until your next shoe falls."

Andy's face showed that trapped rat look again, and Scott tensed, looking desperately for options in case the man started shooting.

"Do you really need all of these Indians?" Darla asked. "What if you let a few go and—"

"Let them lurk in the woods and shoot arrows at us?"

One of the men behind Andy sagged and dropped his light; the point of an arrow protruded through the front of his shirt. Without a word he fell face down on the concrete. His flashlight thumped its way across the room and his pistol fired as he landed. The shot hit a few inches from Scott's leg, sending cement chips flying. One slashed across the top of his foot. He willed himself not to move. The remaining guards looked spooked, ready to start shooting.

Andy yelled, "Get out. Close the door and get the lights off."

One of the other guards grabbed the fallen man's gun and they hustled out, slamming the door behind them. Peter jumped up and quickly rifled the man's pockets. He handed Darla a large pocket knife.

"Hide this where a guy probably won't search if he doesn't know you have it." He emptied the man's pockets and pawed through the contents. He also yanked the arrow out and grabbed the man's shoes.

"That's ghoulish," Scott said.

"But we now have a very slight chance if little Ms. Boardroom Shark pushes her ex-lawyer too hard next time he stops by and he starts shooting."

A couple of gunshots sounded outside, not far from them. Scott peeked out the door slot but didn't see anybody close to the door. "Petey boy is right for once. Your friend Andy was on the edge of shooting us all at least twice during that little confrontation. He would have the second time if our friend in the woods hadn't interrupted."

"I don't think so," Jeni said. "It wouldn't make any sense. He would be trapping himself."

"It doesn't have to make sense; he's not the kind of guy who operates on logic. Otherwise we wouldn't be here. You back him into a corner and he'll do something irrational. It may not be killing you. It may be shooting you in the kneecap. It may be killing one or all of us in front of you."

"If he does that, all deals are off. He gets nothing."

"Are you sure of that?" Scott asked. "More importantly, is he convinced of that?"

"What you want me to do? First Darla jumps all over me for giving in to him on something. Now you're telling me I'm pushing him too hard."

Scott retrieved the flashlight and turned it off. "Just understand that people aren't all logic, even lawyers. They're emotions and self-image and prestige and stubbornness. He was going to shoot somebody. If you corner him again while he has the power to kill us, he *will* shoot somebody. You're on a tightrope. Don't lean too far either way or we'll all fall off."

Another gunshot sounded outside. Scott peeked out the window. Indians out in the field were gathered in tight clumps. "I hope they don't make a break for it; they'll be massacred."

"Nothing you can do about it," Peter said.

"Well, maybe there is." He strode to the window and yelled in an Iroquois dialect, "They can see in the dark." He repeated the message in Sioux, then ducked away from the window and slumped against the wall. "Hopefully that won't draw attention to us."

"I don't see how it could avoid drawing attention to us," Peter said. "But the last thing we need is to witness a massacre."

"You know, the real Bond would've taken advantage of that arrow to grab a gun and take out the lot of them," Darla said. "You're not living up to the image. I'm disillusioned."

"We're not bulletproof."

Scott moved away from the body, as did the others. He tried to avoid staring at the dead man, but his gaze kept drifting across the cell. "Nice people. They didn't even make sure he's dead. Petey, I assume you did."

"Not being a complete idiot, yes, I did. I didn't need to though. He was dead before he hit the floor."

"Still think bows and arrows are toys?"

"In the right hands they can kill. I didn't see you kill anybody with yours."

"I did when they cornered us back in the canoe. Not something I want to think about."

More gunshots rang out in the field, some from the watchtower above them. Scott thought about returning to the window, but the extreme exertions and tensions of the past several days finally caught up with him and he couldn't motivate himself to move. Jeni's head was back on his leg, and her hand rested on his stomach.

When she muttered, "I'll get us out of this," another gunshot from above punctuated her vow.

Chapter Forty-Four

JENI ACTUALLY DOZED briefly, but Andy and his surviving guards came back sometime during the night. According to the dead man's watch, it was three thirty.

Andy gestured to Jeni. "Up. Now. We're going to settle this once and for all."

She stalked to the door. "What do you want me to do?"

"Get the gates open."

"Let some Indians go—women with children, at least. You don't need them and they won't hurt you."

"Fine. Two dozen, and not because I have to. Fewer to feed or hide anyway."

"Make it a hundred."

"Fine. A hundred. I have plenty."

Jeni tiptoed through the muddy grass, her bare feet squelching in the mud. "Well, are you going to let them go?"

"I think I'll wait until morning."

"Okay. And I'll wait here until it happens."

"Don't push it."

"I'm not pushing. I just want to see you do what you said you'd do."

"Fine." He called to the guards on the nearest tower. "Get a couple dozen women with little kids out of there and get them to edge of the compound."

Someone yelled back, "Then what?"

"Tell them to run and never come back."

Jeni waited patiently until the Indians staggered out the gate and on their way. "I'd like to see them actually leave."

"And I'd like to flap my wings and fly," Andy said. "I'll keep my word. No point in not doing it. I have plenty more for my purposes. Now let's see if you keep your word."

"I'll have to get into my house and on the computer."

"That could be a problem."

"You haven't been able to break into the house yet, right?"

"We're working on it. I assume you have some kind of override."

"Maybe. I've never tried to use it."

By the time they reached the house, Andy's men had used one of the electric carts and a ram improvised from a tree trunk to knock one of the doors off its hinges. Andy and a couple of guards escorted her up to her office. "Okay. Turn the computer and electricity back on and open the gates."

She pulled an old laptop out of her desk drawer and powered it up. "I have about two minutes of battery power left on this thing, so we don't have time to argue. You turn your back, and I'll open the gates and bring stuff back online; you don't see how I do it."

"Okay, this time."

Jeni worked quickly by the faint light of the laptop screen. The lights came back on and she plugged the laptop in. "The gates should be open for now."

"For now?"

"Another dead-man switch. You're going to need me on an ongoing basis as long as you're here. You should leave as quickly as possible. I'll set up the severance package. I'm not thrilled about doing it, but we're both logical, reasonable people. We can both leave here free and wealthy—you, me and your people."

"Right now I just want to get some stuff out of here that

neither of us wants the BTI to find."

"Organs? You are a ghoul."

"My sister died of liver failure. They couldn't find a donor," Andy said.

"That's sad, but it doesn't justify this."

"I wasn't trying to. She was a drunken bitch; I'm glad she died. But the cost of dialysis wiped out the last of the family's finances and gave me the idea for this project."

"I always instinctively distrusted you. I should have listened to my instincts."

"Maybe you should have. For now you need to tell the security people in the data center to let me through. Cheer up; my cargo will mean a better life for dozens of people, maybe hundreds."

"I'll do it, but not cheerfully." Jeni tapped in a security code and views from cameras scattered around the compound came up on the laptop. She spotted the Indians and their guards and tracked them from camera to camera as she picked up the phone.

"Speakerphone," Andy said.

"Sure." She turned it on. "This is Jeni. Mr. Hollsworth has packed up a few of his things. You need to open the gate on your side and let him through."

"That may not be a good idea right now." The guard's voice sounded strained. "We may have visitors."

"May?"

He paused, then finally said, "It should be okay. Send them through."

Jeni watched as the guards reached the gate of the compound. She tensed, waiting for them to bring their guns up as the Indians ran out the gate into the surrounding forest. The Indians disappeared, and Jeni let out a deep breath. "Okay. I did my part. You did your part. I'm surprised."

Andy pulled out a radio. "Okay, move the special cargo

through."

"By the way, have you heard anything from Bernhardt?" Jeni asked.

"I don't expect to. He'll lie low until this is over one way or the other," Andy said. "Actually, if anything, he'll help me if I need it. There's no statute of limitations for murder."

"So that's what you had on him. Our screening process really did a great job didn't it? Two murderers in key positions."

"I've never killed anybody real. I don't have qualms about killing someone, and I may do it at some point, but I haven't yet. The way I see it, nobody from Timeline X is real. They're what-ifs. Might-have-beens."

"I don't think a court would buy that."

Andy grinned. "It would be fun arguing that case, as long as I wasn't the defendant." His grin faded when a burst of rapid-fire gunshots sounded from outside, near the house. He ran over to Jeni's desk. "Get up." He didn't wait for her to respond. He pushed her out of the chair. She saved herself from falling by grabbing the side of the desk.

His back turned to her for a second, and she had a wild urge to grab him and crank his head sideways until his neck broke. He turned the chair so he partly faced her as he brought security cameras up on the laptop screen. "I don't think I want you behind me."

"You really don't want me behind you."

Jeni moved so she could see over his shoulder. More gunshots echoed in the room, a curious double sound since she heard the noise both over the laptop's speakers and a fraction of a second later through the air. The cameras showed a confused jumble of muzzle flashes and men running. Andy zoomed in on a face. An oriental man in his early thirties aimed a machine pistol toward the house. Rapid-fire muzzle blasts filled the camera with flares of light, the double reports sounded like stuttering.

"Danny Minh." Andy spun around in the chair. "Don't you have any security at all around here?"

"So asks the guy who did his best to destroy it."

Andy switched rapidly from camera to camera. "We're getting the crap beat out of us." He yelled into the radio, "Send the pixies over to the main house. Everybody you can spare from guard duty too. Come ready to fight. We have a situation."

Jeni glanced at her watch. "It'll be worse in a minute or two. I only brought the security system up for fifteen minutes. You're going to lose cameras and electricity."

"Take care of it. Now."

"Why?"

"Do you think Minh's going to be a better bet than me if he wins? You want me to win this thing."

"No, I don't. Let the Indians go. All of them. You need the guards here anyway."

"They would massacre us and you too. Isn't going to happen." Another burst of rapid fire sounded outside. Sporadic fire from near the house answered back a second later.

Scott had dozed off again in spite of the tense situation, his body desperate to repair the damage from days of stress and heavy physical activity. He woke to gunshots in the distance.

"Is Jeni back?"

"No." Darla answered from the far side of the room.

Scott eased his aching body up and picked his way through the darkness to the faint starlight from the window. "The shooting's quite a ways away."

"They took some Indians out a while back. They're probably shooting them," Peter said.

"Why?"

"Same reason they brought them here in the first place."

Scott saw movement around the guard towers and then

heard the golf cart. "They're pulling guards away. Maybe the Indians made a break for it. Petey, how are you doing on the door?"

"All three of us together could pop the middle hinge if we kicked the bottom of the door at the same time. We would need a distraction though."

"More than we already have?"

"The guards have semi-automatic rifles. They aren't machine guns, but we won't make it across the open field without them shooting us."

Scott stared out at the field. The Indians still sat in little clusters, but most of them were awake. "The warriors are gradually filtering toward the watchtowers. I think they're going to make a break for it."

"They're as dangerous to us as they are to the nutsoid lawyer and his pals," Darla said. "If they get loose, anyone who isn't wearing deerskin will be fair game."

"So we've got to move first," Scott said. "Any ideas?"

"Some," Peter said. "Be ready on the door. Our mystery bowman will probably take a hand any minute now."

They pulled the dead guard into a corner and propped him up.

"I can't believe they just left him here," Darla said.

"No further use to them," Peter said. "One more complication for us to deal with; one less responsibility for them."

The three of them lined up facing the door. "On the count of three. Balls of feet so you don't break anything."

Peter counted off and they slammed their bare feet into the door. It shifted, but the hinge didn't give. Scott cringed at the screech.

"This would be a lot easier in shoes."

"Again. Quick." Peter counted off and they slammed the door again. The hinge side rasped open a half-inch more. "We're pulling the screws out instead of breaking the hinge. Again."

This time the door swung open six inches at the bottom. Peter reached out and grabbed the dangling screws from the hinges. "Now pull it back. Make it look normal in case the guards glance over."

"Any idea how many guards are left?" Darla asked.

"No more than one or two per watchtower, so maybe eight at the most, maybe fewer from what I saw on the other towers," Scott said. "They're not going to be too quick to check on random sounds down here."

He reluctantly stood and worked his way to the window. His shoulders burned, and he loosened them up. His whole body felt sluggish.

And my life is going to depend on moving fast any minute now.

Outside, a man yelled in the Iroquois dialect. Scott didn't catch all the words, and what he did catch didn't make sense. "Something about the moon and a cloud." A couple of shots rang out from the watchtowers, followed by silence. Scott watched a cloud pass in front of the moon and tensed, but nothing happened. He stared out into the field. The Indians seemed to be scattering across the field and lying down. "Nothing happening yet." The moon came back out. Scott watched the towers. The guards crouched with their heads just above the waist-high parapets rather than pacing. As near as he could tell, there were two guards on one of the towers he could see and one on the other.

A steady background of distant shots filled the night.

"Somebody has really naughty toys," Peter said. He cocked his head. "Hear that? That's fully automatic. So that's either the cavalry or very illegal firepower."

"My money would be on the illegal firepower," Scott said. "But what's going on out there? This isn't about catching a couple of dozen Indians. And if they have automatic rifles, why didn't they use them when Mr. Lurks-in-the-Woods nailed them?"

A high-pitched scream, choked off, came from above them. Something fell past the window.

"Speaking of Mr. Lurks-in-the-Woods, Petey, I think there's a rifle lying out there."

"You think?"

"I saw something fall," Scott said. "It was the right size, but I couldn't tell for sure."

More shots rang out from the watchtowers. Scott watched the muzzle flashes, the sounds of the blasts coming just enough after the flashes to make sequence look out of sync. "Nobody shooting from above us."

"You sure?" Darla asked.

"Pretty sure. Did you hear any shots from up there this last burst?"

"I don't think so," Darla said.

The moon drifted behind the clouds again, and suddenly Indians swarmed toward the two watchtowers Scott could see. "The Indians are making their move."

Peter sprinted the three steps to the door and pushed it open. "Stay here and hold the door open." He came back a couple of seconds later with a rifle. "Get down close to the wall by the window. They'll shoot through the window as soon as I start shooting." He ran to the window and fired off five quick shots. A return shot shattered the window and sprayed glass over Scott.

"Time to run." Peter yelled. They ran out. Several Indians were writhing, caught on the barbed wire, but others were already at the top of the watchtowers. The remaining guards fired point-blank, then went down screaming under dozens of Indian attackers. The screams stopped abruptly and the only sound was low moaning from wounded Indians.

Scott stood for a split second, dazzled by the fighting. Peter whispered urgently, "Run. Now."

They found one of the electric golf carts and Scott drove,

weaving wildly through the trees. Half a dozen Indians ran after them, armed with rocks and sticks. Peter aimed the rifle back at them, but didn't fire. They pulled away from the Indians, but with nightmarish slowness, even though Scott had the pedal pushed to the floor.

"Any idea where the portal is?" Scott asked.

Darla pointed ahead of them. "Up there where they're shooting."

The shooting seemed to die down, but there were still occasional bursts.

Darla said, "That's not somebody shooting at a bunch of unarmed Indians; it's a firefight. Both sides have guns."

Scott saw something in the path ahead of them and slowed the cart. As they pulled closer, he recognized Bad-Comb-Over face up on the path with blood leaking from several holes in his chest.

Darla jumped out and checked for a pulse, then nabbed a pistol lying on the path near the man. She searched the body for ammunition. "Four shots left. Better than nothing, I guess."

A burst of shots rang out ahead of them, and one of the bullets spanged off the cart. Two men ran toward them and one fired a burst at the stopped golf cart. Scott rolled off the seat as three sharp reports from the passenger side told him either Peter or Darla was shooting back. One of the men fell on his face. The other turned and ran a couple of steps. Another shot rang out and the man grabbed his thigh, then fell on his side. He rolled over and fired anther burst. Shots ricocheted off the metal of the cart, and pieces of the driver's seat went flying.

Scott tried to flatten himself behind the inadequate shelter of the golf cart. Another shot sounded near him and the firing stopped. Peter ran by and returned a few seconds later with a couple of formidable-looking guns with something of the submachine gun in their ancestry. He held one out to Scott. "Can you shoot?"

"I've fired one a time or two, but I doubt I could hit the inside of a barn from the inside."

"Good. Take one of these. You couldn't hit anything you aimed at with it anyway, but it looks cool and sprays a lot of bullets until it jams after a few dozen shots. Just point in the right general direction and don't expect much." He also handed Scott a pair of night-vision goggles and put on a pair himself. "Both of those guys are Asian. Could be Vietnamese."

"Danny Minh," Darla said. "The guy's a stalker on steroids. What does he think he's doing over here?"

Scott took a quick survey of the golf cart. One headlight was out and both front tires were flat. Fluid leaked out of holes in the front. He hopped in, surprised the cart moved when he pressed the accelerator.

"Are we better on this thing until it dies or on foot?"

"Turn off the light and go," Darla said. "We're not far from the main compound and the portal. If we don't get caught in the crossfire and if the gates are open, we may actually get out of here."

They moved along the path. The cart's whine sounded louder now, though Scott thought that might be his imagination.

Peter said, "Romans behind us. Coming fast. Outrun them if you can, so I don't have to shoot them."

Scott jammed his foot on the accelerator even though he figured the cart was going as fast as it could. He checked the speedometer. "Twenty-five miles an hour."

Darla glanced back."They're gaining."

"I outran three of those things. How can they be gaining?" Scott caught a glimpse of two guys with pistols running through the brush near the road in the opposite direction as the cart flashed by them. Behind them, a man yelled and a single shot rang in the air.

"They stopped," Peter said. "But that gunshot is going to draw trouble. If you see a way to get off the path, take it."

They suddenly broke out into a clearing with a large, elaborate house built into the hill on the far side. A cluster of men by the door turned and fired at them. Peter fired back and Darla joined in with the other submachine gun. Two of the men in front of the house fell, and the other four ran for cover. A shot whistled by and Scott felt a sting along his thigh and then wetness, but no pain. He steered the cart in a zigzag, but Peter said, "Go straight. They'll only hit us by accident, and I can actually aim this thing."

Another of the men by the house dropped his gun and clutched his upper thigh. One of the others called, "We give up."

Scott hit the brakes and discovered they no longer worked. The cart passed the men who were trying to surrender. Peter jumped and rolled. Scott saw him come up on his feet with the rifle pointed at the remaining men. The cart had a lot of momentum. The side of the house loomed. Scott jerked the wheel to turn the cart away from the house, but saw a steep set of concrete stairs going down a hillside in front of him. He turned back toward the house and suddenly the side of the cart was scraping along the stone of the house, with sparks flying back onto his shirt and pants. He yelled, "Jump." and Darla jumped out of the back seat.

Scott scrambled to the passenger side and jumped too. He rolled and came up in time to see the front of the cart explode, sending flames and pieces of cart into the air and into the side of the house. He lifted a shaking hand to discover he'd dropped his gun.

Darla ran to him. "Are you okay?"

"I think so."

She kissed him hard on the mouth. "I love a man who can make even an electric cart go boom."

Chapter Forty-Five

ANDY STUDIED THE monitors, then gestured to Jeni. "We're out of here. I know you have a back way out."

"Maybe. Why should I go with you? Why do you even want me to go with you?"

"There are too many of them. They'll get to us before my guys get here. I'll take your deal. I get the product we've already processed, a hundred million dollars and legal services. My men get a reasonable amount of money and safe passage. In return, you get us out of here. The Indians go free. You won't get that good of a deal from Minh."

"But I don't think you're in a position to deliver, and I'm not either." Jeni watched on the monitor as the two sides blazed away at each other. "Okay. I don't trust you, but I don't want to get caught in the middle of that." She led them down to the basement and to a closet. "The back opens up to a tunnel. It leads to the edge of the compound. And yes, I thought I was being paranoid when I had it built. But now I have a Vietnamese street gang and the Russian mafia fighting over my little getaway retreat and it doesn't feel quite so paranoid."

"Russian mafia? That's a new one." Andy raised his pistol, then hesitated. "How are they involved?"

"Aren't you tied to them? That's what Danny Minh thought."

"No. I collected a bunch of the guys I remembered from pre-med classes who used to spit in other people's experiments to keep them from busting the curve."

"That's a letdown; I guess he was messing with me. Darla said he does that. Oh, in case you're planning to shoot me, you'll want to know there are three steel-core doors in the tunnel, each coded with a separate number. I don't leave much to chance."

"I wouldn't think of shooting you at the moment, unless you forget to do everything I say, no questions asked."

"Yeah. We'll have to see."

Jeni led them down the tunnel, Andy's flashlight guiding her way. As she worked to open the third door, she smiled back at him. "In case you're thinking about getting feisty, there are a few other twists before you find your way out. I used to design role-playing games back in college."

They walked the remaining few feet toward a dwindling night. The tunnel came out fifty yards from the fence at the edge of her compound. Jeni peered out the tunnel and didn't see any motion, so she dashed out, with Andy and two guards following her.

She heard two faint popping sounds and the guards behind Andy fell. He and Jeni turned back to find Bernhardt Sloan, a silenced pistol in his hand. An Indian man stood behind him, an arrow poised on his bowstring. Bernhardt grinned.

"I've always heard there's only one way to deal with a blackmailer, and that's to kill him. I guess there are actually two."

"Maybe you've forgotten something. I can prove you killed your stepfather. If I don't check in, evidence goes to the police."

"I know. And even though I was a teenager and he was abusive, it was premeditated murder. I might plea it down to manslaughter, but my career would be over." He focused on Jeni. "That's why I looked the other way when he used the portal. By the time I figured out what he was doing, I was in deep, but not deep enough I would let him hurt you."

"So what was this uberplan I screwed up?" Jeni asked.

"Pretty simple: wait until he sent most of his people back across and then shoot him and turn myself in for both murders."

"Walk away," Andy said. "You don't have to waste your life."

"Sorry. I can't do that. And even if I did, the guy behind me would make that a moot point. Meet...well, as near as I can tell, his name is Two Eagle. I don't speak the language too well, but I understood that your people killed his father, his wife and his daughter. He's a tad pissed, but he's willing to give you a chance—a fair fight, bow versus pistol. I'll step out of the way and let the two of you work out your problems. You could try to talk to him, but you don't speak the language at all, do you?"

Bernhardt stepped back, his pistol steady on Andy's chest. Andy stared at the Indian, then back at Bernhardt. "What's the point? If I win, you'll shoot me."

"I'll give you a head start."

Jeni stepped aside. "I'll sit this one out."

Andy dodged to put himself behind her and fired at the Indian. Two Eagle fired simultaneously, and the arrow streaked by Jeni's arm before burying itself in Andy's right shoulder. Jeni ducked and ran toward Bernhardt. Two Eagle fired again as Andy grabbed the arrow in his shoulder. Another arrow hit him in the left side of the stomach, below the ribcage. Andy ran for the forest, firing wildly back over his shoulder. A third arrow hit him square in the back and he fell without a cry.

Jeni's arm was stinging. Bernhardt rushed to her. "Are you all right, boss lady?"

She glanced down at a line of blood beading on her upper arm. "I guess the arrow grazed me. If that's the worst I get out of this night, I'll be the luckiest woman alive. We have to get out now. Wait, I left Scott and Darla in a cell back by the Indians."

"We can't help them. They'll have to find their own way out." She hesitated, but he grabbed her arm. "I *am* going to get you out alive."

Chapter Forty-Six

"SOMEDAY YOU'RE GOING to have to give me one of those kisses when nothing is on fire or blowing up," Scott said.

"She won't." A Vietnamese man came out of the house. "She has a screw loose that way. Always has."

"Danny Minh. I get kidnapped into a different universe and still you stalk me," Darla said. "Done shooting the place up?"

"I ran out of people to shoot, unless you count these guys."

"They're fine, but two thousand angry Indians are headed our way. We'll want to be gone before they get here."

Danny nodded. "So that's where he was going to get the merchandise. I traced the earlier shipments back to Hollsworth, but I couldn't figure out where he was getting the parts. Yeah, they'll be a tad pissed." He yelled into a radio, and half a dozen men ran out of the house. A dozen more trickled in from the surrounding area. They sprinted for the portal.

"We need to disappear too," Peter said.

Scott took a step toward the portal. "What about Jeni?"

"Jeni made her bed; she can lie in it," Darla said. "Let's go!"

The sky was getting lighter, though the sun wasn't up yet. They ran across the clearing toward the portal tunnel. Two Romans jumped out from behind a bush and sprinted toward them, swords slashing. Scott caught a glimpse of a sword hitting the rifle Peter raised to block it. He heard three shots close behind him. A sword thrust blurred toward his stomach. He pivoted away, but his body moved in slow motion. The sword suddenly angled up, allowing Scott to duck under it.

Darla clung to the Roman's back, fingers digging into the eye sockets of his helmet. Scott caught the flailing sword arm and tried to break it at the elbow, slamming it down across his shoulder. The elbow didn't snap, but the sword clattered to the ground. The Roman jerked away from Scott and grabbed the hand Darla was using to gouge his eyes. Scott charged, throwing his weight into the Roman's upper body. Any normal human would have fallen, but the Roman just staggered. Scott drove two hard fingers at the now undefended eye sockets and clawed desperately. An armored forearm slammed into his side and Scott fell, his world narrowed to frantic gasps.

The Roman charged.

Scott tried to stand, but his legs wouldn't support him. The Roman kept coming, apparently not seeing Scott. It tripped over him and fell hard. Darla and Peter hauled Scott upright. The Roman lurched to its feet, flailing out wildly, blindly.

Scott wheezed breath back into his body and got his legs working. He grabbed the Roman's sword and searched for the other Roman. It was sprawled unmoving on the grass.

Peter held a finger to his lips. They backed away. Scott and Darla kept their captured swords ready, but the Roman made no move to follow them. It turned its head toward them, and Scott saw blood streaming from the eye sockets of the helmet. He stared back at the sightless eyes until they reached the tunnel.

They staggered through the portal and through the open door on the other side into the nearly deserted data center. The portal doors slammed behind them, the sound echoing. A terrified-looking security guard peeked out of the security room, then slammed the door. Scott ran to a desk and called Chad.

"You'll never believe what I've been up to."

Chapter Forty-Seven

JENI AND BERNHARDT freed her household staff and her pilots. They worked their way to the flying boat and took off as enraged Indians rampaged through the compound. Bernhardt sat across from her.

"Where to?" he asked.

"Rome by way of the Azores. I have a yacht to check on. I don't leave people behind."

She closed her eyes, and her exhausted body forced her into a long and remarkably dream-free sleep. She woke briefly during the refueling and peeked out at the island, still deserted except for the birds. She woke again when they landed off the port town that had become Lisbon in their timeline.

Her yacht wasn't in the harbor when the plane taxied in. Severus met them in a ship full of security pixies dressed for battle. As best she could figure from the minor amount of Latin she knew, he claimed that the ship had slipped out of the harbor at night during a plague, either intentionally or carried out by a sudden storm.

They searched the surrounding coasts and ocean for the yacht or its wreckage until they ran low on fuel. When they finally gave up and flew away, Jeni turned to Bernhardt. She tried to keep her face expressionless, but felt a tear slide down her cheek and swiped it away.

"I guess you called it. When I think with my heart I'm

dangerous."

Scott spent the next few days in the hospital, in part to mend a broken rib. Darla stopped by on day three.

"I'm trying to wrap up my end of this," she said. "How are you doing?"

"I need to be up and running; I miss my endorphin fix. What's going on with the case?"

"Peter flew back to Chicago. Portal gates are still closed. Jeni is apparently still alive. She's established radio contact with the BTI portals and is trying to plea bargain her way out of this."

"How's that going for her?"

"I don't know. I'm shut out of that part of it. I don't even officially know that much."

"So who killed Samantha Murphy?"

"That's the one thing they did talk to me about. Burgen claims Andy killed Samantha and left the body. Sloan initially thought Jeni had killed Murphy or had her killed and was asking him to dispose of the body. He did, but then his conscience got to bothering him and he called in the anonymous tip that led us to it."

"So do you believe all of that?"

"Bernhardt getting an attack of conscience? It's not exactly the picture of him I had in my mind, but I can't think of anyone else who would have the motive and the knowledge to tip us off. He may have thought that Hollsworth killed Samantha on his own. Sloan really is loyal in his own way."

"What about the Samantha Murphy part?"

"Burgen probably didn't do it herself. Did she knowingly have someone else do it? I don't know. With a psychopath like her lawyer around, there's enough reasonable doubt that the district attorney wouldn't want to bring a case against the kind of legal horsepower she could throw against him."

"The cause of death points to the lawyer," Scott said. "He was a paramedic and then pre-med. He would know how to induce a heart attack."

Darla stared down at him. "You actually look good in that dorky hospital gown. And you don't want to believe that Jolene Beck is ruthless enough to order somebody killed. Only she really isn't Jolene Beck. She may have been like that at one time, but money and power and the need to defend both changed her. You saw how she smacked down Andy when he had her helpless and could have shot her and all of us any time he felt like it. He had the guns but she owned him."

"Yeah. I saw how she's been able to swim with sharks. But this whole portal thing was pure Jolene. Or actually Jeni before the money and the power. Do you understand what she was trying to do?"

"Not really."

"Remember what she said when we were in the cell? Bringing together elements of cultures at a similar technological level? That was pretty much it. Trying to play God. Trying to save the Indians."

"Sky nutjob of the Iroquois."

Scott shrugged. "A worthy goal. It wouldn't have worked." A nurse poked her head in, glanced at him and withdrew, leaving a faint antiseptic smell. He asked, "What happened to Andy's shipment of human pieces?"

"They never found the truck, but they found the bodies of three of Andy's men dumped along the road not far from the data center. I'm assuming Danny Minh and company hijacked the truck and killed the people in it. He's probably peddling the organs to rich and desperate people even as we speak. Assuming that is one thing, proving it is another. We haven't found evidence to link him to the bodies or organ running."

"So Danny Minh walks away from this? What about his men

shooting up things on the other side of the portal?"

"We can't even get to the crime scene. I'm not sure who, if anyone, would have jurisdiction over there. Besides, he sort of rescued us."

"Do you think he intended to?"

"Maybe. Me, anyway."

"I'm guessing the organ smuggling prospects had something to do with it too. So why is he stalking you?"

"I've never quite figured that out. It seems to be a mix of obsession and a kind of weird protectiveness. It worked out well this time, but eventually it won't. Did you ever figure out why the Roman Empire and all of the other European and Asian empires stagnated?"

"Sort of. Remember the hobbits?"

"Yeah."

"A primitive, sort-of-human species survived on Flores until surprisingly close to historic times. I'm guessing something similar happened on one of the Mediterranean islands like Sardinia that didn't get attached to the mainland during Ice Ages. When modern humans reached Sardinia, they'd already invented slavery and instead of killing off the locals, they enslaved them."

"Wouldn't that have changed things way before the Roman empire?"

"Locally, yeah. But the interior of Sardinia was pretty isolated up until not long before the Romans started expanding."

"Okay. Why did that matter?"

"The hobbits are ideal for maintaining a static social structure because they're a way out of a dilemma. Slave-owning societies are inefficient. Slaves produce as little as they can get away with unless they get a meaningful share. But if you give your lower classes a meaningful share, that eventually threatens the structure of a society. Lower-class individuals accumulate wealth. They innovate. They change society. Eventually they diminish the status of the people on top."

"How did hobbits change that?"

"They gave the Romans another option. Unlike human slaves in our history, they really are the things that our slave-owning societies claimed their slaves were: small brained, eager to please and not capable of living on their own. They've been bred to perform enthusiastically, like dogs trying to please their masters. They don't need a cut of production to make them work hard. They can't accumulate wealth. They can't innovate. They can't displace the upper classes. At the same time, they let Romans keep the nuts and bolts of technology at arm's length. Most Romans don't have to understand technology and they don't want to understand it because it's stuff slaves do."

"So you end up with a society of wealthy people and slaves," Darla said.

"Yep. There is no social group in Rome capable of technological change or pushing for it. Ordinarily, a society of wealthy people and their slaves would be the perfect setup for an invasion of barbarians. If you don't give the average guy a reason to fight for you—a significant stake—he may still fight, but not very hard or effectively. Plus if there is no way for the lower classes to advance, the wealthy would be stupid to give those lower classes military training. Static master/slave societies are brittle, with a strong army, but little ability to build new armies if the one they have is destroyed."

"Take out the history geek stuff and you're saying the hobbits are basically pit bulls for the Romans." Darla said. "They fight enthusiastically for their masters because they're bred to love them. They keep the barbarians out, and the whole rotten structure just sits there. Nice."

Scott stayed at a hotel near the hospital for a week, resting and getting back in touch with his family. L. J. stopped by with Sara once. The little girl smiled at her "uncle" but otherwise seemed indifferent to Scott. The portal remained closed and Scott's inquiry to Chad about what was going on was met with "You don't need to know, but you do need to back here as soon as possible."

Darla had already flown back to Boston. Scott said his goodbyes and flew home himself.

When he got to the BTI building, Chad met him at Scott's office.

"I've talked to Peter and Darla, so I know what happened. I still haven't quite figured out why. Why did Burgen spend all that money and take all those risks to open her portal?"

"Idealism. Misplaced, but real."

"Okay, but what was she trying to do?"

"She thought it was just a matter of time before someone figured out how to get over there the same way she did, without the huge energy expense. At that point the Indians would get screwed over even worse than they did historically over here. She planned to push their technology development into overdrive so they'd develop technology to let them compete when the two timelines met in earnest."

"How'd she plan to do that?"

Scott sat down at his computer and started through his email, the return to routine oddly comforting. "Remember that theory of hers I told you about?"

"Cross-pollination of technologically near-equal cultures."

"Yep. It might actually have worked given a couple hundred years. In the time frame she was thinking of, it wouldn't have made much difference."

"Why the trips to Rome?"

"She probably wanted to find out what kept them from developing, which I have a theory on myself, by the way."

"What's your theory?"

"Hobbits."

"They don't exist."

"I killed one."

"Right, but they don't exist. If they did, the temptation to do something with them would be too great. And that's a slippery slope we couldn't get off of. So it's a good thing they don't exist."

"What about Jeni and the portal?"

"She's been in touch; I'm sure that much has leaked out. She's a hardball negotiator."

"Let me guess: you want the portal and her portal design. She wants to get off with a slap on the wrist. How is she still alive? Last I heard she was trapped over there with several thousand irate Indians."

"I don't know how she ended up not getting killed. As to the negotiations, something like what you said, only with licensing fees for the technology, we lease her *property* over there, and a plea bargain to a misdemeanor with no jail time."

"Are you going for it?"

"Not my call. Our lawyers tell me she could tie us in knots for years, and the technology she used for the portal would probably become part of the court record, which would give it to a lot of people we don't want to have it, so it's possible. Also, you and Peter might possibly have killed a person or two over there, all in self-defense, but that's a jurisdictional can of worms we don't want to open. One thing, though—based on what we know, we can't prove a tie between her and any of the killings. The question is, was she tied to them?"

"I don't think so. Of course, I'm biased. I like the woman."

"So I hear."

"I didn't sleep with her—at least not in the usual sense."

"I don't want to know."

Scott moved on to new research. The weeks went by. One morning when he went out for his jog, Jeni Burgen met him wearing shorts and a T-shirt that read "I went to Timeline X and all I got was this lousy T-shirt."

"Mind if I run with you?"

"Aren't there legal problems you need to take care of?"

"No. I'm free to be here, and my lawyers tell me that's not going to change."

"You broke a lot of laws."

"Allegedly."

"I don't like the whole 'rich people justice versus poor people justice' thing."

"I don't either, but it's reality. Let's run. We can chat on the way."

As they jogged, Scott asked, "So you did a plea bargain?"

"Pretty much."

"What about your lawyer?"

"Dead. An Indian shot him."

"Sloan?"

"Bernhardt is somewhere in Timeline X. He's helping people who need security. He's not coming back—a little matter of murdering an abusive stepfather back when he was seventeen. He made it look like an accident, but Andy managed to document that it was murder."

"Couldn't he come back and fight it?"

"Maybe, but he doesn't want to. He has work to do over there."

Scott paced her quietly for a couple of minutes. "Who killed Samantha Murphy?"

"Hollsworth. I can't prove it, but he's the only one except Bernhardt and I who could have. We didn't."

"What about the Indians your lawyer and his goons kidnapped?"

"They call themselves the Wenroh. They're back home. They're not secure there, though. They lost hundreds of men, and surrounding tribes would ordinarily take advantage."

"And your plan to help the Indians?"

"Let's just say that the Wenroh may show some extraordinary technology advances over the next few years if my theory is right."

"Ah. So that's where Sloan is."

"Nobody knows that for sure, and nobody really wants to find out."

"And the BTI is okay with that?"

"No. But Andy did enough harm to the tribe that they can justify leaving him to help out, as long as they don't officially know the details. Life gets complicated sometimes, but you do the best you can."

"What about the hobbits or pixies, whatever you want to call them?"

"They were figments of your imagination."

"Not you too."

"Sorry. Part of the deal. They never existed, and if they did exist the BTI would have whisked them off somewhere, except for a few assassin/ninja types that they couldn't find."

"They didn't find stealthy types? That's not good."

"It's not my problem anymore. I never wanted any of them, of any kind, in the first place, especially not a yacht-full of them."

"What happened to your yacht?"

Jeni slowed, then stopped. "Sorry. I've got something in my eye."

Scott turned and saw tears flowing down her cheeks. "Are you okay?"

"They were in Rome. The last message said everyone on the yacht was sick. I stalled the negotiations as long I could, hoping to hear from them, and when the BTI took over they kept listening. Nothing so far. I had a good friend on the yacht."

"I'm sorry."

"Me too. Bernhardt said that when I start thinking with my heart, I'm dangerous."

They finished the run in silence.

When they stopped to stretch, Jeni said, "I don't want to leave. I probably won't see you again. Back to my gilded cage." She grabbed his hand. "I'll always have a place in my heart for you."

"And I'll always have one in mine for you."

"Unfortunately, neither of us has room in our lives for the other."

They chatted a while longer. Finally they drove to Dickey's, taking separate cars. Bill Dickey waved when they walked in.

Jeni asked, "Have you heard from Darla?"

"A time or two. She's living her life. I'm living mine."

"Hmmm. I always thought I saw a spark between you."

Scott laughed. "Yeah. You might say that."

They chatted a while longer. Finally Jeni kissed him, a long, lingering kiss, and walked away.

Bill strolled over as Scott finished his drink. "So, did you get the girl?"

"Not really."

"That would be your fault. She obviously wants you to."

"It's more complicated than that."

"I'm still waiting for us to do the locust thing over in Timeline X."

Scott thought about the towns and villages he had seen, the thousands of Indian men, women and children living their lives in Timeline X.

"Hopefully, you'll be waiting a long, long time."

www.ingramcontent.com/pod-product-compliance
Lightning Source LLC
Chambersburg PA
CBHW030532270626
47155CB00024B/2736

9780984907090